advancing wolf publications

Th
Re
of
Christmas

MEGAN MONTGOMERY

Book Cover by Sarah Jane — @illustriousjane

1st edition 2024

Dedication

This one's for the readers who think *really good men* are just as sexy as the Morally Grey. Because when they finally unleash themselves, it's glorious.

fig.1 Bones of the Skull

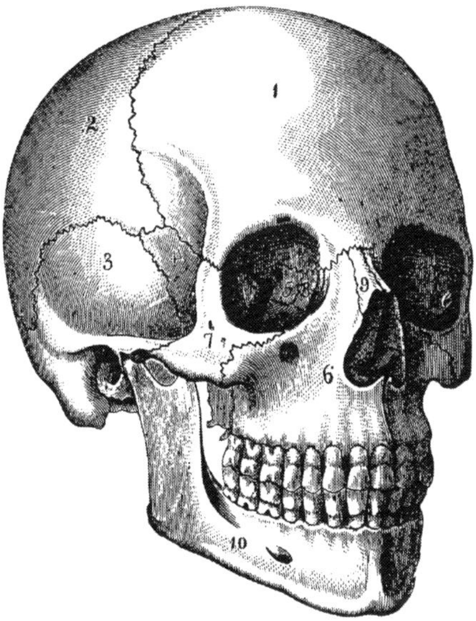

1. *frontal*
2. *Parietal*
3. *temporal*
4. *sphenoid*
5. *ethmoid*
6. *maxilla*
7. *zygomatic*
8. *lacrimal*
9. *nasal*
10. *mandible*

(1–4) *a.* — (1–9) *b.* — (1–10) *c.*

a. calvarium
b. cranium
c. skull

Part One

Chapter 1

Chris

I DIDN'T CARE WHAT was *so fascinating* about this case—no skull was worth the agony of scrotal frostbite.

I'd regretted answering Decca's text as soon as I'd arrived at the site to "lend a hand." A hand which they clearly didn't need, since the place was crawling with deputies and investigators from the ME's office.

I'd finished my first four-shot flat white in the car on the way here. I'd finished my second four-shot flat white thirty minutes after the first.

I didn't have a third.

That was hours ago. We'd been out here in the scrub brush next to the railroad tracks since dawn, bouncing on our toes to keep from freezing our balls off—well, *my* balls—while police assured us that *any minute now,* they'd be finished securing a perimeter around a partial set of human remains.

A cut-and-dried case. Nothing to identify. Nothing to solve. A waste of our time in the bone-chilling cold.

December in Nashville was never this cold.

December was supposed to be mildly cold. Pleasantly cold. The kind of cold where you could get away with a wool coat, a scarf, and gloves if you wanted to look chic in a Christmas tree lot, but you could just as easily wear a hoodie.

This morning, I was bundled for the Christmas tree lot and it still wasn't enough. *According to the New England Journal of Medicine*, it was also a terrible idea to wear boxers in below-freezing temperatures. Yet, here I was.

I fished my phone out of my coat pocket and checked the temperature: nineteen.

Nineteen, for fuck's sake. This was why I didn't do fieldwork anymore.

My colleague and best friend, Dr. Decca Crowley, huddled close to my left, using me as a windbreak. Even without testicles, she was worse off than I was. She'd had to borrow a beanie from one of the cops. Her hand-knit mittens had holes.

She breathed into her cupped hands.

I snapped an extra hand warmer to life. In the decade or so I'd known her, Decca had never come to a scene fully prepared. "Put this in your pocket. At least you'll be able to move your fingers when we finally get to work."

"Th-thank you," her voice shook. "I'll be fine as soon as I get moving. Why is it t-taking them so long? Why did the ME call us out so early?"

"I'm still trying to figure out why *you* called me out here at all—"

"You had nothing better to do."

"—for an alleged skull—"

"Confirmed skull."

"Confirmed calvarium." I argued. "Do you know if there are any facial bones? Dentition?"

"No clue." She shrugged.

A train whistle blew from somewhere not so far away, haunting in the cold, gray, just-past-dawn morning.

In the sparse woods ahead, below a railroad bridge that spanned a gully, a dull, beige-brown parietal bone peeked out from under the leaves, dirt, and decades of trash the wind had collected down there.

It was law enforcement's job to secure the area and figure out the best way for us to descend.

It was our job to posit the age of the *alleged* skull/confirmed calvarium once we got down there.

The remains were most likely historic—more than a century old. A bone lab would determine the details once homicide officially passed the case to Decca, the state forensic anthropologist, or to me and my team at the University of Tennessee's renowned Forensic Anthropology Center, colloquially known as The Body Farm.

"Oh, my God." A white blur floated into my periphery. I pushed my glasses higher on my nose, surprised to find a pretty blonde elf in a cracked black leather motorcycle jacket—a jacket I intuitively knew had no lining and, therefore, offered minimal protection against these nineteen meager degrees. And I'd just given away my last hand warmer.

"Nice car. Yours?" she asked, directing her question to me.

"Yes. Thanks," I smiled and followed her eyes to where they were trained behind me—to my brand-new pride and joy, a satin black AMG Mercedes coupe. Besides my Bösendorfer Grand, it was the only thing I'd ever truly splurged on.

"It's eight days old," I bragged to the newcomer. At least there was someone around here I could impress with my fancy new vehicle.

"That's the new GT, right? I've been following the redesign. Custom?"

"Uh... yeah."

"The composite brake discs were the giveaway. AMG discs are usually yellow. Yours are as black as the car. Nice. Sleek."

I'd seen plenty of women go gaga over a car before, but not quite like this, like a gearhead. I wasn't even a gearhead and I owned the damn thing. I was just sick of the old Volvo I'd been driving since undergrad. I'd done my duty. I'd been committed to carbon emissions-consciousness for long enough. Puttering around in a boxy car for over a decade had been slowly destroying my soul. Now, I was a new man—with a very fast, German-engineered supercar.

"I drive an '87 Firebird. She's rough, but I do all the work on her myself. Well, I used to, anyway. I'm Daphne, by the way. Decca's assistant."

"Daphne," I repeated. My thoughts were unable to move beyond her name, her lilting, lightly smoky voice, and her smile that unveiled a slight diastema and a rotated cuspid I wouldn't straighten if she paid me.

Waves of heat rippled through my body, like I was suddenly standing in front of a roaring fire instead of a clearing in these frozen woods.

She lifted her brows and her pink cheeks grew pinker.

Decca elbowed me in the side and looked up at me with a big, silly grin.

"Daphne, this is Dr. Christopher Carter, the forensic odontologist I've been telling you about. He thinks that fancy car will make me forget he's bringing the remains back to the lab. His lab," she said pointedly, "since I have no time. Not if you want to eat or drink anything at the party tonight."

Like hell was I putting human remains in the trunk of my eight-day-old Mercedes.

"Chris." I removed my glove and stretched out my hand.

"Oh." Her face changed. Her smile dropped. "Oh, wow. You're the teeth guy?" She stared at our joined hands. It was too cold to feel much, but I still hadn't let go. I couldn't seem to remember how.

"I'm just a dentist," I said. Definitely not worthy of an *Oh, wow,* unless it was *Oh, wow, your glasses are really thick.*

"You're more than a dentist. I read your last paper on current trends of bite mark analysis. And the one about facial depth thickness indicators determining masseter tissue strength and their impact on bite mark depth. And... pretty much all your other first-author papers."

I stared at her mouth—at her pointed canines, the slight overbite (God, that was sexy), and the lightly glossed, rose-tinged lower lip she tugged between her teeth as she recited damn-near direct quotes from my papers.

She'd read my papers. Memorized them.

I could imagine her doing it, too.

Her body flung sideways into an overstuffed chair; legs draped over the arm, bare feet swinging. A pen dangling from twisting fingers until she reaches up, absentmindedly, to grip the barrel between her teeth, steadying it with her tongue when she got to Fig. 3c, showing the closeup of an abnormal composite filling that had allowed me to identify a body pulled from the Gulf of Mexico.

"Sorry to be such a fangirl. I think I just made it weird. Did I make it weird?"

"Nope. He's making it weird," Decca said. "Besides, that's the appropriate response. We're all fangirls of Chris's work here. Especially Chris."

Daphne looked nervous the way she rocked back on her heels in those beat-up combat boots.

And cold. She looked very, very cold in whatever she called that scrap of fabric that barely covered the tops of her long, lean thighs in these nineteen-degree temps.

"Um, want me to check in with the Sheriff, Boss? See if we can get an ETA?"

Decca's shit-eating grin stretched wide as she tracked my eyes. "That would be so helpful, Daph. Thanks."

Daphne jogged away, her short skirt swishing back and forth, just under her ass. I seriously doubted those tights were doing anything to keep her warm.

"So. Daphne."

"She have anything to do with why you texted me this morning?"

"I have no idea what you're talking about," Decca said. "This skull's just too much for my current caseload. I need you to take it."

I didn't buy that for a second. Nothing was too much for Decca's caseload. She lived for this. Besides, if these were historic bones, they added virtually no work.

I tore my eyes away from Daphne and the cops who'd suddenly sprung to life as she came toward them.

"You told her about me?" I raised my eyebrow. Decca was a meddler. I wouldn't have been surprised if she'd thrown the skull into the gully just to orchestrate this whole encounter.

She held up her hands in surrender. "All I did was give her some journals I had lying around the office. I didn't tell her to go to JSTOR and look up everything you've ever written. And I swear I had nothing to do with *that*." She pointed to where Daphne had just been standing. "You can't fake that kind of chemistry."

I looked sharply at Decca.

"It wasn't just you, Chris. And that was way more than fangirling on her end. We just saw her internet crush become her real-life crush. You're welcome. I want an invitation to the wedding."

I'd be lying if Decca's words didn't do something to me, but this was getting a bit ridiculous. "I'm not her internet crush. I'm not even on social media."

"Doesn't matter. Your courtroom appearances are basically glamour shots in our world. Remember the Cosgrove trial where you were doing something stupid with your mouth, but you looked really handsome anyway?"

I groaned. "Demonstrating how malocclusion can be ascertained even after soft tissue maceration."

"Whatever. Your blindingly white teeth make an audible little ping when you click on that image."

"Shut up." I said, laughing.

"Seriously though, Chris." She took a deep breath. "Maybe... go out on a limb this time. Open up. And don't let that one get away. Because she's amazing. You both are."

I swallowed hard. Opening up wasn't my problem; timing was. Timing had always ruined everything in the past.

After a quick squeeze of my forearm, Decca left me to go hang out with the cool kids: the investigators from the ME's office and the Davidson County deputies. Swirls of steam rose from their Styrofoam cups. Twangy Christmas music blared out from one of the patrol cars. A few of the deputies were tossing around a Santa hat, until the Sheriff caught it and shoved it down onto his own head.

Despite the season, I wasn't in a festive mood. I'd always been more of an observer, hanging back quietly and getting my kicks by watching others. Part of the crowd, but drifting closer and closer to the fringes each year.

It was a matter of pragmatism. It was harder to keep up with friends when their conversations revolved around their kids' picky eating and travel ball schedules.

It sucked being the man who sobered the room when eyes turned to me, and I had only the same boring career updates. *Yes, the conference in Stockholm went fine. No, I didn't hook up with any hot Swedish girls. Yes, you probably qualify for Invisalign. No, it didn't work out with the girl from the app.*

I'd missed the milestones of marriage and kids. There was no one important in my life. But no matter how much I longed for it all—the wife, the kids, the chaos—I wasn't the settling type.

I needed to *feel* things. And I hadn't felt anything for anyone in a long time.

The wind picked up again, and I shuddered as an icy breeze whipped against my cheek. This was stupid. I could be sitting in my car, cranking the heat if they weren't ready for us. I could thaw my hands and regain feeling in my frozen testicles. Just as I reached into my pocket for the keys, Daphne caught my eye and started to jog toward me. She slowed to walk again when the contents of one of her to-go cups sloshed over the rim.

She hissed and raised the cup to her face before licking her knuckles. It was fucking adorable.

"It's not very good, but it's hot." She offered me one of the cups.

"For me?"

She laughed. "Who else?"

I took the cup and sipped. The cocoa was watery and nowhere near hot enough—it was never hot enough—but she'd thought of me, and that made it all the sweeter.

"So..." she huffed out a vapor cloud. "Something tells me you've never even lifted up the hood of that thing." Daphne nodded to my car.

"If you're trying to insult me, it's not going to work. I admit I know nothing about cars—besides how to drive them."

"How'd you choose the customizations? There are a lot of technical specs."

"I clicked all the boxes."

She smiled like she wanted me to kiss her. Or maybe I just wanted to kiss her.

"I should probably warn you. I don't try to insult anyone, but it does sort of leak out of my pores. I'll say something to make you cringe before the day's over. Just watch. I have a talent for sticking my foot in my mouth and not even realizing it."

"There's no conceivable way that's true."

She shrugged. "Sadly. Spend an hour with me and you'll be ready to choke me."

"Right." *Only if she let me.*

Her face was so vulnerable, so sincere. Like she had no idea what she'd just said—or that her words went straight to my cock, and all that hot blood didn't feel particularly pleasant rushing into ice-cold, spongy tissue.

I made a mental note not to wear boxers and loose trousers next time I had to stand around in nineteen-degree temps.

Shit. *These* were feelings I wasn't at all prepared for. Not today. Not out here in the weak morning light and the gray haze of the woods. Definitely not *in situ*, where human remains had been found.

I ripped my gaze away from where her teeth had been, once again, biting into the pillowy softness of her bottom lip. I exhaled and took my time about it.

Decca's assistant. That made her a coworker of sorts. I probably shouldn't be wondering what it would feel like if those teeth were biting into my lip instead. Even if the flirting and the feelings were sanctioned by her boss, and ours was only the most marginal of working relationships, it was still wrong. Right?

"You look cold," I said unnecessarily.

"We're getting an ice storm." Her voice rose several notes in her excitement.

"You want to get in and warm up?"

"Really?" Her eyebrows shot up to her hairline. She bobbed up on her toes, then deflated again. "Ugh, no. I mean, yeah, I do. I'm dying to see the interior. But... I'm acclimated now. I don't want to get all warm and toasty then have to get out again when they're ready for us."

"Here, let me..." I loosened the tight knot of my scarf and handed it to her.

Her brows pinched together in confusion.

"I thought it might—" I held the rim of the Styrofoam cup between my teeth, looped the scarf over her head, and wound it around her neck. "It might help a little." My breath fluttered one of the tendrils of hair at her temple.

"But you don't—"

"I'm warm enough."

She bit her lip and reached up to adjust the fabric, her bare hand brushing my glove and sending fizzles of electricity straight to my solar plexus. "I can be really dense sometimes." Her smile faded into something quieter. She was dropping her guard and trusting me to see something real about her. "Thanks, Chris. This might be the warmest thing I'm wearing."

How long had it been since I'd felt anything like this? Had I ever?

For me, desire usually built over time, after months or even years of mutual respect that was earned working side-by-side. It had never felt this instantaneous.

But this was something more than desire.

I finished the rest of my cocoa and dropped the cup on the ground to retrieve later. She did the same.

"What got you interested in cars?" I popped the hood so she could take a look. She jumped into action, propping it open. Her face turned serious, analyzing the engine and hoses—or whatever was under there—the way I'd analyze an underdeveloped maxillary arch.

"What? Sorry, I got distracted by this beauty," she said, searching for something in the engine. "Uh… my dad, at first. He made me learn how to change the oil, tires, brakes, spark plugs. He never drove anything fancy that required computer diagnostics or controls. They were all hoopties, so it was a lot easier to learn on them. When I was young, I thought him teaching me was all about bonding." Her face had become a mask of indifference. "Then I realized we were just too poor to take our cars to a shop and it was all a ploy. But I ended up really liking engines. Her smile widened and her eyes danced. "And then I saw the *Fast and the Furious.* I was obsessed with your car as soon as I saw it. Your car in the movie, anyway."

"*The Fast and the Furious?*" I adjusted my glasses, surprised they hadn't frosted over.

"You're kidding? You drive a movie car and don't know it's from a movie? That's like driving an Aston Martin and asking who James Bond is?"

I was in big trouble if I found her this interesting this fast.

"Your car is actually from *The Fate of the Furious;* the 2016 model," she flowed on, her head still under the hood. "But it was so sleek. It looked like driving it would feel like being inside a bullet shot from a gun. Is that what it's like?"

"Uh, yeah. Kind of. Not that I get many opportunities to pull the trigger."

"I'd give anything to drive your car. I didn't get to work on a lot of German cars."

"Work on?"

She gently dropped the hood and crossed her arms, warding off the cold. I did the same.

"I'm a mechanic. It's how I put myself through undergrad. I was kind of a peon. Most of what I did was just lube tech stuff, and we mostly serviced domestic cars at my garage, but every so often we'd get something fun."

God, this woman. "That's… really cool."

"Really?" She raised an eyebrow. "You don't strike me as the type to be impressed by a blue-collar girl."

"That's a reductive way of referring to yourself."

"Trust me, that's not the way *I* think. It's just what gets thrown in my face."

"Competence should be celebrated, no matter what arena it's displayed in. Besides, it's…" I shook my head.

"It's what?" Her eyes lit up with hope.

"Being good at something like that—it's, ah…" I blew out an audible breath. *Don't say it, don't say it.* "Sexy as hell. A major turn-on." *Fuck.*

She smiled wide. I hadn't realized how close we'd been standing, or that I was still facing her, the tips of our shoes practically touching. I could pick out the striations of icy grays in her irises. "I actually had a race car bed when I was a kid." We were so close, her vapor cloud of breath hit me in the chin. "It wasn't one of those official plastic ones. It was painted wood. Blue, not red. My dad built it for me. Before he got… sick."

"Maybe we can—"

"Finally!" Decca cut in. I hadn't noticed her walking back. "They're ready for us."

"Hell yeah!" Daphne said. "I'm excited to see what this teeth guy does with the remains." She bit her lip again, still staring at at my mouth.

Shit, this was big.

I straightened my spine and steeled my mind, preparing myself to enter the sacred space of a disinterment. This wasn't the time to be thinking about my love life. I was here to perform my job.

I was good at my job.

The fact that I wanted to show Daphne just how good was inconsequential.

Chapter 2

Daphne

"YOU WANT ME TO do what?!"

"It's the fastest way down, ma'am," said the officer gesturing to a belay seat I was supposed to strap myself into so I could freaking *rappel* into the ravine under the train tracks.

My forehead felt prickly. I was seconds from breaking out in a sweat, despite the frigid temperatures.

I took a long, deep breath. *Okay. I can do this.* I had to. Only one way down was faster, and that route ended with me never coming back up.

I stepped closer to the edge of the embankment, taking a deep breath and daring myself to look over. It wasn't a ninety-degree drop-off. From here, it didn't even look so steep that we couldn't walk it. That's how the first few officers had gotten down there initially, to confirm the remains were human.

Then again, they were probably very athletic. I was clumsy. I never knew when my joints might decide to roly-poly on me. Because of that, I could concede *strapped in* was a good plan, but *rappelling?*

"Need help?" I spun around to find Chris already in his belay seat and ready to go. It should have looked ridiculous over his fancy wool trousers, but he was too elegant to look ridiculous in anything, including a trouser-bunching rock-climbing harness topped with a fancy wool coat and expensive-looking shoes.

Of course his shoes were expensive. He was a single dentist, professor, and one of the most preeminent forensic odontologists in the world. He was in his mid-thirties, maybe? He probably made bank and had no financial obligations other than to himself. The man owned a custom luxury supercar.

So yeah, why wouldn't his shoes be expensive? I'd have expensive shoes, too.

He reached for my harness and kneeled in the dirt at my feet. Automatically. Like it was nothing to help a helpless plebe about to descend to her death.

I focused on his fancy shoes instead of my impending fall and severed spinal cord.

He didn't wear them like they were expensive. He wore them like they were just shoes. Ordinary, everyday shoes. Like how I wore my Army boots.

He was probably so accustomed to the finer things, he didn't even notice how fine they were. He didn't strut around like some men, showing off the one faddish, semi-luxury item they owned, blasting it in your face like you should be impressed they bought some expensive, but still very mid shit.

Chris didn't have to flash his wealth by making a show of looking at a blingy watch. He'd lent me his cashmere scarf and fur-lined gloves after knowing me all of ten minutes, as if they were disposable. I would have had to save up for the better part of a year to buy a cashmere scarf, and even then, I probably would have used the savings to buy something more practical—like food, or a phone that held a charge longer than two hours.

He didn't fuss or fidget trying to keep his shoulders erect in his expertly tailored coat. All his clothes were surely about to be ruined, and he didn't seem to care at all.

This was more than dentist money. This was old money. The kind of quiet luxury the rich didn't even notice.

Maybe he'd fallen through the cracks of time and was really a peer of the realm from Regency England.

"Step in."

"You know what you're doing?" I asked him.

"Yes."

"That's it? Just 'yes'? You rappel into a lot of odontology cases?"

"Right leg through here," he said calmly, holding the loop open for me. "Not for the job. I've just climbed a lot."

Hmm. Rock climbing could also be old money. No one I knew did it, so that automatically made it feel like an activity for wealthy people.

Chris probably did dressage or show jumping too. And fencing. Definitely fencing.

Now I was imagining him in a fitted black jacket, tight-ass riding breeches, and knee-high, shiny leather boots, and I didn't want to see him in anything else. I bet his thighs would look amazing in riding breeches.

"Left leg."

"Did you ever fence?"

"What?"

"Fence. You know—en garde? *The Princess Bride*?"

He looked at me quizzically. "No. Decca has a friend who does, if you're interested. She's the only person I know who fences."

"Ride horses?"

"Daph, put your other leg through." He tapped my calf. "Once. And I don't want to repeat the experience."

I stepped into the second loop, trying to ignore the easy way he shortened my name. As if it was a term of endearment rather than an ordinary nickname. It was like he'd been saying it forever, had known me forever.

"Archery, maybe? Or, like... flintlock pistols? I think that's what they're called. Do you use those?"

He laughed. "For what? Dueling Aaron Burr? What's with the questions?" Good. At least I hadn't offended him.

"I'm trying to figure out what you were like as a kid."

"You thought I..." He said something under his breath before shaking his head and smiling up at me. "The guns sound cool, but the only swords I've held were probably... I don't know, toy lightsabers. I don't know what sort of impression I give off, but I'm from Nashville. I played soccer. I skateboarded. Video games."

Okay, so he maybe wasn't a nineteenth century duke who'd fallen through a wormhole into a twenty-first century not-quite-a-crime scene. That just meant I hadn't found the right archetype for him yet.

"Are you disappointed?" He said it like a joke, but the nervous way he was avoiding my eyes was sending my insides on a roller coaster loop.

"That you're normal? No. I'm glad you're real. I just wondered how you became... you."

Chris took a breath and focused entirely too hard on strapping me in. He pulled the loops up over my knees but stopped just short of adjusting the flat rope across my upper thighs. "Uh, maybe you want to do this?"

My cheeks grew hot from the way he looked at me from behind those glasses, sincere—*always sincere*—and a little embarrassed to be touching me in such an intimate place, even if it needed to be done. The harness hadn't been an issue for Decca; one of the officers had gotten her done up in no time at all, without the red cheeks and stuttering and sudden inability to make eye contact on either end.

I inched the harness into place over the bunching sweatpants I'd borrowed from one of the male officers—luckily, since I wasn't about to dangle from a rope on a freezing cold morning in just my tights and a miniskirt. Decca had called me up this morning, and I'd rushed here. I was dressed for Christmas shopping and caroling at Mom's house this evening, not rock climbing.

"I play the piano," he said quietly as he tugged the straps around my inner thighs tighter, strategically un-bunching the fleece so it wouldn't twist while I was on belay. "Stop fidgeting."

"I can't help it."

The way he was bent over, tightening and adjusting the harness and keeping his fingers carefully away from my crotch and my ass—even though that was exactly where they were supposed to be—was... hot. It also meant his face was directly in line with mine and only inches away. I could lean forward and brush my lips across the hollow of his freshly shaved cheek. I could probably smell old money cologne if I inhaled deeply enough. Whatever that smelled like.

I leaned closer, as close as social decorum would allow me get to an almost-stranger. But all I could smell was... woods. Dirt. The briny scent of incoming snow.

He tugged some more, practically wrestling the harness into place over the giant pants. When he swallowed, his Adam's apple bobbed. I wanted to run my tongue down his throat, along his strong square jaw, and close my mouth just there, where his heartbeat pulsed. If he didn't step away in about five seconds, I'd do it, too. Once an image popped into my head, my impulse control plummeted right off a cliff. Which, incidentally, was the action my real-life body was about to imitate.

"I wanted to be a concert pianist," he said.

"Oh." I basically breathed out the word.

He looked at me. At my mouth. Then went back to his task.

"I thought that might tie in with your hoity-toity perception of me."

"Oh! No. You're not hoity-toity. Well, not in a bad way. You're a duke. Sorry. It's silly. It's just a thing I do. I... rearrange people into different eras and archetypes, and it's... really embarrassing and classist. I was imagining you as a historic manorial landowner. A Mr. Darcy type, working the fields alongside your tenants."

He cocked his head in surprise. "Darcy wasn't a lord, but I'm flattered by the comparison." He stood up. "Well, that's about as good as it gets."

"That's not at all reassuring."

"Ready?"

"No way."

"Go behind me." He smiled his lopsided smile, the one that was making my insides twist in the most wonderful way. "I'll catch you if you fall."

"ALRIGHT, FOLKS. I'VE GOT halls to deck and wassail to brew," Decca said, once we'd retrieved the remains and the cadaver dogs had swept the area.

"What even is wassail?" I asked Decca.

"It's what you drink on Christmas," Chris turned to me with his lazy smile and mischievous eyes. "If you're a duke."

Oh. I was in trouble.

"I'm officially turning this case over to Dr. Carter. Daph, do you mind assisting him?"

Sure. If by "assist," she meant tripping over my own feet and boring him to death with my nonsense factoids and inane questions. But that wasn't the real issue. I took a deep breath, about to show my underbelly to the woman who was my idol.

"Uh, actually, I was hoping to catch a ride with you. I don't have a car."

"How'd you get here?" Decca asked.

"Uber."

"You Ubered to a crime scene?"

"It's not a crime. They're historic remains. Never mind. I'll ask one of the cops to drop me off at a library or something, so I can ride-share from there. It's just like... twenty miles back to Franklin."

"What happened to your Firebird?"

"Everything happened to it. I couldn't afford to drive it home, so when I got into town yesterday, I drove straight to the junker my dad knows. He gave me barely enough for it to cover gas and the two cases of oil I had to put into it on the way out here."

"Shit. How are you getting back to Knoxville?"

"Dad'll pick me up tomorrow. When my stipend comes in, I'm going to use some of it for a down payment on a slightly less-used treasure that was once someone's trash. Hopefully old enough that I can still do the maintenance on it myself. I don't trust modern cars."

"Modern cars? Please at least get something from this millennium." Decca grabbed my phone out of my hand. "And use my Uber login. As your former lead on this case, I insist on covering your transportation while you're in my town. I don't want you to be stranded anywhere." She looked at me with concern. "I'll have Chris drop you at your mom's when you're done here. Don't worry. He'd never do anything that wasn't one hundred percent gentlemanly." She gave me a pointed expression that seemed to mean more to her than it did to me.

"I'm sure he's got stuff going on. I don't want him to feel obli—"

"Hey, Chris..." Decca shouted to where he was hunched over a table, pushing up his glasses in a way that made him look like a little boy. Something happened to my cheeks whenever I looked at him. To the casual observer, it would look like I was merely blushing, but I knew better. If you looked deeper, it was like I was being x-rayed. Only, instead of seeing my bones, it was all my sexual fantasies playing on a flickering film reel. And when it came to Dr. Christopher Carter, I had a big canister of film hidden inside me.

Chris looked up, his eyebrows shooting above his eyeglass frames in question.

"Give Daph a ride home after?"

He didn't move a muscle. Didn't even drop his brows. He held that shocked little boy expression as he glanced at me, then quickly back to Decca before nodding once and returning his attention to the skull.

That was odd. But it meant I got to ride in a brand-new AMG GT, so...

"I'll see you later, doll. Try to be at my house by eight o'clock if you can't make it by dinner. We're playing Dickensian party games. You won't want to miss them."

"The Minister's Cat?"

"Of course!" She shouted back, over her shoulder.

I knew who was coming to Decca's party, and I suspected she and I would be the only willing participants in tonight's revelry.

I scooped up the packing material Decca had left for the remains and started to organize it below the table. We'd found a few more bone fragments besides the skull, although nothing helpful like a femur—something that could help us accurately guess the decedent's height. All in all, the remains included a complete skull with mandible—detached, of course, but that it was there at all had been a nice surprise. The jaw was usually carried off by animals. Decca had assured me the three-inch-long one on the table was a third metatarsal. Because it was almost the same length, and had the same facets as a first metacarpal, I couldn't yet eyeball the difference like Decca or Chris could. There was also a spinous process, broken off from one vertebra, and a few small unidentified bones—although I'd go out on a limb to say one of them was a superior articular process of a different vertebra.

Chris was examining the cranium.

We were so lucky to have an intact skull.

"What do you make of it?" he asked, not looking at me as I stood at the plastic folding table opposite him.

"Um..."

He nestled the cranium into its jaw like a lopsided frame. "Age, sex, race? Anything interesting?" He gestured to the nearly toothless grin.

"Oh." I focused my attention down. "Uh... male."

"Yeah." He shrugged. "Any of these cops could probably tell you that. What else?"

"The brow ridge is very... um, overly... prominent. And straight. More so than average."

"Is it?" He was studying me now.

"I think so. Um." *Stop saying um.* "Getting a date on the skull will be difficult. It's been partially buried face down for a long time. That's why the parietal bone is bleached and the facial bones are brown. The back of the skull was exposed to the sun and the elements."

"Why?" He drilled.

"Animals?"

"Most likely. It accounts for why we can't find the rest of him. Animals gnaw on the skull last. Hard to get their jaws around it. It's a lot easier to take off with a femur or a rib. Which is partly what led us to believe these are historic remains. They must have been buried so long, all organic matter was completely decomposed long before he was unearthed."

"If they'd been uncovered sooner, before total decomp, they'd have more teeth marks?" I asked.

I'd read that information so many times. It made sense in the textbooks, but this was my first time seeing it in situ. Things were clicking into place, but I knew I wasn't about to flood him with the heat of my competence this time. I just tried not to sound like a total noob.

"Yes, and you were right earlier, too. The brow ridge hasn't changed that drastically in modern history. He was a weird looking dude, even before 1920."

Okay, what else? "Caucasian. The nasal spine is broken, but there's a narrow nasal opening and interorbital breadth, plus the sloping eye orbits."

"Good."

My body flooded with warmth from his praise. *I needed more.*

"Age..." I shook my head. "May I?" I gestured to the skull.

He nodded, watching me intently, with a curiosity that thrilled me.

I gently gripped the cranium by its temporal bones, which didn't appear as fragile as the rest of it. It easily lifted off the mandible, since there was no tissue connecting the bones.

It was the first time I'd held human remains in my bare hands. Even during undergrad, I'd worked mostly with plastic replicas, since the real human teaching skeletons were expensive, and they rarely let us undergrads play with them. On field studies, and working with Decca, I'd never actually had the authority to touch anything.

Letting the weight of this moment sink in, I saw myself in my career for the first time. This was exactly what I was born to do. Maybe I was rushing it. I still had another two years of learning—tramping over bloated corpses at The Body Farm, learning how to do this stuff without Chris or Decca prompting me. But soon enough, I'd be able to tell a third metatarsal from a first metacarpal with a single glance.

I carefully inverted the cranium and looked at the few intact teeth. "Wisdom teeth in place. Wear on the bicuspid. There's enough remodeling to suggest he lost a lot of his teeth premortem. I don't know—sixties? Seventies? His underbite game was strong, like a bulldog. You can see the grinding here." I pointed.

"Underbite game?" He raised an eyebrow.

"Mesiocclusion," I rephrased.

"Thank you."

My thumb brushed across a series of shallow ridges on the squamous part of the temporal bone.

"What's..." I squinted but couldn't see much. "This feels... anthropogenic." *But that couldn't be.*

"Where?" He grew serious.

"Left temporal. Right above the zygomatic arch. It's too even, too perfect. You can feel it better than see it. Here." I held his hand and placed the pad of his finger on the exact spot I'd felt the marks. But he wasn't looking at the skull. He was looking at me with that same odd blend of curiosity and fire. His chocolate irises darkened as his chest rose heavily.

"It's... uh, probably nothing." His mind seemed elsewhere, but I could tell he didn't sound convinced either. "More teeth marks. Maybe from a premolar." He took the skull from me, his thumb brushing mine across the orbital socket as it slipped from my hands. "I can see why Decca hired you. You know what you're doing."

He said it more to the skull than to me, but it was the best compliment I'd ever received.

Once we'd packed up, Chris gestured awkwardly to his car, as if my heart wasn't racing just thinking about nestling into its creamy leather seats. There was an odd moment where he hesitated and veered to the passenger side before straightening again. Was he going to open my door? Why did this feel like a date? Did it feel that way to him, too?

He tucked the small box of carefully packed human remains into the trunk. The scent of leather and new car that wafted out made my knees weak. I couldn't wait to get in, feel how she drove, feel how *he* drove.

"I feel like classical music should be pumped in wherever you walk. Like a tiny Bluetooth speaker. What am I going to discover when you start the car?"

"Never know. Could be Mozart. Could be Mahler." He raised his eyebrows. The brown of his eyes flashed for a second, but he didn't even quirk a smile before folding his long body into the small car.

I moaned once our doors shut. "I forgot what it was like to be out of the wind."

He pressed the button, and the engine purred to life.

"Oh, I don't know about Mahler, but this is the soundtrack of my heart right here. I could listen to this all day." I jerked my head toward him, my joints not fully thawed yet. "Did you know that Carl Benz was about to give up on his invention of the first internal combustion engine when his wife, Bertha, stole his car and drove it cross-country through Germany as a PR stunt?"

"I heard something like that."

"She was an engineer as well, even though she wasn't allowed to study in school. She came up with the idea for brake pads. And she invested her own money in her husband's company, but her name never made it on the books because wives weren't able to be listed as investors then. She's kind of my hero."

"I can see why," he said quietly. Everything about him was quiet and still, opposite my frenetic verbosity. Being near him even made me feel calmer.

When the music roared to life, it was decidedly not classical. It was... rap. Something about Wu-Tang. I'd heard of the Wu-Tang Clan but had never actually listened to them. It was raw and powerful—nothing at all like what I would have pictured from his old money shoes and tortoiseshell eyeglasses.

"Not classical. Still out of my wheelhouse. And my generation. I like it, though."

He smiled patiently. "It's before my time, too."

"Is there a story behind it?"

"Yes and no. I listen to all kinds of music, so this isn't out of my norm. But there was a man who worked with my parents—Darius. When I was a teenager, I really looked up to him. He became kind of a second father to me. Always had Wu-Tang playing. When I come home, I get nostalgic, I guess."

"How old are you, Chris?"

"Older than you."

"Oh, come on. I'll pick your pocket and sneak a peek at your driver's license," I said, giddily.

"Thirty-six."

"Oh. You look thirty-six."

"Disappointed?" He seemed amused rather than offended. Good.

"Only because I missed the chance to prove to you that I could, in fact, pick your pocket."

"I've seen your nimble fingers. It doesn't surprise me you have a gift for sleight of hand." He merged onto another road and accelerated effortlessly, flicking the paddle with his pretty hands. "So...?"

"So what?" He was melting me into the seats and rendering me incapable of following my own train of thought.

"How old are you?"

"Oh. Twenty-four." Would he think I was too young?

Chris wasn't that much older than me. He certainly didn't feel it, despite his air of general ducalness. Quiet and composed did not equal old. I'd known plenty of kids who were quiet and composed. *I'd* been quiet and composed as a kid. But everyone knows how to play when they get comfortable. I suspected, deep down, Chris knew how to play. He'd just been kicking at the loose rocks on the playground until the right person came along to chase him onto the monkey bars.

He wasn't even the type who needed me—your stereotypical ADHD manic pixie dream girl—to show him how to let his hair down and roll with the punches.

He was a bone geek, a death worker. His hair was already down. He rolled.

There'd always been a disconnect with my dating life, and it was one hundred percent because of me.

The unfairness of it all was that my neurodivergent, trauma-informed brain made me impulsive, up for anything, great in emergencies or morally ambiguous situations, but I didn't get any of the fun parts. I wasn't a free spirit; I was riddled with anxiety. My life wasn't a playground; it was a hellscape where I'd been left alone to parent myself from a young age and never given the tools to do it.

I looked like trouble, but I was traditional. I'd been blue collar, but I liked bougie. I liked security, warmth, and home. My goals involved one day having a closet full of black sheath dresses and season tickets to the symphony.

Something about Chris and his untapped boyishness made me think he might be the one to see me how *I saw me*. He just might be my opposite—the Mercedes to my Benz. Here he was, in his car that was fancy, but not flashy—which obviously meant he valued quality craftsmanship—yet he was accelerating into traffic like an Indy driver instead of a hesitant old man.

He wore exquisitely tailored, side-buckle trousers and a cashmere pullover, but I hadn't once seen him brush off the dust or the mud flecks. Plus, we were listening to some pretty hardcore nineties rap.

And I was pretty sure he was doing some heavy flirting on an almost-crime scene.

Maybe he was my manic pixie dream boy.

Maybe we could teach each other how to live and be and love.

I reached for the knob to turn up the music at the same time he reached for the heat controls. The backs of our fingers bumped, and I quickly shoved my hands between my thighs.

"Are you cold?" A line formed between his brows, as if my comfort were the most serious thing in the world. God, he was handsome. His sincerity, his style, his silly droopy smile, the way his elegant hands curled around the shifter panel, easing through the gears with the tips of his fingers.

Every now and then, his eyes drifted over to the strip of sheer black tights between where my skirt ended and my thigh-high socks began.

I hid my smile.

The rest of the drive was filled with companionable silence. Under normal circumstances, I'd be nervous as hell, compulsively picking at my black nail polish that hadn't yet started to chip. I was no good at flirting or banter. I'd rather spew random facts about the Gilded Age or talk about how Mercedes Benz was the first automobile to develop four-wheel suspension than pretend I was incompetent just to stroke a man's ego. But being with Chris made me feel different—mature and grounded. Comfortable.

I could get used to this.

Chapter 3

Chris

Daphne's cool blue eyes met mine across Decca's hot and crowded kitchen.

She smiled and lifted her fizzy water in acknowledgment, continuing her conversation with one of Decca's friends. The rest of the party suddenly faded into oblivion.

Only Daphne's wide, unapologetic grin remained in my consciousness, and her silvery hair, glowing like a halo beside Decca's Christmas tree.

I tightened my shoulders and cracked my neck, testing the motion. My body felt unfamiliar. I didn't know what I was feeling. So much at once. Like something was braced against my chest, dragging my body down into some dark obscurity, while an opposite force filled my lungs with something so weightless it let me float up and up.

Her eyes were so light, the blue so unsaturated, they were practically gray—the reflection of stars on inky oceans, belying the cold, murky depths underneath. Getting lost in them would doom me.

But oh, how I wanted to be lost.

Something hit my back, jolting me headfirst into reality. The din of conversations roared back to life. I blinked, surprised to find myself still sitting at this rickety kitchen table, still holding a drink that was now more melted ice than bourbon.

Decca trailed her hand across my shoulders before she shoved her deceptively strong body into the kitchen chair with me. I winced as my right ass cheek slid off the seat, forcing me to uncross my legs to steady myself.

Her breath smelled like whisky and orange rind from the cocktail in her hand. She must have had quite a few—Decca only got touchy when she'd been drinking.

"Bethany wants to sing Christmas Carols," she said.

"Are you prohibiting her from doing so?" I sipped my drink.

"Well, she can't just break into song a cappella, can she? She can't even hold a tune with proper accompaniment."

"Accompaniment would be a bonus." The wool tweed of my jacket pulled tightly across my back as I crossed my arms.

"We have a piano." Her eyebrows raised suggestively.

"You do," I agreed.

"If only someone here could play it." She tapped her chin.

"Dec, you don't have to dance around it. Just ask."

She clasped her hands together in front of her chest. "Please, will you play some Christmas songs for us?"

I stood, removing my jacket, pushing up the sleeves of my sweater, and unbuttoning my cuffs. "Consider it your Christmas gift."

“You already gave me a Christmas gift. I’m drinking it.” She lifted her Manhattan to her lips. “Thank you again, by the way.” She sipped.

“That was your hostess gift. My mama taught me better than to walk into a party empty-handed.”

“Ah yes, the quintessential Southern gentleman.” She shook her head. "Thank you, Mr. Southern Living."

"You want me to take the scotch back?"

“Don’t you dare.”

Someone clapped anemically as I sat at the piano and raised the fallboard. The keys were dusty inside, as if no one had thought to cover them until they realized the piano hadn’t been played in years. Curling my fingers around the first few chords, I gritted my teeth against quarter tones that weren’t supposed to be there. *Eesh.* Probably been out of tune even longer than it had gone unplayed. Hopefully, Decca’s guests were too filled with the holiday spirit—and spirits—for their ears to be offended by the discordance.

Without thinking, my left hand began an arpeggiated jazz intro to “Angels from the Realms of Glory,” a hymn that wasn’t particularly well known as a sing-along carol, but had always been a nice, peaceful opener to my old set list—the same one I’d performed countless times in high school, when my parents made me spend my holiday breaks volunteering at the nursing home instead of video gaming.

After the first verse, I transitioned into an uptempo, but rather burnished “Deck the Halls,” and the infectious joy almost drowned out the horrid intonation of the piano.

It had been a long time since I’d played in public.

Long ago, I matriculated to college as a piano performance major, which meant I never *just played*. I *practiced* pieces that never got good enough. I *performed* them for dour-faced committees. There was no happy medium. My instrument had quickly become a stressor.

I hated it. I burned out. I quit.

Majored in Biology instead. Something where the answers were objective. A clear right or wrong. Not another "you're almost there."

Sometime during the last five or so years, I'd started playing again. Really playing. Focusing on nothing, just zoning out to the rhythms, improvising like I'd never done before, and relishing what it felt like to create beauty.

There was a tactile satisfaction to making music: the buoyancy of the keys, the extension of my muscles when my hands stretched to span a tenth, the tension of the sustain pedal under a leather-soled Oxford.

I could close my eyes and hear the notes bloom in ways that were altogether different from the past. Most people didn't talk about how good it felt. How fun it was to savor those tiny, sensual pleasures.

Now, I played to relax or to navigate my feelings. It was the one thing I did solely for myself. My therapy. It was what I did to avoid a different kind of burnout: the compassion fatigue that crept up insidiously on deathcare workers.

But tonight, it was nice to play with others again. Their happy voices, lubricated by alcohol, and the kind of laughter that only came with friendships that were deep and long-lasting. It warmed my insides, being a part of it—even if I was only a tiny part.

Halfway through "O, Holy Night," which Decca's husband, Gus, and his brother were absolutely killing in the vocal department, I caught Daphne's figure out of the corner of my eye, blotting her eyes with the sleeve of her light blue sweater.

Crying. *She couldn't be crying.* I couldn't stop to console her.

I flubbed a chord, my fingers getting lost somewhere along the way. Watching her become emotional made me lose all concentration.

What was it that made her cry? Where was her family? She mentioned something about her dad. *Before he'd gotten sick.* If he was still alive, whatever it was must've happened a long time ago, since she'd mentioned it in the same breath as her childhood race car bed.

Oh, Lord. It was cute as fuck that she'd had a race car bed. I never even had a race car bed. And I had... well, everything.

I transitioned into "Silent Night," the universal last carol. Daphne seemed better now, holding one of Decca's hands and sipping her pink can of bubbly water with pink-painted lips through a pink straw.

"Thanks, Chris. That was a nice surprise," Gus said, reaching out a hand for me to shake. We'd had words earlier. It seemed my playing had been a step toward healing the strain I'd caused.

"Yeah, man. Great playing." Waylon, the detective who'd been holding a baby on his hip most of the night, also reached out to shake my hand after Gus.

"Tell me again why we joined a hockey team instead of a band?" Gus asked Waylon.

Waylon shrugged. "We don't have a drummer?"

"I could take drum lessons," Soula said.

"No, you can't. Remember when you were fourteen and you wanted to learn the hammered dulcimer? You made your teacher quit," Gus said.

"I don't ask so many questions now. I can read the room."

A look passed between Waylon and Gus. "Can you, though?" Waylon kissed the top of his wife's head.

I left the siblings and their spouses to their conversation and snuck away to check on Daphne.

There was a flash of blue outside, next to the raging bonfire that looked almost hot enough to chase away the frigid temps—now negative four.

I pulled on my coat and stepped outside.

The air bit into my skin where it was unprotected: my face, my hands, my neck. Daphne still had the scarf I'd looped around her neck this morning and the gloves I'd later lent her. I didn't have the heart to ask for them back. I didn't *want* them back. My lizard brain wanted her to keep them, let them comfort and warm her body, so she'd think of me every time she wore them.

She didn't turn at the sound of my footsteps, not even when I stopped next to her in front of the fire. As hot as the blaze was, she shivered and folded her arms across her chest.

I slipped my coat off and draped it over her shoulders. The air was so cold when it hit my back that it sucked the breath from my lungs. She smiled sadly in thanks.

"You play beautifully," she said finally. A slight smile stretched across her mouth as her eyes met mine. "Not like a duke at all. You play like... you."

"What was it that made you cry?" I asked.

"I wasn't *crying* crying. I just..." She shook her head and let out an exasperated groan. "When you dropped me off at my mom's earlier, I was supposed to go caroling with them."

"Them?"

"My mom and stepdad, stepbrother, and sisters. Twins. I can't carol—I can't carry a tune in a bucket—but the point is, we'd made plans. They left without me."

"Were you alone? If I'd known, I would have brought you with me to my mom and dad's for lunch." I faced her, rotating my body to warm my backside. The position gave me a better view of her face, still open and vulnerable, even with whatever she was thinking about. The flames danced in her downcast eyes.

"No, my stepbrother didn't go with them. We watched Die Hard."

"Ah. For the record—not a Christmas movie."

"Agreed. Still good, though. Listen, I'm sorry to be a downer. I just get a little melancholy this time of year."

"I know how you feel."

Dozens of questions popped into my head. I wanted to know everything about her. I wanted to pry it out of her so I could make it better.

But I kept my mouth shut. It wasn't my business. She didn't owe me her life story. She didn't need me to save her, as much as I wanted to.

Jesus, I'd never even thought about saving anyone. I didn't know why her vulnerability cried out to me.

"I don't know what it is about Christmas," she continued. "Maybe it just highlights how I thought life should be: warm and cozy and bursting with love and acceptance. And mine never was. It wasn't bad. It just... they try to include me—my mom's family—but I add a weird formality to the dynamic. My stepbrother and my sisters—they're always on their best behavior whenever I'm around. I think I would have preferred fighting." She sounded tired. Her voice lacked the emotion it usually carried. *Usually.* As if I'd known her longer than—I glanced at my watch—fourteen hours. God, this had been a long day. A thrilling, eventful, life-altering day. But only a day.

"I used to hope somebody would adopt me. A lovely older couple who'd low-key hate me at first, but they'd whisk me off to Prince Edward Island, and soon, they'd grow to love me so hard they couldn't imagine their lives without me."

"I can't imagine anyone wouldn't immediately love you," I said to the fire. I hadn't meant to say it out loud, but I had, and I wasn't even that mad about it. Something about this woman made me abandon my senses.

I couldn't tell in the moon and firelight, but she looked like my words had hit their mark, like they'd meant something.

"It doesn't do anything to complain, I know. But when I have kids—*if I have kids*—I'll never let them think they aren't the most important things in my life."

"What about your dad? He's the one you lived with, right?"

"Dad's fine. He's just... I don't know, haunted. He was in the army. A mortuary officer. He'd seen too many bad things to be there for anyone else. Especially an eight-year-old daughter. He couldn't really handle the family holiday stuff, so the years I wasn't with Mom, Dad and I didn't do anything. I'm grateful. Really. So many people have it so much worse than I ever did."

She laughed like she was embarrassed, and raised a hand to cover her eyes. "Don't look at me like that. I know I sound like a spoiled brat. I am. I'm a spoiled brat. Let's just go back inside and pretend I never said any of this. I'm not a terrible person, I swear."

She leaned into me, whether it was for physical warmth or companionship, I didn't care. Her nearness made my nerve endings explode. I'd take any bit of that feeling I could.

The logs in the fire shifted off-center, sending sparks eddying up into the night sky.

"I used to wish I'd been adopted, too," I said. I had no right to complain, but I hoped it would make her feel less alone. "I hoped that one day, my real parents would discover where I was, and they'd come back for me. And I'd have three brothers and HBO so I could watch *Fraggle Rock*, like my friends. I don't think you can call yourself a real kid unless you've considered what it might be like if you were born into a different family."

"What was your childhood like?"

"Not bad, just unusual."

"Because you're rich?"

"Why do you think that?"

"Think what? That you're rich? Because you are. Obviously."

I looked into eyes filled with mischief and challenge. "You're very perceptive. It's not obvious to most people. In fact, I pride myself on how well I usually disguise it. You caught me on an unusual weekend. I was in town for brunch with my parents when Decca called me out on a case she said I'd enjoy."

"Did you enjoy it?"

"One part of it," I admitted. Her teeth scraped across her rose-stained lower lip, but the look in her eyes was anything but coy.

"So, what do The Rich do for the holidays?"

"I don't know about the rest of the one percent, but I spent most holidays working in my parents' charity kitchens," I said, stoking the fire back toward the center of the pit. A welcome blast of heat wrapped around my body as the logs locked into a new position.

Her eyebrows raised as she moved even closer.

"Did you lack for love?" she asked. I could see the change in her when she was no longer in the spotlight. She became brighter, empathy shining out of her as she turned her light on me. This was what she needed. Plumbing the depths of my disappointments seemed to work like a shut-off valve for her own.

"I lacked for nothing. It's just... my parents like to give back. Christmas was hectic with charity work, on top of our regular giving. Sometimes it would have been nice to have Christmas dinner on Christmas. Decorate the tree as a family rather than leave it for our people while we ran around, frantically trying to feed the entire homeless population of Nashville. There was this never-ending need to be useful to everyone else, while ignoring the special, quiet moments I saw others have. It made the holidays sort of sad. Anyway, first-world problems." I shrugged. "I'm not traumatized, just annoyed."

"It doesn't mean your feelings aren't valid. Same as mine. You're just as entitled to a little seasonal depression."

"Thank you, but you've seen my car. I have a tremendous amount of privilege. My parents love me. I know that. I have everything I could possibly want." *Or, I did until now.*

Daphne's hand brushed my elbow before running down the sleeve of my thin sweater. Icy cold met my hand. I looked down to find her fingers lacing between mine.

"I always wondered what it would be like to have that greeting card commercial Christmas. Where everyone piles onto a couch with hot cocoa and watches movies under a shared blanket. Or cookie baking that erupts into a flour fight. I think it's okay to mourn the loss of our... I don't know what they are. Presumptions? Misconceptions?"

I swallowed hard, forgetting to breathe for a few moments. Forgetting to move. Forgetting everything but the feel of her fingers in mine, as cold as we both were.

I wanted to warm the side of her body the fire wasn't reaching, to feel her frozen lips pressing against mine, her breath on my cheek, my hands tangling in the soft-looking strands of her hair.

My left arm was pressed into her side, and I'd never been more aware of the skin on that limb. Electricity shot through my entire body, beginning with those points of connection, making my heart jolt from her nearness.

She made a sort of moaning sound in agreement.

I clasped her hand tighter, pulling it into my chest, turning toward her and bringing her closer to me.

"Chris?"

"Yes." I looked into her eyes. One, hot and fiery. The other shrouded in the cold blue from shadows the light couldn't touch. I was desperate to cling to this tenuous moment without knowing how.

"I'm sorry." She shook her head. "I hope I didn't ruin the happy party vibes."

I smiled. "You couldn't ruin anything."

Pulled her closer, holding her elbows. Her eyes never left mine. What was she seeing? It was probably only the fire reflected in my glasses, but surely there was something more there. My desire. Our chemistry. It was impossible to hide my own fire for her any longer.

Her lips parted, but no words came—only a thick puff of vapor. Her breath was barely warm against my mouth as I leaned in. Closer. So slowly. Not because I was hesitant, but because I needed to stretch this moment out like taffy.

Her eyes, her cheeks, her aquiline nose morphed with kaleidoscopic symmetry, the surreal image shifting into a new pattern with each millimeter closer. Our warm breath collided, hinting at the fires burning big and hot inside us both. My lips just barely brushed hers when her eyes fluttered closed.

"I don't remember a winter this cold. Ever," said an obnoxiously loud voice. "Where's your—oh my God, sorry guys."

I sighed and pinched the bridge of my nose under my glasses, expecting Daphne to jump out of my arms. But she didn't pull away. She smiled warmly, as if she hadn't been embarrassed at all to be caught with me.

I dropped my hands, still taking in a delighted Daphne for a few more seconds.

I'd wanted to extend the moment. My wish had been granted. Our lips had barely touched.

"I'm sorry I ruined your moment," Decca slurred.

"It's time for me to head out, anyway," I said to Daphne. "I'll be back tomorrow morning. Is seven too early? I'd like to get to the lab before noon."

"Yes," Decca said.

"No," Daphne said simultaneously.

The two women looked at each other.

"Why don't you take Daphne home with you. Have you got a place for her to sleep? That way, you can just leave from there and already be closer to the highway."

I nodded. "There's a bed for her." Her pupils widened.

Oh. *Shit.* I didn't mean it like *that.*

Something was wrong. This was too good to be true. Something had to go wrong. I racked my brain for potential complications. "My parents aren't home. I took them to the airport this afternoon. They're traveling for the holidays. It would just be me. And you. Would that make you uncomfortable?"

Daphne's lips quirked up. "No." She said it like a dare.

A thrill rushed through me, the exhilaration of the cold mixing with the way she was biting her lip and threading her fingers through mine. This was happening.

I squeezed her hand. I couldn't wait to get out of here.

I'd woken up this morning with a summons to work.

My dental practice was closed between now and New Year's. The school and the lab were closed even longer between semesters. I'd been thrilled for my parents when they'd asked if I minded them finally taking their trip to Germany this Christmas, but that meant I was now looking at weeks curled up alone in my apartment. More alone than usual. Reading, writing up some overdue research, cooking a single Christmas salmon filet, exchanging gifts with Nubi—and I already knew she was giving me a Montblanc chronograph and matching fountain pen this year. I'd had to wrap them myself, since feline paws weren't exactly deft in the arts of folding and taping.

My holiday vacation would be cozy enough, and I enjoyed being alone. Like I'd told Daphne earlier, Christmas was more a time for being "on duty" rather than gathering with loved ones in front of a tree.

Like a geek, I'd been grateful for the distraction of work. Like a man, I'd been even more grateful for the distraction of Daphne. I was eager to spend more time with her. All the time with her.

The promise of Daphne spending the night with me, even if it was in only in one of the guest bedrooms in my parents' house, was intoxicating. A three-hour drive to Knoxville with her, where I'd get to hear more of her smoky voice as she teased me about my lack of mechanical skills and talked about my research and hers, flooded me with happiness. It did so much more than waylay those solitary hours I'd be spending over the next couple weeks.

These were the feelings I'd been waiting for. Holy fuck.

I'd never felt like this before. I'd never met someone and known almost immediately that they were important. Daphne was a respite. The first drops of a perfect cabernet. This was more than just three more hours of distraction. It was like being saved from a disaster I hadn't known I was experiencing.

She was pulling me from a building filled with carbon monoxide, and I was suddenly breathing oxygen.

Chapter 4

Daphne

CHRIS TURNED INTO THE driveway, and the tall iron gate opened automatically. Minutes later—*whole ass minutes!*—the house, if you could call it that, came into view.

It was low but sprawling, and completely gorgeous. This wasn't some boring, cookie-cutter McMansion. This was an old money home, its design somewhere between Southern charm and English country manor. A winterized fountain stood in the center of the circular drive we bypassed before parking in an adjacent coach house.

Suddenly, Chris felt like he was on the opposite end of a ridiculous spectrum of humanity from me. It was odd that I'd gotten as close as sharing an almost-kiss with someone who lived like this.

Inside, the house was cold, empty, and dark. The only light seeped in from the fluffy swaths of lit garlands that hung outside each window.

In here, it was a ghost of Christmas. The cool blue of night with only a dim glow around the edges.

I didn't have to see much to know I'd never been in such an opulent space before. But quietly opulent, where real people lived and presumably did normal-people things like eating, and bathing, and pretending to watch a movie while zoning out on their phones.

What were these people like—living here, spending the holidays in Germany? Chris's parents. If Chris was any indication, they probably weren't as snobby as this place looked.

There was a generosity of spirit in him I wouldn't have expected if I'd met him in this mansion instead of on the train tracks. It went beyond his occupation. There was a sense of softness, of sadness about him. Maybe because he'd spent so long in forensics. Maybe that'd happen to me, too, once I worked in the field as long.

But there was that kiss.

It was everything I dreamed an almost-kiss could be. It was a fire that burned through my core and weakened my structure, leaving me a burned-out hull on Decca's patio. Something ravenous lurked inside the softly sad man with the cool glasses and crooked smile.

"Want something to drink?" He shrugged out of his coat and hung it up on a real hanger in a real closet, instead of a hook behind the door. As an anthropologist, I was always interested in how different societies lived. This was as foreign and as fascinating to me as an ancient civilization.

"I don't suppose you have any hot cocoa? This doesn't really seem like a Swiss Miss packet kind of place." Chris hung up my beat-up thrift store biker jacket next to his and smiled that adorably crooked smile that turned my insides to goo.

"I'll see what I can scrounge up." He moved his hand to the light switch.

"Oh no. Don't turn them on."

"Why not? There's no one to disturb. We're the only ones here."

"It's just... I'm afraid to see how big this house really is. What if I like it too much? All this wealth and luxury. What if it's so much I start hating you for being rich when you've been so nice to me?"

To his credit, he laughed. He was so much more down-to-earth than he had any reason to be, and it—*oh, God*—it squeezed my heart. "Are you holding that against me?" Something in his eyes almost looked worried. "Should I start behaving like Scrooge, throw you out in the snow without a tuppence?"

"I don't think you could be a Scrooge if you tried."

The kitchen was surprisingly not huge. It was also homey, or at least it looked that way in the blue light from outside.

Chris stood in the yellow glow of the open fridge door, looking for something. "You drink dairy?"

"I drink and eat everything."

He smirked. "Noted."

After setting a pan of milk to heat on the gas burner of a huge French stove, he rummaged through cupboards until he produced a fat bar of fancy-looking chocolate and began chopping it into shards on the antique butcher block island. The crunch of the blade reverberated through the silence of the empty house. I studied him, entranced by the way he'd moved through the kitchen. His steps seemed choreographed for the most efficient, elegant paths around the island, fridge, and stove. His knife skills made him look like a chef.

When I stepped closer, that smirk ghosted his lips again. Without looking up, he pinched a perfect square of chocolate between his fingers and held it in front of my mouth. He nudged his glasses up with the wrist of his knife hand before finally bringing his eyes to mine with a sighing breath—as if it hadn't been his idea. He was forced to do this by a secret flirting compulsion.

My heart beat faster. My body was melting as fast as the candy in his hand. I had two choices. I could open my hand, holding my palm under his to catch the chocolate he'd probably intended to drop into my hand as a kindness. Or I could… not.

I leaned closer, parting my lips, holding his gaze even as his eyelids drooped seductively lower, his own mouth falling open with mine.

He placed the candy in my mouth, drawing his fingers slowly off my tongue as I moaned. Swallowing hard, he pressed his lips together, and went back to his task, only he looked… lost. His hands supported him as he leaned forward, gripping the edges of the island with the knife clenched in his fist.

His chest rose and fell as heavily as mine, blinking at his pile of chocolate shavings like it was something foreign. Whatever was happening between us was big. Deafening. Consuming.

I could barely taste the chocolate melting on my tongue. Tasting would mean focusing on a sense Chris wasn't sharing with me, and I wanted every part of him with me right now. I wanted to experience all of him everywhere. Not just sexually, just… him. His spirit. His Chris-ness.

I took one tentative step closer.

"Oh, fuck," he whispered. The knife clattered to the island, and all at once, his arms were around me, his lips pressing against mine, his warm body pushing me back against the counter.

He caressed my lips with his, digging his fingers into my hair with a desperate wildness.

Part of me couldn't believe this was happening. I wanted to breathe him in, get lost in his kiss. When his tongue slipped over my lower lip, heat ripped through my body. I groaned, deepening the kiss, needing more. His hands slid behind my thighs, gripping the backs and pulling me up, up and onto the counter, stepping into the space between my legs.

I rocked my pelvis, needing contact with him, but he wasn't close enough.

My legs wound around him, pulling him into me. He sucked in a breath of air when we made contact. In seconds, his cock went hard, pressing against the pleats of wool trousers, hitting me right where I wanted to feel him. The way he'd lost all control—so thoroughly, so fast—was intoxicating. I was out of my body but feeling everything: the heat of his mouth, the strength of his hands kneading my thighs, the strong square shoulders under his black sweater. Joy and pleasure and hope radiated through my body, bursting out like an explosion of light.

Then, I felt nothing.

Chris pulled away from the kiss. He inched his pelvis away from mine. Dropping his forehead, he adjusted his glasses again. A pained expression crossed his face. "I got chocolate on your jeans."

"It'll wash out," I said stupidly.

He spun around and turned off the flame under the milk, dumping the chopped chocolate into the pot.

"You're just going to go back to the cocoa after that?"

"I shouldn't have done that. You're a guest. I didn't want you to feel like you couldn't say no. There's a power imbalance."

"That's sweet, but who's on what side? Because it felt pretty fucking powerful to feel your cock get that hard the minute you were between my legs."

He bit his lip to stop his smile. "You think I'm being an ass?"

"Kind of."

"Okay."

"Okay?"

"I know better." He smirked. "But I'm choosing to believe you." He poured the steaming cocoa into two mugs and handed me one. "What do we drink to?"

"To this not being a blue Christmas."

After he'd given me the official tour of the *family side* of the house, we stood at opposite ends of his bedroom. His murky brown eyes were black as he looked at me across his childhood bed.

His king-size childhood bed. Something about it seemed so lonely—his mom and dad reading him stories and tucking him into this enormous bed in this enormous room.

The whole house was huge and lonely, as if it was only meant to be used for parties. With just the two of us here, it was an empty rib cage with no heart lub-dubbing away inside. He'd noticed my discomfort with this insane level of luxury: room after cavernous room of king-sized bed suites. He'd offered me his room if I'd wanted it. It was cozy, dark, and hugged me like I was inside a womb.

I did want—and more than just the room. I wanted him in it with me.

"I'll leave you to it, then. I'm just next door if you need anything."

In front of me on the bed, Chris had laid out a pair of his boxers and a neatly folded Harvard t-shirt, well-worn, its crimson faded to the pinky-brown color of a healthy liver. Obviously, it was a favorite. And maybe a flex, although I'd memorized his C.V. and already knew that was where he'd gone to dental school.

"Well..." He nodded once, definitively. He looked like he was about to leave, but he didn't. He hesitated awkwardly.

"You know..." I started.

A single eyebrow rose over the frame of his glasses.

"There's really no need for your parents to have to wash two sets of sheets when we leave. This bed is too big for me anyway. You could... sleep here, too. It's your bed, after all."

His mouth dropped open and an audible breath escaped. Pushing his tortoiseshell glasses higher onto his nose, he glanced at the bed. "My parents don't do the laundry." The light was dim, but I was pretty sure his cheeks were reddening. "They have someone."

He stood in place like he'd been stunned.

"Of course they do. Still." I dug my toes into the plush navy rug. The room was decorated floor to ceiling in a space theme, but this was more than just a comforter and matching rocket ship sheets. Standing in one corner was a blue velvet armchair, retrofitted into a scaled-down replica of the lunar module. An actual piece of one of the Mercury ships lay under thick protective glass on the bureau, and above us, a mural of celestial bodies mimicked the night sky.

My dad was a big space geek. One of our only vacations was to the Kennedy Space Center when I was twelve. It was the most hot and bored I'd ever been in my life. Between that excruciating visit—seriously, why couldn't we have gone to Universal Studios?—and all the NASA documentaries I'd been forced to watch, I knew way too much about a subject I intensely detested.

Maybe I wouldn't have hated it so much if I'd known a space aesthetic could be this pretty.

In honor of the season, someone had even decorated a Christmas tree with twinkling silver garland, blown glass stars, space shuttles, and satellites, topped with a gold beaded crescent moon. That might have been the saddest part of all: the idea of his *people* decorating a child's Christmas tree. His own solitary little tree. Except it wasn't little—it was full-size.

My heart ached for little Chris, tucked away in here with his space books and toys instead of a big, raucous family.

Then again, just because you were poor or you came from a big family didn't mean you had love, either. Maybe Chris and I were two loveless sad sacks destined to find each other.

I could tell he wasn't going to make the decision for us. I'd have to do it, even if asking for what I wanted made my skin crawl.

I closed the distance between us and reached out, covering the back of his hand with mine. I threaded our fingers together. "Please? Stay and cuddle with me?"

He looked down at our fingers as if they were something foreign to him, but he nodded slowly. "I'm trusting you on this. That you don't feel like you're being pressured to do this."

"Do what? It's just sleeping."

"Right." He let the delusion play.

"Is it okay if I shower first? I'm sure you have a guest bathroom somewhere on this property stocked with girl shampoo and conditioner. Maybe even a razor?"

"There's girl shampoo in the bathroom in the bedroom next door. To the left. Just open the drawers. Anything you need will be there. I'll take this one. It only has shampoo that identifies as male." He gave me one of his droopy smiles.

"Can...? Never mind."

"What?"

"I was going to ask if two people can shower at the same time, but in this house, it feels like a really stupid question."

"Why wouldn't we be able to?"

"That's what I mean. Stupid question. Obviously, you've never lived anywhere with a tiny water heater."

He smiled at me fully, bringing out more of the lopsidedness of his mouth. He seemed embarrassed about it earlier, looking away and letting those big smiles dissolve almost as quickly as they'd come out, like the sun going behind a cloud. Now the sun was bright and shiny. And he made me bright and shiny, too.

"Enjoy your shower. I dare you to use up all the hot water. Or get pruny trying."

I DID ENJOY IT. The shower alone was practically the size of my bedroom back home, and it took what would have been all the heat in Dad's hot water tank just to steam it up enough so I wouldn't freeze once I stepped around the glass partition.

I found fancy shampoo and conditioner, razors, softly fragranced, fine-milled soaps, lotions and oils with minimalist labels, and extra toothbrush heads for a high-end, sleek-looking electric toothbrush. Well, I should've expected that with Chris being a dentist for living people as well as the dead.

The scalding water bit into my skin. I stood under the downpour, letting the searing heat turn my skin pink, giving my body the sensation it craved.

When I padded back through the hall, wearing Chris's Harvard t-shirt under a fluffy, white robe (there were freshly-laundered guest robes hanging in the linen closet, just begging me to slip my arms into), his door was shut. When I knocked, there was no answer. I peeked in. The shower was still running in the en suite bathroom.

Damn. Apparently, he was even more desperate for the hot water than I was.

The room was darker, too. The overhead chandelier was off. The only glow came from the lamps flanking the bed—not rocket ship-themed, thank goodness.

I let the robe fall off my shoulders and pool on the floor, then pulled back the piles of blankets and the embroidered velvet duvet and sank between layers of pristine, ironed cotton.

The pillow was the perfect level of firmness to curl around my shoulders and allow my big head to sink into. Just for a minute, my eyes drifted closed. I didn't want sleep to overtake me. I didn't want to miss a moment of this hedonism. If this was what it felt like to be rich, I could definitely adjust my prejudices.

The bed moved, and my eyes opened. Chris was lying on his side facing me.

"Hi," I said sleepily.

"I didn't mean to wake you." He reached toward me and brushed his thumb across my cheek.

"I wanted you to. You promised you'd cuddle."

"I did."

I scooched closer. It was difficult under the weight of the covers and how tightly the sheet corners were hospitaled.

"Wait here."

He got up, and my eyes drifted closed again. It was euphoric, being in this bed that I imagined smelled like Chris, even though it hadn't really been *his* bed since high school and I doubted he smelled the same back then. Feeling the soft jersey of his old t-shirt slip against my perfumed skin, awaiting his arms to settle into. Hopefully, I could convince *more of him* to settle into me.

Even if he didn't want to... this night was still perfect. The whole day. I'd competently worked in the field, been the first person to handle the remains that were who-knows-how-many-years-old. I'd shared a meal with Decca and her friends, and now I was here.

For the first time, my future actually felt as bright as my teachers had always promised it would be. The prickle of anticipation was almost too much. My eyes grew hot as tears of gratitude pooled, leaking out the side onto the pillow.

"Hey," Chris said, kneeling on the bed. "What's the matter? I can sleep..."

I grabbed his hand. "Stay. I'm just grateful. Overwhelmed with it."

He stared down at me with a curious expression, not daring to move a muscle, even when I squeezed his hand. "Daphne," he said. It was a statement, like he just needed to say my name at that particular moment. Not to get my attention or change the subject. Just to feel the shape of it on his tongue.

"Water can only get so hot." He smiled, breaking the moment of reverence. It was a relief. I was liable to feel too much. I already was. He was, too. Wonder and excitement, curiosity and lust poured off him in waves. I absorbed the feelings into my body, taking them in, using them to strengthen me. I could conquer anything like this.

Stretching out his long legs, he tucked me against his side. Heat ran down my back, my waist, my hip, and thigh. "Look up."

With the flick of a switch, the ceiling transformed. The mural had been elevated from a pretty painting to a firmament. Tiny glittering lights—real lightbulbs—formed constellations and dotted paths across the trompe l'oeil night sky. I would have gasped if there were any breath left in my body. "Oh, Chris. This is heavenly."

"I guess that's the idea."

"Is that the Big Dipper?"

"Uh-huh. And Orion. Ursa Major. Cassiopeia." He pointed. "This was my nightlight. It's not mapped out accurately. That used to bother me.

Dumb to think about something like accuracy when you get to sleep under the stars every night."

I turned my head to watch him. He'd removed his glasses. I'd never seen him with them off. The handsomeness of his face didn't come as a shock. He was clearly a good-looking man, but without his tortoiseshell shield, he looked even more boyish. More vulnerable.

I moved a bit farther away, leaning on my elbow to see him better, and ran my hands through the damp tufts of his short, dark hair.

"I don't think it counts as cuddling unless you're on my arm." He grinned.

"Are those the rules?"

"Yes. And I'm sorry to say you're breaking them."

"What if I want more than cuddling?" I asked.

He took in a breath. "You'll have to be specific."

"Kissing?"

"I wouldn't mind kissing you again." He made no move to do it, though.

"And maybe... touching."

His eyes flashed. "I guess it depends. Touching who? Where?"

"Me. Touching you. On your chest... your arms... your thighs." My hands followed the path my words had cut. Goosebumps erupted when I traced his biceps under the sleeve of his t-shirt. He let out a pleased breath when I got to the line that ran down the side of his quads. "You. Touching me. Anywhere... everywhere."

"Mmhmm." He nodded. "We can amend the plan to include kissing and touching. Is there anything else you want to add to tonight's agenda?"

"Well, since we're already here, sharing this big bed. Under the stars. And we have this chemistry. I think... sex would be nice."

"It would be nice. As long as you're sure you don't feel pressure."

"Chris?"

"Mm?" he intoned drowsily.

"I already know you're a great guy. You can stop it with the power dynamics. It's really hard for me to ask for what I want. This is me basically begging you at this point, okay? *Begging.*"

"In that case..."

"Chris, I'm going to kiss you now, if that's okay."

"No." He raised an eyebrow. His fingers threaded into the wet hair at the nape of my neck, scratching through my scalp, pulling me toward him until only our breath was touching. "I'm going to kiss *you* now."

My eyes closed at the moment of contact. His full lips were hot on mine as he pressed me against him, softly but with enough pressure to let me know he was the one in control. He was the one guiding me.

I hadn't expected him to be like this—without hesitation or doubt, just straight in for the kill—although the kitchen should have given me a clue.

His lips cradled mine, gently and softly, nestling in but going no further. He planted kiss after kiss, small and warm, plotting my mouth like a map, in no hurry and with no particular order.

I nudged his lips apart, in a rush to deepen the kiss and taste that strong peppermint of his industrial-strength toothpaste, but he held back. A low chuckle rumbled near my mouth. His tongue stroked my bottom lip before pinching it between his own and lavishing all his attention there. Still so in control.

My body moved of its own accord, inching closer to his and grinding myself against him.

He reached down and found my knee, pulling my leg up and pressing his body down against mine, hard, exactly where I needed him to be.

Tearing himself away from our kiss, he moved his face back, trying to see me clearly without his glasses. His eyes were wide, almost crazed, nostrils flared, lips reddened and swollen from my bites and tugs. Oh God, he looked feral. For me. Ravenous and ready to plunge forward.

He rolled his hips against mine, tentatively at first, staring into my eyes as he did. I moaned. He did it again, stroking himself against me, feeding my desire. His teeth were bared and gritted, as if this was something primal.

Besides my shirt—*his* shirt—I wore nothing. I hadn't wanted to dirty my last pair of clean undies before the drive home tomorrow, and I'd really hoped we'd be doing exactly this, so I hadn't bothered with the boxers he'd lent me. Only, I didn't think *he* had any idea how close we actually were. How the friction from his cotton jammie pants was rubbing directly against my wet clit. How any minute now, his erection could slip free and we'd be skin to skin.

We needed a condom. Like now. Damn, this escalated fast. It was exactly what I wanted, but he seemed more like the third-date type.

Whatever. We'd fuck after our third date, too.

I brought my hand between us, squeezing his cock through the soft cotton. He thrust slowly into my hand. Lust-drunk eyes held my gaze.

"Can you even see me without your glasses?"

"W-what? Uh... a little." He squinted.

I smiled. "Do you have a condom? There's some in my bag. I don't care if you dig."

He stilled, seeming to need a moment to understand words. How had this brilliant man been reduced to this? Had I done this to him? Or was this just how he was with sex? Did he go feral for every woman?

I didn't want to think about him with other women.

He swung off the bed and put his glasses back on before rifling through my overnight bag.

"This is a big box."

I shrugged. "Have you seen you?"

"You bought these for me? For... us?"

"I had a feeling."

He looked... I couldn't tell if he wanted to throw up or hit something. He rocked back onto the balls of his feet and stood effortlessly. Staring at it like it was evidence instead of contraception, he precisely placed the box on the nightstand before looking at me.

And that was all he did. He looked. And kept looking. As if trying to solve me.

Just as I was about to check in with him again—at that point, buying a box of condoms *just in case* felt like more of my typical wishful thinking—he came back to himself.

"I don't know where you came from," he took a deep breath, "or much else about you. But I feel like there's something..." He paused and looked away, as if trying to find not only the right words, but the right sentiment, the right ideas to express, "...happening here. I know this sounds like a line; I don't even know you at all yet, but I feel like I've known you forever. I've never felt more myself with anyone than I have today. With you. Do you—you feel this too, right?"

I nodded, unable to say anything. He'd already said it. The uncanny *knowing* that this was... something.

"Chris." I reached for him, needing him close the way I'd never needed anyone before.

He crawled onto the mattress and pulled me on top. His fingertips burned as he gripped my waist, just feeling my skin under the shirt. I straddled him, reaching forward to pull off his glasses.

"No." He shook his head. "I want to see you. I want you on top so I can see every face you make. Every breath that flutters the hair around your temples." His hands skated under my shirt and cupped my breasts, rubbing my nipples with his thumbs. "Every wrinkle on your pretty nipples as they harden."

I rocked against him, arching my back until my boobs filled his capable hands. Delicate, elegant hands that fixed kids' teeth and expertly stretched across the piano keys, not twisting greasy bolts of an old car, like mine.

Slowly, I lifted the hem of my shirt and drew it up over my head, tossing it onto the floor.

He sucked in a breath. "God, you're beautiful."

I wouldn't have believed him except he'd said those words with such awe.

I leaned forward to kiss him, gaspingly deep.

"You're a succubus. That's what you are. Stealing my soul. I'm undone with you. I've never..." I rubbed my pussy over his erection that was peeking out from his open seam, and a sound escaped from the back of his mouth. "Never felt like this. Out of control. Owned. I apologize in advance if this isn't going to be good tonight. I have no idea what I'm doing with you."

"You think I have any clue? I've never been so turned on. Just promise you'll be honest. Tell me what's happening as it's happening. Even if you don't know what's happening." I moaned into his kiss. "I will too."

With his help, I shimmied down his pants and rolled the condom on. He sucked in a breath, bracing himself. I laughed at the monumental feeling of it all. "We've got to stop this. Both of us. It's just fun."

I tweaked his nipple hard to punctuate my point. Then I leaned over and soothed it with my mouth, staring up at him while he bit his lip to stifle a groan.

His body felt so good under mine. Lean but strong and every bit as warm as the scalding shower I'd just taken.

Wrapping his hands around my waist, he rocked me against him, robbing me of the strength to stay upright. I was already close by the time I rose up onto my knees and took him inside, agonizingly slow, swallowing his cock, inch by inch, allowing us both to adjust to the thrill of our joining.

The muscles in his stomach and chest rippled as he breathed and fought to hold himself back.

“Open your eyes,” he said. “Look at me.”

He looked so different beneath me, inside me, than he did on the scene, standing in the cold, reluctantly taking care of everyone around him. This morning he’d immediately struck me as a handsome man. Now, like this, he was mine. Like he’d always been mine. There was never a time before when he wasn’t; we’d just been waiting until now to find each other.

His face was so familiar; the angular cut of his prominent zygomatics, the plump lips that widened into a lopsided smile over perfectly straight, white teeth, his large warm eyes shadowed by a strong, straight brow ridge. I’d already memorized his face.

One hand came up to cradle the back of my head, lacing his fingers into my hair, tugging me where he wanted as he rocked his pelvis against me. Oh, God, it felt good being controlled by him. His pubic bone rubbed my clit just right. Sparks shot off all over my body, running down my arms into my fingertips. I felt the pleasure down to my toes as he repeated the motion.

There was no rhythm, no repetition. No propulsion toward a pinnacle experience. It was quiet and profound as both of us sank into the feeling of our bodies joined together.

He kissed me softly and reverently. I rocked my hips and he moaned into my mouth, his enjoyment deepening my own. Already, I felt my pussy growing heavier.

"Jesus Christ, you feel good." He said, through gritted teeth. It was clear he was holding back, but I didn’t urge him to let go. I selfishly enjoyed the way he tortured himself. For me.

His fingers trailed down from my head, lingering for a moment on the outer curves of my breasts before gripping my hips, fisting the flesh, urging me deeper onto his cock, rocking me harder against him.

His painful grip was enough to pull my attention to the sensations of my body, and I let myself go, chasing the pleasure as it built.

"Yes, sweetheart, come for me. Use me. Get yourself off."

Words hitched in my throat, caught between grunts and hoarse moans. My head whipped back as I arched, leaning away from him and using his thighs to bolster my momentum.

"You're a fucking goddess, Daphne." His hands came back to my breasts and he teased my rock-hard nipples, sending more sensation to my clit. A low wail escaped from deep in my chest as my orgasm built and built. It wouldn't stop. The pleasure came in waves, until all at once, it exploded out of me from every nerve ending.

My body shook, crumpling like a dried leaf, pulling him down with me. He kissed me hard as he pumped into me with a jerking, shuddering motion, and came with a grunt right along with me.

He stroked my hair as his cock pulsed inside me, telling me sweet words I couldn't quite understand. Fucking beautiful. Something about watching me come over and over again.

The mattress jostled, and a few seconds later, I heard the click of the bathroom door. I could still feel Chris inside me, filling me so completely, giving me his tenderness and compassion and admiration with every thrust.

I could barely move. I didn't want to move. My celestial view was all I needed. They could bury me here, naked and splayed on his bed under these incandescent stars.

When the bed dipped again, Chris was moving me, pulling me against him. He said nothing. He didn't have to. It was proprietary. I was his now. I belonged to him.

"I wish I could feel this forever."

"Feel what?" His voice was deeper, gravelly in the aftermath of his orgasm.

"I don't know. It's just... good. Right." Perfect was what I wanted to say, but that was jinxing it.

I'd never been more in tune with my body and at peace with my soul. It was like I needed him to become fully myself. Maybe he did too.

"Maybe..."

He lifted his head off the pillow as he absentmindedly traced my nipple with his middle finger.

"Maybe we could stay here for Christmas," I said quietly, my head resting against Chris's chest. I felt his deep breath.

"We have the skull."

"One more day? Please, Chris? I'm not ready to leave this bed yet. The stars are too beautiful. Let me see what it's like to be old money for a day."

He chuckled underneath me, but his silence made me nervous. I had two choices; I could let myself be dulled, wondering if I was overstepping somewhere; or I could continue to be my full, unapologetic self and pretend not to care what he thought of me.

I chose the latter. Better to show my true colors, even if they were a manic pixie rainbow, than try to live in black and white for a man and still fail at it.

"You've spent every holiday working your tail off in a soup kitchen somewhere. I got to watch my brother and sisters celebrate Christmas from the sidelines. We've got a lot of work to do, Chris."

"Work?"

"Yeah. From now on, we're making our own holiday traditions."

Chapter 5

Chris

I STRETCHED MY HAND across the bed, searching for the warmth my body was missing. I'd fallen asleep curled protectively around Daphne. Now she was gone.

The bed was still warm where she'd lain. I opened my eyes to a blur of glare as light streamed in through the open curtains. A figure stood next to the Christmas tree, looking out onto the leafless landscape below.

I groaned, turning around, checking my phone on the nightstand.

Seven-thirty.

Plenty of time to have a leisurely morning and still make it to Knoxville before noon.

I put on my glasses so I could see Daphne; not just her dark silhouette. She hadn't turned yet. I didn't know what caught her attention out there, but I was grateful for the opportunity to take her in.

Her back was to me. Her head turned in profile, highlighting her prominent nose. I loved her nose. It was too large, too Roman to give her face that generic beauty of an Instagram model. It gave her character, and added to her allure. *Patrician.* That was the word for her. With her creamy pale skin, that deep cupid's bow of her lip, her striking cheekbones, she could have been honed from marble and crowned in laurel, the frozen representation of a mythological goddess. *Daphne,* her namesake. Her long, blonde hair, still snarled from sleep, looked almost white in the early morning light. When she hugged her body, the motion pulled her shirt tight across her back, revealing the nip of her waist and elongated curves of her hips under the crimson t-shirt.

Finally, she turned, her face exploding into a wide, toothy smile and eyes that crinkled in the corners. Oh, God. To wake up every day to that look... it would be worth all the pain, all the heartbreak I'd ever experienced.

She ran over and hopped onto all fours on the bed. "Merry Christmas Eve Eve." She leaned over and gave me a chaste kiss on the lips before I'd had a chance to respond.

"I don't think that's a thing."

"Who's to say it can't be though? Except, once it starts, where does it end? Merry Christmas Eve Eve Eve? Four Eves. Fifteen? All the way up to Thanksgiving, and Halloween, the way the retail stores are going. Okay, I see your point. I'll save it for tomorrow."

She yelped as I put my hands on her waist and rolled her beneath me. "Do you ever stop talking?" I asked, looking down into her soft gray eyes.

"Only in my sleep. Sometimes not even then. Only I make even less sense. It's always cheeseburgers taking the alligator for a walk and—*Oh!* There was one time I got shot in a dream and it felt really good. Losing all that blood felt relaxing, like sinking into a warm pool."

My glasses slipped off my ears as I kept my body dutifully away from hers. Last night was last night. It was magical. It was spiritual. But maybe sex was always magical and spiritual for her. We hadn't talked about anything continuing beyond a single encounter. I didn't want to presume.

"Do you think it really feels like that? Like stepping into a warm pool?"

"What does?"

"Getting shot."

I looked at the empty pillow beside her. My brain had automatically assigned it as *her pillow*.

"Um..." I shook my head, trying to pull the brakes and stop the train of thought my body had been following. "I think... getting shot feels like your skin exploding, shattering your nerves, but not enough to render them incapable of sensation. Bones crushing, splintering apart as the path of the bullet snakes through your body, rupturing and bruising tender organs. And if there's an exit wound, more skin ripped apart, as if an animal is clawing its way out. But it happens all at once, and you'd feel it for at least twenty to forty minutes until you've gotten to an ER and the docs have administered the first dose of morphine."

"Mm. That's the opposite of a warm bath, then."

"So much for that dream. Our pool is heated, though. You can go for a swim later. Is that bougie enough for you." I shot up. "I'm going to brush my teeth."

"You're coming back to bed, right? I've already brushed mine, I thought you'd appreciate the effort before I kissed you."

"Do you want me to come back?" My dick throbbed inside my boxers. Her eyes tracked down my body.

She sat up, nodding with a hungry smile, as she flipped the t-shirt over her head, baring a vast expanse of gorgeous, naked breasts and pebbled pink nipples.

Fuck, I needed to be inside her again, immediately.

I brushed my teeth for the required two minutes. The time had never passed that slowly. I counted the seconds with my breaths. Daphne naked. In my bed. Waiting.

"I'm already starting," she called from the bedroom.

White foam trailed from the corner of my mouth. My eyes closed. She was touching herself. Daphne was in my bed, touching herself. My dick throbbed again, painfully. I swore it was sentient when it came to her. It reacted uncontrollably. I'd never been this fiendish before.

I spat into the sink. "Tell me what you're doing."

"I'm pinching my nipples."

Oh fuck. Those nipples. Those big rosy peaks that had felt so perfect rolled between my thumbs and forefingers last night. Standing so proud on my tongue. I couldn't wait to taste them again. Taste the rest of her.

I braced myself on the edge of the marble countertop, letting my head drop between my shoulders. My cock was so heavy and thick with blood, it almost pulled me down. She was going to be the death of me.

The toothbrush shut off in my hand. I had to restart it to actually finish brushing.

"Move your right hand lower. Touch your pussy. Make yourself wet. By the time I get out there, I want you glistening."

There was a breath and then, "I already am."

Ow. Fuck. The toothbrush skidded across my incisors, and stabbed the inside of my cheek.

I cupped my cheek with my other hand and continued the path across my front teeth. Brushing had never been such torture.

Finally, the toothbrush shut off. Daphne moaned quietly.

I spat out the remaining toothpaste and wiped my mouth.

"I thought you'd never be done."

I said nothing. When I came around the corner and saw her, my heart was skipping into arrhythmia. Her head snapped to the right, and something like relief spread across her face.

I threw back the covers, my eyes immediately locking on her delicate fingers teasing herself. I watched her work, studied the way she dragged her middle finger straight up through her center before tracing a wide circle around her clit. She did it slowly, her hips moving in rhythm with her hand.

"Chris," she said with need in her voice.

"What is it, sweetheart?"

"You're here now. Touch me."

I shook my head slowly, still unable to tear my eyes away from what she was doing to herself. She was so free with her body, so generous in allowing me to see so much of her. "I want to watch you come."

She moaned. "I need you."

"No. You can do this all by yourself. Look at you—so wet, so beautiful. Give me this, baby. Please?" I kissed her forehead.

She reached lower, dipping her middle finger into her vagina before bringing it back up to swirl over her clit once more. Still agonizingly slowly, she brushed the pads of her fingers over her lips with the lightest touches. Maybe she was sensitive. Maybe any more pressure and it would be too much. I tried to memorize the pattern she was creating, imagining it was my tongue and not her fingers.

It would be soon enough.

"Will you touch yourself? Come with me?"

I swallowed a laugh. "I might come just from this... watching you."

Her fingers worked herself a little faster and her legs fell open. My eyes were ready to pop out of my skull when her inner lips spread like butterfly wings.

Her arousal soaked her beautiful cunt.

Her mouth was open. Panting. Her back arching off the bed. When she looked at me, there was uncertainty in her eyes.

I'd give her certainty. It was only a matter of saying out loud what I'd already been thinking.

"Your pussy is fucking beautiful, Daphne."

Her ribs flared out on an inhale, plump breasts bouncing as she fucked her hand. Those eraser-head nipples pointed toward the sky.

I squeezed my dripping cock. "It's taking everything in me not to sink to my knees and rub my face all over your perfect cunt."

"Please," she whimpered.

I nodded. "After you come."

"I n-need you."

"You don't." I stepped closer, still standing over her, staring down. "Show me, darling. Show me how you come. Let me see how perfect you look."

Her toes scrunched, gripping the sheet, upper back arched off the bed as her orgasm gripped her and possessed her body. Her breath was ragged and she came with a deep moan, as if nothing could possibly bring her more pleasure. God, even her noises were perfect.

It was the most beautiful thing I'd ever seen in my life. And I'd been to Rome, Florence, the Alps.

Daphne's face as she came made all the vistas and artistic masterpieces seem banal compared to the way her body jerked as pleasure coursed through her.

And I planned to give her a lot more pleasure.

I was a patient man, but I'd waited long enough. Her scent was filling the room and driving me insane with want. I grabbed the ankle closest to me, twisting her body and dragging her closer to the edge.

I dropped to my knees, taking a moment to appreciate the slowing pulses of her pelvic floor as she pumped out more moisture. Moisture that I was about to lap up and swallow down. Then I'd beg for more. There'd never be enough of her. I'd never be through with this woman.

She lifted her head, glancing down her body toward me before raking her fingers through my hair and pushing my face into her pussy. "Already?" I smiled, lazily flattening my tongue just below her clit.

Her head dropped back with a moan. "Oh God that... Wait a min ute..." her head snapped up again. "Ah! Your tongue is freezing."

I chuckled. "Toothpaste."

"Ohhh..." she wailed.

I licked a slow, lingering swath through her slit, feeling every fold and ridge, every delicious texture, following the path I'd seen her own fingers tread, before spreading her wide open, stroking everywhere, everything, concentrating my peppermint-cooled tongue on her clit.

"Oh my God, Chris!" She moaned and writhed under me, her feet slipping off my shoulders, scrambling until her thighs closed around my ears, pulling me closer as her fingers pulled my hair at the roots. Greedy girl.

My cock throbbed. It had worked its way out of the fly of my pants. A thread of pre-cum stretched to the floor.

I dropped my hand from where I'd been kneading her ass and squeezed my dick. Just once.

I just needed a moment of relief to stop this ache. But it wasn't just my cock; it was my skin, my heart, my blood. Every bit of me needed to consume every bit of her.

"Yes, please. Touch yourself," she said, noticing where my hand had gone.

"Oh, no. Not yet." I shook my head and smiled against her pussy. My whole face was covered in her. I needed both of my hands to hold her open so I could catch every juicy drop of her.

I moved lower—stroking, circling, leaving behind a wake of fiery cold.

My scalp burned as her fists tightened in my hair, her clit throbbed out a rhythm on my tongue as she came, milking out more precious fluid I lapped up with a desperate sort of hunger.

And fuck, I didn't think it was possible for my cock to get any harder. But it hurt now—oh, God—it hurt. It fucking... So angry and purple, pulsing from the engorgement of blood and then, *oh fuck, oh fuck* I was coming. Thick spurts of cum painted abstract streaks on the navy rug as I watched helplessly with my hands still between her legs, pulling her wide open.

I nuzzled her softly, kissing her cunt until her both of our orgasms faded completely.

Daphne was exhausted. Her legs hung loosely off the bed, her arms straight down at her sides.

"Now you. I can't move, but I want you inside me."

I laughed and kissed a path down her thigh. She didn't realize I'd already... but that didn't stop me. My cock had never softened and I never wanted her more.

I grabbed a condom and rolled it on. Daphne still hadn't moved a muscle. She lay on the bed, groaning anemically, muttering words I couldn't make out.

I laughed. "You sure you want more?"

There was a sleepy smile on her face. "Not more for me. Seriously, I can't move." She let out a shocked laugh. "I've never been able to do that... twice. What did you do to me?"

I loved how unashamed she was. So open and free, like she was just as delighted by her body as I was.

Seeing her like this, exhausted and immobile from pleasure—pleasure I'd wrought—carved something deep into my chest. The beauty of her openness, the willing exposure, not just of her body, but who she was underneath all that flesh and muscle—it was doing something to me, changing me, rebooting components that hadn't been updated in years.

God, this woman.

I pulled her legs up to my shoulders, kissing the inside of her calf and stroking her thighs.

Slowly, I pushed in, little by little, hissing through my teeth as I teased into her wet heat. It was torture, but she was too much to take all at once.

She sank further into the mattress and her legs fell open at the knees.

Sweet Jesus, she was a ragdoll.

I caught her thighs, and the motion seated me fully inside her. A long, low-pitched moan escaped from deep inside me. She felt as good as I'd remembered.

It was exquisite watching her lying there, limp and dripping, unable to move, unable to do anything except fuck me.

Or be there for me to fuck.

I dragged myself out and eased back in. Her slick pussy made it so easy, too easy. I was already on the verge of coming.

If I could make her come one more time, feel her pulse around my cock the way she had last night, that'd be it.

Jesus Christ. Fuck. Fucking her like this—so excruciatingly slowly, watching my cock disappear into her, her clit growing harder as more blood filled the sensitive tissues in her pussy—it was the prettiest thing I'd ever seen.

"You're so fucking perfect. I want you to come again. Tell me what to do to make you come on my cock. I need to feel it again."

"Chris, I can't."

"Let me try. Please, baby."

She smiled. Her arms drifted to her belly, smoothing over her skin before pulling my hand to her clit. "Press," she said. "Don't move."

I pressed my thumb there, lightly. Using the momentum of our slow fucking to provide stimulation.

This had to have been the longest stretch of her not talking since I'd met her yesterday. *God, was it only yesterday?* So much had happened and nothing really happened. Just that I'd met her, and that, in itself, was magic.

My head rubbed a spot inside her that made her gasp. I focused all my attention there. Her head rolled back into the tangle of sheets.

"Ohhh," she breathed.

"Like that? Is that where it is, sweetheart?" I rocked my cock back and forth, right where it made her breath catch.

The sounds we made together were wet and sloppy. I could hear her moisture when the suction broke. She dripped onto the floor and my feet.

"Um, Chris, I don't know... I think... something's diff— I'm... I'm gonna..."

"Let go, sweetheart."

And holy fuck, she was... *Wet.* Everything was wet and hot. "Oh, shit." I froze, trying to figure out what was even happening. "Daphne, you..." God, she wasn't just coming on my cock; she was fucking soaking it.

Everything was covered in drops of wetness and she was squirting out more. "Fuck. Baby. Look at you." She looked down just as she gushed on my dick as I pulled out, watching her make a mess all over us, all over everything, the bed, the floor...

"Chris, what did I do?"

I was in awe. Her body was made to be fucked.

"Daphne. You're so perfect. You're so beautiful when you come."

I pushed back in as the last of her orgasm clenched around me, milking my cock and taking me right with her. My breath escaped in a ragged huff as I spilled into the condom.

I was as wrecked as she was. More so. After that, I couldn't conceive of fucking anyone else. She was mine. Maybe she didn't know it yet, I still didn't know why, but this was more than sex; it was a bonding.

Hours and countless orgasms with several clean-ups later, she lay still in my arms. Comfortable and complete, like she knew she belonged there.

"Were you going to be alone for Christmas?"

I laughed. "It's fine. I don't always come home for Christmas, anyway. When I do, it's just for volunteer work. But now that Darius has passed, it's hard."

"Tell me about him?"

I groaned. "He was the best."

"What made him important to you?"

I reached for my glasses on the nightstand, and slid them on. "My parents run a nonprofit called Nourishing Nashville. It's a huge conglomerate now, but it started as a community kitchen. Darius was one of the first people they hired. Just for odd jobs, mostly. Their first location was a church basement and there was this old upright piano there. Every time I'd come in with my parents, Darius would drag me away and teach me the ragtime and Dixieland jazz tunes his granddad had taught him. He loved music—all kinds—and he gave me an ear for it. Loved food, too. He had a picky palette. After he complained enough about the quality of the food, my parents found him scholarships and grants for culinary school and eventually put him to work as the head chef, but he was always more like family. I was more afraid of disappointing him than I was of disappointing Dad."

My throat grew tighter the more I thought about him. I took my time kissing Daphne on the top of her head, waiting for the ache to pass so my voice wouldn't hitch.

"His food was amazing. It's why we needed to finally expand this year. Even though he's been gone for several years, he left that legacy behind—that even the unhoused deserved good cooking."

"I'm sorry he's gone. I think I would have liked him."

"Everyone liked Darius, but he would have loved you. His wife, too. She's still on our board of directors."

"Hmm. I think that would be a nice way to spend the holidays—helping others in a tangible way. Just maybe not every holiday."

She nuzzled my neck. It tickled in the best possible way.

"It was Darius who showed me balance. You can go home and leave your work at work. There will always be someone hungry. Someone in need. Missing persons to find. You have to learn to find joy, even if you feel you haven't done enough. Because it's never enough. Not for one person." I drew circles on her shoulder.

"Have you found that joy, Chris?"

There was no point in playing coy anymore. I tipped her chin up to look into her eyes.

"I think I'm starting to."

Chapter 6

Daphne

"Food," he said, standing in front of the open door of the fridge. "There's got to be something we can make for dinner."

"Dinner? We're staying?"

I hopped up onto the counter.

"I called my neighbor. She's thrilled to cat-sit another day." He stepped between my legs and gently kneaded my thighs.

"I saw a Chinese place in the strip mall on the way here."

"Oh no. It's Christmas Eve Eve. It might not be a real thing, but if we're going to start making our own holiday traditions, we may as well start here. And we're going to do this right."

I kissed him chastely on the lips and reached my hand out for his.

"Cookies?" I asked.

"I think I can throw together a batch of something." A seductive smile played on his lips as he touched our fingertips together, playing with my hands.

"Gingerbread? I've never had gingerbread."

"Gingerbread it is, then."

"Sugarplums?"

"I'm not convinced those are real." His fingers slid down my palms. Intensely provocative for a nonsexual gesture. A shiver went up my spine.

"Movies?"

"Whatever you want, sweetheart." He tugged me closer.

"Charlie Brown. I love the music."

"I can play the music," he actually sounded excited by that.

"Oh! Play for me!"

"Of course." He nipped at my lips.

"This is dangerous, Chris. You're going to spoil me."

"Only a little."

"What if I turn into a brat? A Veruca Salt. *I want it now... Daddy.*" I said in a terrible Veruca Salt accent.

His face was inches from mine. He'd been leaning in to kiss me again—or so I thought—and then he stopped. Pulled back. Dropped his hands. His face was... was that horror, or desire? *What did I—?*

Chris actually squeaked before he looked down and cleared his throat.

I felt like I'd stepped in something and tracked it all over the carpet.

"Right, uh..." He licked his lips and came back to himself. "Follow me." He spun around and opened the door into a room behind the kitchen. Sunlight shone on black and white marble tiles laid in a harlequin pattern. Black slate countertops housed rows of mixers and toasters and other fancy appliances I couldn't identify. There were beams in the ceiling. *Beams.* In a closed-door room. Rows and rows of fancy wicker baskets lined thick, solid wood shelves on one side, while the other side appeared to be reserved for glassware. They must have hundreds of every type of glass, meant for every type of wine or cocktail.

"You have another kitchen behind your kitchen?"

"It's the pantry."

"A pantry isn't something that's decorated like a Victorian-era pastry shop. A pantry is a closet barely big enough to store a few bags of potato chips and some old phone books from the nineties. You have two sinks in here. Another fancy stove and a fridge bigger than the one in the display kitchen."

"The only kitchen. A-ha!" He produced a vacuum-sealed package from the freezer and held it up like he expected me to understand. "It's not a turkey, but these'll thaw in time for dinner."

"What is it?"

"Quail. I think." He looked at the package again. "Maybe partridges. I'm not sure. Anyway, they're basically the same."

"From a pear tree?" I scrunched up my face. "Oh no. I don't think I can eat a bird."

His lopsided smile was loading. "You eat chicken."

"Yeah, chicken's a food bird. Those are like, power line birds."

"They're food birds. You'll see."

"I can't cook."

"I can."

I narrowed my eyes at him. "Don't you have people for that?"

His lips quirked. "I love cooking. Mom and I cook our family meals. It's the one small holiday tradition I'd like to keep."

He rooted around in the various baskets meant to organize dry goods; essentially hiding them from view, as if it were uncouth to display anything useful, even behind a closed door.

I'd said I wanted bougie, but being in here was showing me just how uncomfortable I was with the idea of having money. I was someone used to pumping two gallons of gas at a time; just enough to make it to work and back. I would splurge on a Happy Meal when I wanted takeout. I'd gotten good at doing the math so that I always had three dollars in my bank account to cover my $2.99 Apple bill that hit right before my paycheck came.

Hiding the label on a box of pasta was solving a problem that didn't exist. It wasn't that I didn't appreciate the beauty or extravagance. I knew people like the Carters were vital to their communities. If no one could afford to buy these expensive-looking, artisan-crafted baskets, they'd stop from getting made and more people would be out of jobs.

This pantry was great for the economy. It would just take me a lot longer than one day to get used to the affluence.

He pulled out a jar of almonds, a tomato sauce with a Spanish label, and cured meats and cheeses from the industrial fridge. "Grab those potatoes there, would you?"

"Where?"

"Behind you, sweetheart." He pointed.

"These?" I held up a long, purple finger. "Oh, no. Potatoes are big, brown, and used as vehicles for chili. These are not potatoes."

"These might just blow your mind." He reached behind me, pulling out the basket at my hip, kissing my neck as he brushed past. His lips anywhere on me were a direct line to my clit, my heart, my brain. Everything he did was a turn on. He must have felt it, too. The food fell out of his arms onto the counter behind me as he pressed into me, gripping my waist and kissing his way along my jaw, trailing searing lips up to mine.

My fingers threaded into his hair as I pulled him harder against my mouth, desperate for more of him. As much as I could get. My body felt empty without him inside me; my legs were made to be wrapped around him.

He broke off our kiss with a groan as he shifted his hips away from mine and pressed his hand flat against his sweatpants, adjusting himself with a wince. "Fuck, I'm sorry. I can't stop myself with you. I swear I'm not usually like this. I get one taste of you and suddenly I need the whole fucking feast."

"I don't want you to stop. Not ever. As soon as you pull away, I need more." My words spilled breathlessly out.

"But I want to know more about you. I want to get to know that beautiful brain inside your body. I can't just..."

"We'll have plenty of time for that."

He nodded, still staring at me wild-eyed behind his glasses. I reached up and adjusted his slightly skewed glasses. "Daphne, I need you to know... even though I'm having a very hard time keeping it in my pants, I really like you. I think we could be—"

"Me too." I nodded. For a moment we both stared into each other's eyes. I was analyzing the exact shade of chocolate behind his tortoiseshell frames. It was some kind of milk chocolate. A warm brown, not a bittersweet brown, and darker at the outer ring of his iris, before fading toward a more honey hue near his pupil, even as dilated as they were.

His gaze floated over my hairline, my eyes, my cheekbones, my lips, as if studying me. It was up to me to break this seriousness spell. We had a lifetime to be serious together. Right now, I wanted to give him excuses to play.

"Hey." I smacked his elbow. "Don't you have any normal food?"

He reached over my head into one of the woven baskets on the tall shelf and tossed me a familiar glossy blue bag of salt and vinegar potato chips. It wasn't my favorite flavor, but at least they weren't cooked in tiny batches and flavored with truffles harvested by pigs in the forests of France.

"I don't know if salt and vinegar counts as normal, but at least you have one thing from a real grocery store. Where's your wine fridge, Fancy Pants?"

His smile fell. "Uh..."

"Don't tell me you don't have a wine fridge." I arranged my face into a horrified expression.

"The basement."

"Oh, of course it's in the basement."

"No. It *is* the basement."

"Oh no. Don't tell me."

"Sorry," he said, looking smug.

"You may as well show me. I'll need something to wash these down."

"As long as we're celebrating Christmas Eve Eve with tapas, we may as well find a bottle of cava."

"What's that?"

"Champagne from Spain."

"Isn't it called sparkling wine, then?"

"Yes. I didn't know how much you knew about wine."

Ingredients for tonight's dinner tumbled out of his arms onto the kitchen island.

He pulled me by the hand across the room, through another room, across an expansive hallway, and down the steps into the basement. It took us minutes just to traverse a quarter of the main floor. My legs would be sore after today.

"I'm really not much of a drinker at all. I think I only know the sparkling wine thing from memes. I'd love to be a whiskey drinker. Someone sophisticated but chill, who knows exactly the right unpretentious words to describe the smokiness of the whatever, or the butteriness of the tannins."

"Yeah, those words don't go together."

"See what I mean?" Chris tugged me down another set of winding stone steps.

"I want to like some kind of cool alcohol, but that takes time to appreciate and a lot of drinking, which I don't enjoy. And money, of course, not that I have to remind you. Because even *I'm* aware I can't learn to appreciate fine spirits when they... oh..."

We turned the corner and all I could do was stare. I didn't have to know anything about wine to be awed by the room I was standing in.

Stone walls surrounded me, encrusted from floor to ceiling with racks of bottles, their plump bottoms facing me, daring me to race around the room and run my fingers over their dusty smoothness. But that wasn't what a cool alcohol girlie would do. She'd probably read the labels and comment appreciatively about dates.

What the hell. I wasn't her yet.

I didn't run, but I took a meandering path around the room. I touched stuff, too.

Wooden racks at the center held even more bottles. There was barely enough room to squeeze through the rows and rows of jewel-toned bottles, all lit from some unseen source that glowed from below, as if the foundation had cracked and light streamed in from a fantasy world.

The magical realm of Vintaelia.

"Cava's a great place to start learning about wine. It's dry but not too dry, citrusy but buttery. It's accessible." Chris startled me as he brushed the hair off my shoulder, his warm breath hitting my neck just before his lips did, making me break out in a fit of giggles. "Sorry. Try that again. I'll stay still."

He didn't exactly kiss my neck; he just ran his lips across my skin. My knees bent and I crumpled in another fit, unable to stop laughing. I wanted to like it. I really did. From an outsider, I could see how sexy it would look. But I didn't find anything sexy about a laughing fit where I was liable to snort at any minute.

"I'm sorry. I'm so ticklish." I laughed.

He grabbed me by the neck and spun me around to face him. He loomed over me, looking down with wild eyes. His clenched teeth showed through his parted lips, almost in a sneer.

Slowly, so slowly, he leaned forward, his hand still gripping the side of my neck, his thumb trailing firmly down to my collarbone.

In the span of a breath, Chris had turned into a beast, and I'd lost all sense of autonomy. My heart pounded in my chest; I could feel every squeezing beat circulating the blood in my vessels. When he scraped his teeth along the sinew, it took every ounce of concentration to remain standing.

Nipping and biting his way down to my collarbone, his hot breath no longer tickled to the point of making me want to claw my skin off. Now I needed more of it.

He picked me up and walked with me, kissing me until my eyes closed and I didn't care what happened to me. I'd already given myself to him. I was his to play with however he wanted. He could be gearing up to throw me into a bottomless pit and I'd smile and moan on my way down.

I was lifted even higher and placed on the thick slab of solid wood.

"I want to taste you again."

"You're wild. You know that, don't you? Out of your mind." I bent toward him, hovering my lips over his as I spoke.

"For you." He kissed me deeply, messily, intoxicatingly. Then, he drew back, his eyes even blacker than before. "Can I?" His face was eager.

"Here?"

"God, yes. Here, upstairs. Everywhere. Every second of every day I want you on my tongue or on my cock."

His words sent a shiver down my arms into my fingertips. My skin was on fire for him. "That's impossible. We need to eat. Food. Real Food. We need to work—well, I do. You could very well exist in this wine cellar for years without needing to surface."

He pulled me into him. My back arched in response, giving him more access as he pressed firm kisses along my jaw and neck.

"Is this my cue to shut up?"

He drew back, pulling my head away like I was a puppet. My body was his to control and I couldn't think of a better feeling than being moved and shifted and positioned by this man.

"Not at all. I love the way you talk. I'm just going to get you naked while you do it."

Slowly, he lifted the hem of my shirt up and over my head. His eyes lingered for only a moment on my bare breasts—I hadn't seen the point of subjecting them to the confines of a bra since there was a high likelihood it would end up removed and flung somewhere for the cleaning crew to find. His eyes sparked as they looked up into mine, keeping contact as he leaned in and sucked an already hard nipple into his mouth.

"Oh, God." I cupped the back of his head as he swirled his tongue around the firm peak. "I love the way you do that."

He groaned and sucked harder, using his lips to coax my nipple into an impossibly elongated peak.

"Is that what you want me to talk about? The things you're doing to me? How they make me feel?"

He reluctantly moved away from one breast, fixing his gaze on its twin as if it was a prize he'd won. "It wasn't what I had in mind, but it's a very good surprise."

He closed his mouth over my other breast, palming the first, his thumb mirroring the motion of his tongue. I arched my back and widened my legs. Every lick. Every swirl of saliva sent longing straight to my clit. Even my pelvis canted and writhed with every flick of his tongue.

His mouth popped off my breast and he stood, his lips wet and eyes crazed. "Stay here." He trailed a heavy hand down my thigh as he left, as if he couldn't quite decide whether he wanted to leave me here or not.

I groaned in complaint. I was cold, naked, and wet in several places. I hated to think about the pool I was leaving under my ass, my arousal soaking into his family's unvarnished bar top.

I heard bottles rattling from across the room. "Chris, hurry."

There was a chuckle as he came back into view, pulling a champagne flute from somewhere behind me. He came around the front again, stopping between my legs but otherwise ignoring my presence.

"Now," he said, placing the glasses and second bottle on the bar. "There was something you said upstairs." He twisted the cork in the bottle of sparkling wine that could very well be real actual champagne but I couldn't see the label. "I think I liked it. I think I need to hear it again."

I leaned back on my hands, displaying my boobs, while he poured a glass of glittery bubbles.

"Was it about the potatoes?" I reached for the glass but he didn't give it to me.

"No."

"Hmm... It was partridges in pear trees, wasn't it?"

"No."

"What is that you're drinking? Are you going to pour me a glass?"

He tilted his head back and sipped, thoughtfully, clearly savoring the taste of the wine. He shook his head slowly. “It’s cava. And no, I don’t think I will.”

I pouted, knowing full well what he wanted to hear. *Veruca.*

“I want it.”

His lips quirked a bit on one side. God, he was sexy. I never thought that about anyone, but it just poured out of him. And he had no idea. I couldn’t believe I got to be the one to flip this switch in him.

He took another sip and stepped closer. “I think you can do better than that.” His breath was hot on my lips as he spoke, our mouths not quite touching, but close. It gave me the courage to say what he wanted to hear from me again.

My voice was low. I could only whisper. “I want it... *Daddy.*”

He smiled his crooked smile, but instead of kissing me, he tipped his glass back again and sipped slowly, staring into my eyes.

He held me by the neck, pulling me down until my mouth was beneath his, and the sparkling wine poured from his mouth into mine. His kiss stifled my cry of shock as the dry bubbles fizzed between our tongues. A deep rumble of laughter resonated through his chest and into mine. As he pulled me closer to the edge, I couldn’t help but rock my pelvis against his belly.

“Uhn uh. I’m not done playing with you.”

He raised his glass again and tilted it toward me. My head jerked back as a cold trickle of cava rolled down from my sternum, between my breasts, diverting across the folds of my abdomen before pooling between my legs.

Chris’s breath escaped in a shudder as he watched. “Jesus Christ.”

He was rougher when he pulled me closer, using more pressure as he scraped his teeth over my areola and sucked my nipple so hard I gasped for relief.

He moved lower still, kissing down my belly as his hands came up and kneaded my calves. Suddenly, he stood, his eyes wild as he looked into mine, needy and awed. I moved against against nothing but air, frantic for him to relieve me. I had never needed my pussy touched so badly. I'd give him anything, anything, anything to satisfy me.

"What do you need?"

"I need you, Daddy."

"What part?"

"I need your tongue."

"I need your words, baby. Keep talking. Promise you'll keep talking until you can't anymore." He ran his hands up between my breasts and pushed me down flat on the bar.

"Words," he reminded me.

"Lick me, Daddy. I need to—" His tongue flattened against my pussy in a broad stroke from my vagina to my clit. I cried out. "I need you to make me come."

"God, you taste good." His words came out as if they were on fire, singeing his vocal cords with each syllable.

"I love the way you tease my clit. The way you stroke me up and down, slowly, with your tongue." He did exactly what I liked. Just the way I said I liked it. "Am I doing well, Daddy?"

That word! Why was it rolling off my tongue so easily, so shamelessly?

"You're doing so well, darling."

With his filthy-sweet words, I felt another gush of fluid pour out of me, spilling onto the bar.

He poured more wine directly from the bottle onto my clit, washing me with its intoxicatingly cold tap on my nerves while he drank it up from below. The sight of him using my pussy as a luge for his wine had me seconds from orgasm.

My body jerked off the bar, my legs shaking.

He put the bottle down as he kissed my inner thighs. “Look how beautiful your body is. So wet. So perfect. Can you come already, baby? Talk to me.” He pushed two fingers inside me as he lapped greedily at my clit.

“Oh shit.” My legs started shaking harder.

“Say it,” he said through clenched teeth.

“Ah— I’m coming, Daddy.”

“Give it to me, I feel it. Such a good girl, letting me get you this messy.”

“I need... I need..." But I was too brainless, too weak to say what I needed. To know what I needed.

“You need me to fuck you?”

I nodded. “Yes, Daddy.”

“Fuck. Every time you say that I get even harder. So hard, it hurts. I’m going to come as soon as I’m inside you.”

I nodded again. “I just need to feel you.”

I vaguely registered the sound of a condom wrapper before he pulled my boneless body off the bar and lowered me onto a stool.

He circled my clit with his thumb, but he didn’t need to. I was already on the precipice from the way he talked about my body—what I did to him, and how well I did it, even though all I did was lie there and let him give me another amazing orgasm.

He rolled the condom on, then dropped his forehead to mine after a sweet kiss.

“Daddy. Fuck me. I need you inside me.” It took all my strength to keep myself propped on that stool, my legs wrapped around his hips. I was on the brink of collapse. He still wore his t-shirt and sweatpants, only his cock was pulled free, but that only made it even more obscene, considering I was completely nude, wet, and wine-soaked, with my legs wide open for him.

I gripped him and pulled him close, rubbing his cock up and down my pussy, soaking the condom in my juices. I hadn't squirted again, but I was still ridiculously wet.

In a single decisive stroke, with his eyes burning into mine, he drove himself fully inside me.

And God, he felt good.

Was it the angle that made my eyes roll back in my head? Was it the shape of him that fit perfectly inside me?

Holy shit, sex never ever felt like this. The buildup was so intense, like I'd be climbing forever with no relief. My whole pelvis was tight and straining with need. If it didn't happen soon, I'd explode and then...

"Fuck, yes, you feel so fucking good inside me, yes, fuck me harder." It was meaningless—a slew of filth that poured out of me. "Harder, oh God, yes touch my nipples, it feels so fucking good... fuck... yes... feels... uhn... Chris, Daddy, I'm coming."

His hips jerked, and he made a guttural noise. He pulled out abruptly, ripping off the condom, and stroked himself, his eyes transfixed on the fountain that gushed out of me. "Sweetheart. Look at you. You're amazing. Your body is amazing."

My fluid was soaking everything. I could hear it raining down from the high-top stool onto the concrete floor. Chris came closer, slickening his hand with my wetness to stroke his cock harder until his hot cum was spurting onto my belly, and it felt like I was made just for that. Just for fucking him.

I slumped forward, and he caught me in his arms.

I kissed him lazily, drunkenly.

"I love the way you go all limp after you orgasm. Love the mess you make for me."

"Only you." Releasing, cleansing tears streamed down the sides of my face as I fought to remain present. I searched for his eyes. "Only ever for you."

He wiped my tears away as he held me tenderly. "I know sweetheart. It's going to be only us for a long time."

Chapter 7

Chris

I'D SEEN THIS EPISODE countless times, but it was so nice to laze on the library couch and zone out to throwback TV with a laugh track and commercial breaks. It gave my eyeballs something to do while I tried not to think, feel, or catastrophize while Daphne took another of her scalding showers.

For two days I'd been floating. If I didn't touch ground soon, I might lose sight of Earth and exit the atmosphere.

Alone was my ground. I was used to alone. It centered me, even if I resented it at times.

In this short time, Daphne had become an immediate and unusual companion. Being with her felt like being alone. Just as pressureless and easy. But *so right.* She filled my world with easy laughter, rich conversation, and so much sex my dick felt almost bruised. It was heaven.

I wanted this. Everything about this. So why couldn't I trust it? Why was it so much easier to accept the hardness, the sadness, the loneliness, than to even consider things might be working out for the good?

Yesterday morning, our hands had touched, and I could feel something. Her cold fingers had brushed mine across the frontal bone, and I didn't move my hand away. I knew it wasn't exactly professional. I should have pulled away as soon as she had a grip, but I'd felt the blood rushing through my fingers, so close to hers, and I was paralyzed. When her finger slid further down and pressed against my thumb, neither of us looking at each other—both of us staring at the skull, wondering what in God's name was happening—I knew she'd felt it too. Whatever force had slammed into me, knocking me askew and hurtling toward Daphne had also slammed into her.

I willed my hands to stop shaking. To keep myself from reaching toward her, pulling her into my body and wrapping her in my warmth, covering her mouth with mine.

Out in the woods, we'd found every possible reason to touch. For those touches to hold longer than necessary. Each one was electric, flooding my body with energy.

This had never happened to me before. I'd had plenty of girlfriends. I liked all of them. But it was always just... nice. No flood. No electricity. No caged beast energy. I'd never wanted to simultaneously rip a woman's clothes off and fuck her in the middle of a crime scene while vowing to be her protector. No one before had ever made me feel like I needed to shield them from everything bad in the world. I wanted to fight dragons for her.

I was deeply afraid.

Even when I'd been with Decca, my emotions had been complicated, but there'd never been this feverish *need*.

I pushed up my glasses and scraped my hand over the scruff that was forming on my chin.

Decca and I had fallen into bed blind with desire—not for each other, but to forget our work and our troubles. Sometimes it was blessed relief at the end of an emotionally crippling case, other times it was just blowing off steam with someone trustworthy, yet ultimately disposable. There was never an *us*. It was war-zone sex, a tool we used to cope. Decca was just... there. As I was for her. That was how we could so easily fall back into friendship with no bitterness or resentment after I learned she'd not only never cared about me like that, but she'd married Gus out of the blue.

For a couple weeks after Decca's announcement, my ego had been bruised, my hopes dashed that a romantic love might someday develop between us. But after seeing her again, it was like we'd never gone to that dangerous, fuck-buddy territory in the first place. My friend was back and our relationship was just as strong and platonic as it had always been.

With Daphne, it was the opposite.

I needed sex because I needed to consume her and be consumed by her. To be as close as possible. From that first hour, it had somehow felt like we were one, and being separated from my *one* was akin to torture.

But it had all been too easy.

And I didn't know what that meant.

I wasn't the scary, toxic, afraid-of-his feelings man. At least I tried not to be. I always wanted feelings. I welcomed them. I craved them. But at this point in my life, I'd recently started to believe I'd been sold a bill of goods about love. That I'd been waiting for something that didn't exist.

Mid-thirties weren't exactly old, but it seemed like I should have fallen in love by now. The fact that I hadn't—unless you counted my elementary school crush on Sarah Childs, or my sixth grade crush on Eboni Turner, or my seventh, eighth, or... okay, I had a lot of school crushes that felt a lot like love when they were nice to me, or a lot like heartbreak when I saw them holding hands with other boys instead.

By college, the crushes had stopped. And when my friends had aged out of hookups and they'd started finding the people who would become their partners, that hadn't happened for me, no matter how much I tried to force it.

Had it happened now?

It was probably just chemical. Hormones. My body received dopamine from her oxytocin, which flooded her system with every orgasm. Our hormones were dancing and I was following her lead.

Except I didn't think love was just a feeling. It was a choice. And I found myself making the choice. Deciding to love.

And it was just the slightest bit terrifying.

"I looked up your home on Zillow." Daphne's voice startled me from somewhere behind.

"It's worth forty million dollars, which means you're stupid rich. Probably a billionaire. Where are you?" She spun around, searching for me.

"You can't trust Zillow. And I'm not a billionaire." I groaned as I shifted, propping my head on my hand to see her over the back of the couch. "I'm a dentist."

My gaze went cold. My whole body froze. A wicked smile spread across her face. "I wandered into a whole room dedicated to gift wrapping."

Her wet hair was parted down the center and pulled into two low pigtails, each tied with thick red satin ribbons.

She wore a plain white t-shirt, so thin I could see her nipples underneath. The dark shadow at the apex of her thighs.

Like a package just waiting for me to open.

She sipped her cocoa from the mug I'd left on the bathroom counter for her, resisting the urge to join her in the shower—this time.

Her nipples poked through the threadbare material—she must have really dug deep in my closet to find it—and made my mouth water. I wanted to burst from looking at her.

"I was going to try not to touch you until tonight."

She came closer and leaned over the back of the couch. "You don't want to?" She pouted.

"I do want to. I've been laying here, arguing with my cock, telling it to calm the fuck down, trying to prove I wasn't a lecherous man incapable of keeping my hands to myself."

"What if I don't want you to keep your hands to yourself?"

"Come here."

She sat crossed-legged on the other end of the couch—too far away—tugging the hem between her legs to cover her exposed pussy.

I looked anyway.

"First, tell me how you became a dentist with a billion-dollar trust fund." She tucked my legs around her like a blanket.

"A dentist with a trust fund and a social conscience. My parents aren't even billionaires. You can stop hating them before you even meet them."

"I'm going to meet your parents?" She placed her mug on the coaster and widened her legs, grabbing my t-shirt to pull me toward her, between her legs. I was frequently finding myself between her legs. Not that I minded in the slightest. If I could live here, I probably would.

"As soon as they get home," I said.

Visions danced in my head. Daphne helping serve at our annual Thanksgiving feast, dolloping extra helpings of sweet potato casserole to anyone who flirted with her. Daphne helping small children compete against their older siblings at the annual Easter egg hunt on our expansive lawn. Daphne in a big, white dress. Or a tiny white dress as we hopped a plane to Vegas to avoid the big wedding my family would want from us.

I was getting way too far ahead of myself.

I sat up and nestled back. "Come over here."

She crawled toward my lap, lifted her leg over mine, and sat, biting her lip and looking at me from under lashes much darker than her hair.

I pulled her lip out from between her teeth and leaned forward to nibble it. She tasted like crisp peppermint toothpaste and hot cocoa. A combination of sensations rather than flavors.

"Did you enjoy your shower?" I slid my hand inside her t-shirt in search of her nipple.

She moaned as my fingers teased circles around her puffy areola. The telltale sign her nipples would soon be huge and hard as rocks, jutting up from the tips of her perky round tits. My favorite fidget toys. "I even had to turn the cool water on at the end. I was as red as a lobster when I got out."

I traced her lips with my tongue, before kissing the outer corner of her mouth.

"My parents are going to get back from Germany and find their water bill as high as their beer bill. When no one was supposed to be here."

"Your parents drink beer?"

"It's Germany. Of course they do."

"But they're rich. I don't imagine rich people drinking beer."

"Know a lot of rich people, do you?"

"Only you."

"Mmm." I pulled her off my lap so I wouldn't be too distracted to get out what I needed to tell her.

Who I really was.

"I live off my dentist's salary and whatever I earn as an assistant professor," I said. "I realize that's already a lot higher than the median income, but it's not rich like this house is rich. I purposely don't live like this for a reason. My place in Knoxville is small. I live downtown not because it's fancy, but so I can see other humans when I'm not working with the dead. Even if I'm just watching my community from the window, I know they're out there, living. Drinking and eating in the plaza, walking their dogs, playing in the fountain when it's hot. Sometimes that makes a big difference in my mental health when I come home from a case.

"I saved money to buy my car. It didn't take long, and it wasn't much of a hardship, but some small sacrifices were made.

"I have a small library of first editions I'm proud of, and a watch collection I'm embarrassed about, now that I think about it. But so do men without trust funds."

Without meaning to, I rubbed the crease where her skin folded at her hip. It was just too hard not to touch her somewhere.

"I'm not telling you this to change your mind, or to convince you I'm some kind of a hero for living within my ample means. I just want to lay it all out there and clear up any false expectations you might have.

"And yes, on a yearly basis, I'm awarded my interest dividends from my trust fund. Which is not billionaire huge, but it's still mind-bogglingly huge. It's huge enough that if I allowed myself to take it, I could buy fifty Mercedes AMG GTs every year, and it wouldn't hurt to make the wire transfer. It's huge enough that my children won't have to work, my children's children, nor their children. On and on down the line of my descendants, until one of those idiots decides to squander it all and invest in something stupid, in which case, I will float out of my grave and haunt him for the rest of his days."

"So, you admit you're rich."

"I never said I wasn't rich; I said I wasn't a billionaire. And I'm not. Year after year, those funds go into a separate account managed by my lawyer and after my standing pledges are distributed to the right charities, whatever's left goes to new projects I want to support. My ethics always take priority."

"What did your people do to acquire all this money?"

"Not by prioritizing their ethics, that's for damn sure."

Her face registered shock now, and this time, disapproval. I sighed and sat up.

"The usual way: by exploiting any and everyone who crossed their paths."

I'd been hoping to avoid the unavoidable, but it was better she learned where I came from before she read about it in history books. "There were a lot of income streams. The largest was the L&C line. A transcontinental railroad that displaced a lot of nations out of their ancestral lands and forced low-wage, dangerous labor on immigrants and the formerly enslaved. I'm pretty sure the only thing my ancestors weren't guilty of is actual enslavement, but then again, I could be wrong. We don't have many records that aren't in the public domain. There was a fire in the twenties. Conveniently got rid of a lot of evidence when my great-great-grandfather was facing federal charges."

"Chris?"

Reluctantly, I met her eyes.

"You are not your ancestors." She cupped my jaw and pulled my face to hers.

I wasn't expecting that. I was expecting disapproval. Condemnation. Especially from someone with a heart like Daphne's.

Part of me felt like I deserved the wrath she wasn't dishing out. It wasn't my fault, but it was still a hard pill to swallow, being born into privilege that was built on the corruption and greed of robber barons, the stripping of raw materials from the earth, the exploitation, pain, and terror of men, women, and children. It wasn't something I thought about all the time. For all I knew, my ancestors had lovely personalities and made their money with perfectly respectable and upright business and legal dealings. But it was unlikely. It was a source of shame, and one I couldn't hide from Daphne. She deserved to know why my parents and I tried so hard to atone for the sins of those who came before us, who'd passed down the name.

That was why I'd grown up in kitchens and was asked which charities I'd like to give an extra gift to instead of what I wanted for Christmas. It wasn't that I lacked anything, even emotionally—though thirteen-year-old me was super annoyed when I didn't get the Xbox all my friends had. But in my parents' determination to raise me as normally as possible, they sometimes went a little overboard with their restrictions.

She pulled me back down and widened her legs, settling herself comfortably under me. "I'm proud of you. You're a good man, Chris Carter. And I'm proud to know you."

"I could be telling you what you want to hear."

"You're not. I might not have known you long, but I know your heart. I see you." She got that look of wonder in her eyes again. The one that made me want to get lost in them.

In this position, my glasses were sliding off my face. As much as I wanted to see her, I didn't want to hit her in the bridge of her nose with a pair of heavy frames. I took them off and tossed them on the coffee table.

She didn't even let me kiss her slowly, she met me more than halfway, sucking my lip desperately into her mouth with a moan. God, I loved her moans. My tongue reached out to slide along her lip, coaxing them apart to feel her breath. This wasn't her usual fever of a kiss. It was languid, lazy, as we nipped and licked and sucked.

Her hands made their way under my shirt. Fingernails raked over my chest and stomach, sending shivers down my spine. Underneath me, her hips writhed and her legs wrapped around me.

My hands were back on her tits, always her tits, as I coaxed the hard peaks even harder. Her skin was still warm from the shower—was it still red, too? Jesus, how hot was that water?

"You know..." I pinched her nipple, and my body melted from her gasp. "There's hot water at my place, too. You don't have to keep binge-showering here, like you'll never encounter a tankless water heater again."

Under my hands, her body froze. I adjusted my head to see her better.

"Am I...?" she started. "Are you inviting me over... when we get home?"

"Did you think we wouldn't be together after this?" I put my glasses back on and sat up. I needed to see her eyes to say this. "Daphne, it's taking all the strength in my body not tell you that tomorrow, when we get home, that word will mean something different to both of us. That we'll spend tomorrow afternoon packing up your things at your dad's house and moving them into mine. That you'll never have to take another rushed shower again, because even in the event of an apocalypse, when running water is only a figment of the imagination, I would spend all my time boiling your water and McGyvering your camp showers, just so I could make you happy.

"I'm dying to tell you that you'll always have real Mountain Dew—not Mountain Thunder. And hot cocoa made with warm milk and Valrhona chocolate instead of powdered packets—as long as you promise to brush your teeth afterward

"And that I'll take care of you and you'll never have to work, unless you want to, and I know you want to, and I respect you for that. But if you want to stay home with our kids in the future, that's okay, too."

Daphne's breath hitched as she inhaled. The edges of her mouth turned up into a tiny smile. There were the beginnings of tears in her eyes.

"But I can't say that yet. Because all that is crazy. It's insane to ask someone you just met yesterday to move in with you tomorrow. And neither of us are insane. So, in the meantime, you'll just... be my girlfriend?" I smiled. "Until it's not insane to be my wife."

Her nostrils flared as she dove in to kiss me. I tasted salt and wiped her tears with my thumbs.

"You can't tell me all that and not fuck me afterwards," she said against my lips.

"I wasn't exactly planning on doing my taxes after all that."

I ran my fingers down her wet clit and speared her on my fingers. Two fingers, pumping in easily with her flood of moisture.

She whimpered as I slowly worked my fingers in and out. "Are you sore, sweetheart?"

She nodded. "But it feels good. I like it. I like that you made me sore."

My dick jumped and pre-cum leaked out. I was going to have to take her soon, or I'd be coming in my sweatpants.

But no, I wanted to go slow. Take in every moment of this experience.

"Chris." She grabbed my wrist. "I don't want to squirt everywhere and get this pretty room all gross."

I'd almost forgotten how much of a mess she made—a delicious, erotic, mind-numbing mess of fluid that came out of nowhere. Technically, it was mostly lymph fluid from her urethra, but the fun part was knowing I was the one who got to make her body do this insanely cool thing.

"Please don't let me ruin your mom's sofa. It probably cost more than my student loans. I couldn't bear it."

I groaned but sat up, pulling her with me.

"Actually, I had something different in mind," she said, sinking to her knees.

Her hands ran along the waistband of my sweatpants, playing with the elastic.

"I'm amenable to different."

I glanced down as she teased my cock through the fabric. I'd foregone my usual boxers and as my cock hardened inside my pants, the soft fabric brushed my sensitive skin and felt like heaven.

She tugged the fabric down and pulled out my cock, stroking it greedily. The show was almost as good as the sensation.

"Can I?" She licked her lips.

"Baby, that's not a question you ever need to ask."

She lowered her head and licked it tentatively.

God, my cock looked good on her tongue. The way she stuck it out so naively, kissing the tender frenulum before opening wide and diving down as far as she could take me.

I held her pigtails while she started a nice, slow rhythm. With her head bouncing on my cock and that desperate gleam in her eyes, she was an adorable mess.

My adorable mess.

It wasn't fair to think it. Not yet. But I wasn't giving her up. I spread my legs further and jerked my hips, fucking her mouth as she moaned.

"Oh fuck, Daphne." I was already on the brink of coming down her throat. "Where?"

She faltered for only a moment before popping off my dick and sinking to kneel on the floor between my knees. She tugged her shirt over her head and pumped my cock adoringly, aiming the explosion at her perfect tits. "Here, Daddy."

Jesus. Yes. I couldn't even remember coming. Only the thick ropes that shot out of my cock, striping her pink skin.

She looked so pleased with herself, kneeling at my feet with a goofy grin and large, steel gray dinner plates for eyes. The only thing I loved more than her naked tits was seeing my cum dripping off the peak of her hard nipple.

Holy shit, who was I? I wasn't this guy. I never got this lucky.

"WHY DOES THIS FEEL so good?" she asked later that evening, after gingerbread cookies had been made and eaten and two different versions of *A Christmas Carol* had been watched. She was treading water in the center of the pool, looking happy in the pure peace of the quiet night.

"It's a luxury. Swimming when it's this cold. The way the warm water relaxes your muscles. All luxuries feel good."

"I don't mean swimming." She drifted closer to me. "I meant us."

I knew what she'd meant. I just didn't have an answer. Not one I was ready for.

"I don't know." I stared up at the starry sky. Not the faux stars of my bedroom, but the glistening balls of gas punched out of the cold night sky. I told my body to enjoy it. Relax into the wonder of feeling the warmth of the water and her naked skin slick against mine, of the genuine openness of her soul, of her curiosity and the bright glow of her mind as it leapfrogged from one thing to the next, pulling me along behind her.

Remember this moment.

There would come a time when I'd need to remind myself that perfection existed. If a career in death had taught me anything, it was that life was too fragile. It could all come crashing down, leaving beautiful people to rot in the rain and wind and scorching sun until nothing was left but a handful of teeth and bones.

"Can we trust this?"

"I've been asking myself the same thing."

"I mean, this feels like toxic relationship good. Without the toxicity. Everything seems so right, but also good and wholesome. And still really fucking hot. Is that what... I haven't really had an adult relationship. My only boyfriend was in high school, and no one could classify that as serious." She dipped her head back in the water. "Is it always like this?"

I was quiet for a moment, warring with myself over what to tell her. I tried to think of all the reasons this wasn't real. Our feelings were lying to us. We were too much, too fast. It was all just because we were both alone on Christmas, or that women were more likely to feel bonded to someone when they experienced orgasm because their bodies released oxytocin.

But I couldn't say any of it. Because I didn't believe it anymore.

"It's never like this." I lifted her legs and wrapped them around me, her weight buoyed by the water. "Not for me, anyway."

Maybe something loomed on the horizon. Something insidious that threatened to destroy even the memory of these thirty-six perfect hours together. But tonight, I refused to let these thoughts take over.

Tonight was for creating new holiday traditions. And from the way her hand was pumping my cock under the water, it seemed our Christmas traditions would include fucking in a heated pool under the stars while snowflakes melted into the water around us.

This was going to be a merry Christmas.

Chapter 8

Daphne

"I've decided I'm going to start answering the phone 'Ahoy, ahoy.' It's what Alexander Graham Bell advocated for when he invented the telephone."

"Bell wasn't the only one to invent the telephone though," he said, glancing in the rearview mirror before stepping on the gas.

The G-forces pressed me deeper into the seat as he shifted into a higher gear, passing a semi. The sound of the acceleration was so delicious I wanted to drink it.

"No, but his name is on the patent. Every invention is built on the backs of someone else's research and technological advances. Innovations don't happen out of the blue. Unless you're Isaac Newton."

"You really like factoids, don't you?"

"I have an insatiable intellectual curiosity. That's what my teachers always told me."

"I believe that's called being a nerd. And you won't hear me complaining."

I grinned. I could tell it was goofier looking than I intended based on the small laugh that shook his shoulders when he glanced over at me.

We drove in silence for a few seconds.

I loved watching him drive.

He was not at all tentative.

Then again, he wasn't tentative with sex, either.

He drove like he fucked. He knew exactly what his machine was capable of, knew where he wanted to go, his right hand competently gripping the gearshift while his left teased the wheel by millimeters. He was polite in traffic, waiting his turn, then took it ravenously when there was an opening. I was getting turned on already and we'd barely merged onto the highway.

I squeezed my legs together and squirmed in my seat. Chris's mouth quirked a little as he looked down. My arousal had not gone unnoticed.

I talked about the invention of the telephone for seven miles. Well, not just the telephone, but outdoor electric light bulbs, the hot dog, the Ferris wheel, peanut butter, and several of my other favorite early twentieth century inventions before I realized I was reciting factoids again.

"You're awful quiet," I said.

"Huh? Uh, yeah."

"What's the matter?"

"Nothing. I'm..." he paused, thinking about his next words, "happy. I'm not used to that."

Tension had never built up and released so quickly in my guts.

"Me too. Fair warning though, if you don't start talking, I'm probably going to monologue the whole way to Knoxville."

His lips parted as if to say something before changing his mind. His eyes moved back and forth between my face and the road, as if he couldn't decide what to say or think or do.

"Threatening me with listening to you talk for the next three hours while I get to drive this high-performance machine." He shook his head. "I can only think of one better way to pass the time."

He smiled that crooked smile again. The adorable one that warmed my heart. Only this time, it was softer, more to himself, as if he was lost in his thoughts.

My cheeks grew hot as blood rushed to my head. I squeezed my lips together so I wouldn't blurt out the incomprehensible syllables that were flooding my brain. Being with Chris felt so much *more*, so much *bigger* than any other emotion. I was proud when I'd graduated summa cum laude from a tough program, at a tough school, while working full-time, but even then, I wasn't bursting with feelings like I was with him now.

Maybe it was the car. How tiny it was. Maybe I had too much spirit for this car to contain.

Except I'd felt this way at his parents' house, too. And Decca's back yard. And in the woods, almost as soon as I'd met him. I didn't exactly know what I was feeling for him. Because of him. Maybe it was that we were so sexually compatible. Maybe it was some cosmic connection, but I couldn't contain the energy that was exploding out of me.

"Can you imagine what they thought?" I asked, trying desperately to stop myself from writing his initials inside hearts all over the notebooks of my mind.

"Who?"

"All the people at the 1904 World's Fair, looking at a cityscape entirely illuminated by electric lights. During that era, you were lucky to have gas lines in your home so you could turn on and off the chandeliers with a key. Then suddenly, bam! A single switch is thrown and the whole exterior of a building is glowing!" I could see it in my head as clearly as if I was actually there, rather than imagining it from blurry black-and-white photographs in books.

"I think it would be scary to see something like that for the first time," I continued. "Like the world was poised for change. Sometimes technology can be so big, it grows and grows and gets out of hand before humans stop to consider whether or not they should use it. Look what happened. Less than a decade after electric lights, there were armies lining up in the fields of Belgium, just like they would if they were going to be loading muskets, only the new weapons didn't take three minutes to reload anymore, and instead those poor boys were mowed down by Howitzers."

"That's where your mind goes?"

"Sorry. I think it's a default setting of being raised by a military history buff. War is pretty much the only thing I ever talked about with my dad."

"I don't mind. Besides, the ethics of technology is always a timely argument."

"How so, now?"

"Everything. Look at artificial intelligence. We were all so keen to explore its development for jobs we considered unworthy of human skill. Now it's creating art instead of cleaning up trash."

"Don't get me started on AI."

"It'll take over our jobs one of these days." He shrugged.

"Not if I have anything to say about it."

"Where does your interest lie? In the tech, or turn of the century history?"

"You mean the turn of the nineteenth century?"

His jaw ticked as he gritted his teeth. "Yeah. That one."

"I like all of it, I guess. History. Science. The history of science and the way society adapts as a result. The early twentieth century is a time when so much comes together cohesively. For the first time, we have a wealth of primary sources written by the losers as well as the winners, so we finally got a clearer picture of what life was really like for marginalized people."

He nodded to show he was listening, but he didn't seem to have anything to add.

Damn. He really *was* going to let me talk the whole way to Knoxville.

"Blame Daniel Day-Lewis for my latest special interest. I watched *The Age of Innocence*, and I fell in love with Newland Archer, but I needed to read the Edith Wharton book to get Daniel Day-Lewis's voice out of my head, and that led me down a research rabbit trail about the Gilded Age, and now I'm slowly moving through the decades. In the last month, I think I've read about six pretty thick books, not counting Wharton. Now I'm in the 1900s. Once I start school, I won't have much time to research new interests that crop up. I've been taking full advantage of not having a course load for the first time."

Chris froze. He hadn't been moving much to begin with, but now his stillness was shouting at me. Even his chest seemed to stop moving up and down. "When you start school... what do you mean *start school?*"

"Grad school? Forensic Anthropology. The Body Farm. Remember me, out there in the field the other day, helping you and Decca? I mean, so much has happened between us now, I wouldn't blame you if you forgot."

"No, no. You're Decca's assistant. The people she hires have already completed their education."

"I must be special then."

Chris didn't react. Not outwardly, anyway. His eyes flicked up to the rear-view mirror, his foot grew heavier, and the car accelerated to speeds closer to what it was built for. He passed cars on the left and the right as I listened to the purring engine do what it was built for.

The seat hugged my body close. I looked down to find the side panels automatically shifting to keep me from sliding around on the leather. I'd read about the dynamic seating, but now I was going to be obsessed with its engineering.

We passed a green exit sign. He moved the wheel to the right, pulling into the rest stop and jerking to a stop, perpendicularly across spaces meant for big rigs. Man, I wanted to drive one of those. Maybe I could take a class in my spare time. Get my CDL. Then I could drive the refrigerated body trucks if they ever needed—

"Tell me again. Everything." He spoke in a measured voice to the windshield, his hands still gripping the wheel at ten and two. "I need to make sure this was just a momentary hallucination. You didn't actually say what I think you said." His hands choked the wheel as he twisted them, squeezing tighter.

"What's the matter? Don't you want to..." I pointed to the spaces reserved for cars.

"Daphne." He warned me through gritted teeth.

What was his problem?

"I—I don't know what you want me to tell you. I finished undergrad last May—Biological Anthropology—but it took a while. You know I had to work. And I had to take some time off to care for my dad... I mean, he's capable, but you know I live with him, and sometimes he—"

"I don't give a fuck about your dad." His eyes were wide as he spat out the words. He swallowed and took a breath. "Sorry. I'm so sorry. I'm sure he's a... I just need to know about school."

"I'm starting my master's in forensic Anthropology. At the University of Tennessee," I explained slowly, enunciating perfectly. I twisted in my engineering marvel of a seat to face him. "What's got you in a tizzy?

Isn't it obvious, especially after I was there helping you all day with the remains?"

"It wasn't obvious you didn't already complete your education," he said quietly, breathing it out more than speaking.

"I've been told I'm precocious," I explained. "I studied everything I could get my hands on, on top of my assigned projects. What's the matter with you? Are you okay?" I reached for his hand, still gripping the wheel. My fingertips brushed across his knuckles. He watched for a moment, his face softening. Then something shifted, and he jerked it away.

His eyes shut tight.

"I teach there, Daphne. Didn't you realize that when you read my publications? Didn't Decca tell you? What lab did you think we were going to?"

"Yeah, of course I know that, but... Oh. Shit."

His words slammed into me like a big rig. I stared at his profile. Neither of us moved.

I tried to breathe but my lungs wouldn't inflate. My medulla wasn't regulating like it should. This should be easy. I'd been breathing for years. I'd never had any trouble before. I tried to remember the mechanism. I visualized my alveoli filling with air, knew my ribs should be expanding to accommodate it, but I couldn't figure out how to make it happen.

No. That wasn't true. I'd walked Dad through enough panic attacks to know that wasn't true. It was just my body creating helpful solutions to problems that didn't really exist. I could hack this.

"We can't be doing this, can we?"

He shook his head, slowly, his expression blank except for his eyes frantically darting over the car, as if it held the answer somewhere.

Something shook loose inside me, and I sucked in a gulp of air to calm myself.

"Okay, let's look at this rationally. A: we didn't know, so we can't possibly be culpable."

"It doesn't matter. I'm faculty. In your program."

"What actually do you teach? You're the teeth guy. I'm not studying dentistry or odontology. There's our B."

"Everyone studies teeth eventually. I come in for things. Comparative Osteology and Odontology. It's a short practicum. Teaches you to discern the difference between human and other skeletal remains as they pertain to teeth and the jawbones. I don't teach a full course in the FAC; I primarily teach at the dental school, but I am a lecturer and I have lab hours there if needed. I have an office there. I take on grad students. I could be your boss if you're assigned a case under me."

"That doesn't seem that bad."

"It might not seem that bad. I could very well avoid you for two years. I may never see your face, though it would be unlikely."

"Then—"

"If I'm working on a case, you wouldn't be allowed to participate. It could potentially cut down on your field hours."

The weight was beginning to lessen. Really, this wasn't that huge of an issue. "Oh. Then Decca could make up for them."

"Yes. She could. But that's not even the biggest problem. Oh, fuck." He exhaled slowly.

"What is?"

"The real world is the real problem. I'm an expert witness. If anyone finds out, it could be used against me in court and could sway a trial." He rubbed his eyes under his glasses. "Shit."

"No one has to find out. I won't tell anyone. Decca suspects, but I think she was not-so-secretly hoping this would happen. And she won't tell."

He closed his eyes as he dropped his head back against the headrest. He shook his head against the leather. "They'll know."

"Why? If you and I both keep this under our belts—"

"They'll know because I'm going to disclose it. It's better that way. I can preserve whatever dignity I have—"

"Sleeping with me is not an indignity to you."

Finally, he turned to look at me. "Sleeping with a student is ethically reprehensible. That is the definition of undignified."

"So now I'm just a student. Last night, it was goddess and sweetheart. My pussy was made to sheath your—"

"Enough. I know what I said." His hand hovered over mine like he wanted to hold it, but now he couldn't. Because of stupid rules. "Yo u're… all those things. Except that last one, because you can't be… we can't…"

I shrugged. "I'm glad you're going to disclose it."

He looked at me for a minute, his mouth in a grim line. "You are?"

"Yeah. If you disclose it, there's no reason for us to stop. We couldn't possibly get into deeper trouble than we're in now."

"That's not how it works."

"Well, figure out how to make it work. I have to go to the bathroom."

Chapter 9

Chris

SHE GATHERED HER THINGS and took off into the rest stop.

As soon as her door slammed, I sucked in a breath. And again. And again. Each time, the air felt thinner, barely able to sustain me. A long, slow exhale wracked my body and my arms shook from where I still gripped the steering wheel.

I stared straight ahead, not really seeing the side of the tractor trailer parked in front of me. There was just a sea of dirty white nothing in my field of vision, like the end of my career leering back at me.

I'd worked so hard for everything I'd achieved in my career. For almost twenty years I studied and tested and published and worked long days in multiple jobs; volunteering, forgoing a social life, family obligations, and relationships to get to where I was now: at the top of my field, making a difference in the world.

Now it was all about to be worthless. I'd have to start over again from scratch. I'd retain my dental license. I could move away, open a family practice somewhere where my reputation was still intact, but that wasn't the career I wanted. It wasn't what made a difference. It only made more money.

Pressure built inside my chest, enough to shatter my ribcage. I sat, imagining how my body would look if anthropologists picked through my remains after all this emotion surged out of me like a bomb—fragments of ribs and vertebrae scattered across the highway, down embankments, and nestled in the dried brown grass. The team would consider it the work of an animal, maybe a wolf or a mountain lion; something strong that could crack a rib in its jaw and drag it away from the rest of my bloody corpse. No one would ever guess my feelings had grown so big, so insurmountable, they'd blown me into bits.

I punched the steering wheel until my knuckles throbbed, screaming into the windshield.

A shadow darkened my window. I raised my eyes as a man walked up beside the car, bending low to see beyond the tint.

"Heard you honking." He shouted into the car. "Need some help?"

"Sorry man. I'm good. Appreciate it." I waved and tried to smile. His brows pinched in the middle, obviously unconvinced, but he nodded and headed back to his cab.

Great. Now I felt like a lunatic on top of being a disgusting asshole who'd fucked a student.

Of fucking course she'd be a student. The first woman I'd been completely and utterly enamored with, and she was untouchable.

Oh, but I had touched her. Every silky inch of her. Inside and out. That was the worst part. Knowing what she felt like under my hands, how she moved her body under mine, how she moaned when I kissed her neck and licked her clit. Oh, God, I couldn't stop thinking about the feel of her clit on my tongue. My hands had already memorized the feel of her. My nose knew her scent.

I'd only gotten a few moments of her and my body cried out for hers. Now I had to give her back. It was unfair and cruel.

And where in the ever-loving fuck was she? Did she hitch a ride with someone because I'd called our situation undignified? We'd driven ahead of the storm, but it would be on us again if we didn't keep going.

I unclicked my seat belt and stepped out of the car. The cold smacked me in the face and stole my breath.

The vending machine alcove on the side of the building was empty, so I waited outside the women's restroom for several more minutes, watching people come and then go, giving me suspicious looks when they realized I was camped outside the door. I wandered inside the welcome center. It was the only place left to check before I'd call the cops and start the search.

Sure enough, there was Daphne, standing next to a Middle Tennessee carousel, clutching a stack of maps and brochures for tourist attractions she'd probably been to a million times, smiling with a man in plaid flannel and a baseball cap with a fishhook on the brim.

When I stopped next to her, the man's face became much less friendly. "Oh, hey!" she said when she saw me. "I was talking to Jeff, and he says we should go to this place." She sifted through her brochures until she found the right one, and thrust it in front of my face. "Fiddler's Grove Historic Village."

I raised my eyebrows at the uncharmingly rustic barn on the front of the brochure. "I presume you're Jeff?" I nodded once to the man.

"And you're Chris, I can tell by the scarf."

I shot a look at Daphne. "And you thought no one would find out."

Her eyes widened with the realization. "Sorry. He asked what brought me here."

"And you told him about us?"

"Well, not us us. Not exactly how... involved we are. Or were."

"Excuse me, ma'am. I better be on my way." He tipped his Cabela's cap to Daphne and gave us a wide berth.

"It was nice meeting you, Jeff. Good luck with your baby."

"Thank you, ma'am."

I stared down at her, unmoving.

"What?" she asked.

"Are you ready? Or were you planning to move in? There's a fireplace, at least. I know how much you like those." I stormed off across the parking lot.

"You don't have to be so grumpy," she hollered after me.

"I think I have an excellent reason to be grumpy. We've just lost twenty minutes because you were in here collecting brochures for places we're not going to. Do I have to remind you not to talk to strangers? That guy was hitting on you."

"No, he wasn't. His girlfriend's about to have a baby."

"That does nothing to prevent him from hitting on another woman."

"At least someone was interested in me," she grumbled under her breath.

I stopped walking and her head ran into my back. I turned. Raised my arm to tip her chin up to me before I remembered my new no-touching rule and let it drop again.

"It's not lack of interest, Daphne. It's ethics." I took a deep breath, inhaling the smoky, woody fragrance of a nearby campfire. "I won't budge on that. No matter how tempting you look when you sulk."

"I'm not sulking."

I narrowed my eyes at her.

"Okay, I am. But now that I know it tempts you, I probably won't stop."

"Oh, Lord," I groaned. The next three hours were going to be hell.

"I may as well warn you, I won't stop trying to convince you that we should be together. We have something really special, Chris, and it's not because I'm young and starry-eyed. I know you feel it, too. Why should we let an institution dictate our future happiness?"

"Because what we feel is insignificant when it comes to a breach of ethics. That institution prohibits relationships between faculty and students. I can be fired. Other schools might be more lenient, but not this one."

"Okay."

"Okay?" Something told me she wasn't okay with my decision.

"Okay." She smiled confidently. "I know better, but I'm choosing to believe that you *think* you know what's best."

It was almost word for word what I'd told her two nights ago, about the power imbalance I *thought* would be our biggest issue. I took a deep breath. "Why does that sound ominous?"

"Because your beliefs can be incorrect. Haven't you ever gone to therapy?"

"No."

"Well... me neither, but I have friends who go to therapy and that's what they tell me. Your belief in a thing doesn't validate it. You have to consciously examine your false beliefs."

"Tell that to the employee handbook."

Part Two

Chapter 10

Daphne

"THE NEXT EXIT IS Fiddler's Grove. It's the one for the fairgrounds," I said quietly, dropping him the info so he could make the right choice.

"I have a GPS to navigate for me, thank you, and we're not stopping until we get to the lab." His voice was hard and unrelenting. "That would be on the campus where *I'm* faculty and *you're* a student, in case you've forgotten already."

"It's still early. We killed a whole day at your house. There's no reason to rush now."

His eyes closed momentarily on a sigh. "Maybe not for you. I've got a date with a firing squad."

"All the more reason to prolong it just a bit longer. You said no one's going to be at the lab on Christmas Eve. That probably includes your executioners."

His face remained still.

"Please? It's my lifelong dream."

"Getting a man fired from a career he's spent the last eighteen years building?"

I did the mental math. "Sixteen. At most. You started as a music major."

He grumbled.

"Stop at Fiddler's Grove," I said.

He turned his head to narrow his eyes at me. "Fiddler's Grove is hardly worthy of a lifelong dream."

"You won't know until you stop, and I don't mean that place in particular. I mean a road trip. A real one. Not just driving at breakneck speeds to cover two hundred miles as fast as possible, but one where you stop at the welcome centers. You pick up brochures for cheesy places like the World's Third Largest Worm Farm and you go there, and take pictures you'll put in albums and laugh at for years to come."

"The World's Third Largest Worm Farm is probably at The Body Farm, which you're slated to become intimately acquainted with soon enough."

"But does it harken back to days of olde, like the one-room schoolhouse, blacksmith's shop, and funeral parlor at Fiddler's Grove Historic Village? Oh, come on, Chris! It'll be so fun."

He clenched his teeth and his jaw froze. "We've had enough fun." He moved into the left lane.

He really wasn't going to budge on this ethics thing. His attitude had taken me by surprise. Here I was thinking he'd known the whole time, and he thought I was *tricking* him.

And he'd lose his career over this. Over me. I wasn't worth it. He didn't have to tell me in words. Of course I wasn't worth it.

My chest tightened. I pinched my lips together as sudden tears pooled in my eyes. Oh, God. This is what I get for thinking I was living out my fairy-tale, happily ever after dreams. It was all a façade. My throat grew tight.

"I wasn't tricking you," I said, dabbing at the corners of my eyes. "I didn't know you didn't know. I never even knew to think something like bureaucracy could come between us. I'm sorry." I sniffed and wiped again.

"I..." he shook his head. "I didn't think you'd purposely withheld the information. It was so nice not talking about work yesterday, it didn't occur to me to ask about yours or to... get the timeline of your life hashed out. I thought that would happen slowly, organically. I'm sorry for lashing out."

"I'm still the same person I was last night. We have the same connection."

"I know you are. I know we do. It's not you, or us, it's... there can't be an *us*. That's what makes this so fucking miserable. I—Fuck." His eyes flicked behind him as he swerved into the exit lane. "Tell me where to find this Fiddler's Village."

My eyes widened. "Really?"

He sighed and shook his head. "Like you reminded me, no one will be in the lab on Christmas Eve anyway. Nothing's pressing that can't wait until this afternoon."

"Oh my gosh, they do a special thing for Christmas Eve. Caroling and cocoa. Make a right. Follow the fairgrounds sign. Oh, this is going to be great. The perfect holiday tradition." I gripped his hand on the shifting paddle and he winced like I'd burned him. "And afterward, we can see the Merry Lights of Christmas, Tennessee's largest drive-through lighted Christmas display. You can't complain about that because it won't even take that long."

"It has to be dark to see Christmas lights. We'll be in Knoxville by the time the sun goes down."

"Oh." I deflated. "Still, I'm so happy you stopped. I think you're really going to love this."

He threw the car in park. "Something tells me this is going to be a bad idea."

"LOOK! THERE'S A WREATH making workshop!"

"Kind of late for that, isn't it? You don't have a wreath by now, it's probably not a priority."

"I don't have a wreath and it's a priority, especially if I can make my own. When I have a home of my own, I'm putting one on every door." I moved closer to the sign. "Oh, good. It starts at ten thirty. We didn't miss it."

Slipping into the line, I nodded to the older women standing in front of me.

"First time?" she asked. "We do this every year." The woman shivered in her thick blue coat, almost the same blue as her eyes that sparkled with the joy and anticipation of wreath-making. "It's family tradition to come to Fiddler's Grove on Christmas Eve. I'm Patty. This is my granddaughter, Eva."

"Hi, Eva. I'm Daphne. Are you going to make a wreath too?"

The girl smiled politely until her eyes widened at something behind my shoulder. "Oh, he's with me. This is my friend, Chris." I leaned down to whisper conspiratorially into her ear. "I think your wreath is going to be ten times prettier than whatever Chris tries to pull together. I'll even judge the contest. Give you five dollars if you win."

She humored me with a smile.

"I already have a wreath, thank you," Chris said.

"Like Patty said, it's a family tradition. Remember our plan to rebuild Christmas the way we never got to experience it growing up?"

"Does that mean we have to come back here to... wherever we are... every year?"

I looked around, at the bundled-up revelers sipping cocoa from steamy paper cups, at the Gilded Age post office and dry goods shop, strung with turn of the century electric Christmas lights. I sighed. I didn't even mind the anachronisms here. "I wouldn't mind that."

"You're in Lebanon, dear," Patty told Chris. The apples of her cheeks were reddened from the cold and smooth as polished marble. With the twinkle in her eye, and the white puffs of hair coming out from under her hat, she was giving Mrs. Claus vibes.

"Lebanon. Great. It took us an hour to drive twenty miles."

They started letting people into the building. As we ambled closer, I saw the price of the workshop. Somehow, I'd missed it before.

Fifty dollars.

I stopped short, holding up the line that had formed behind me. I couldn't afford that. I still had to pay my share of the gas money, and I hadn't budgeted for Fiddler's Grove. Spending time here would also mean I'd need to buy food at some point. And it was only right to pay for Chris's workshop, since I'd goaded him into participating against his will.

It was fine. The house had gone this long without any Christmas decorations. Having a pretty wreath on our rust-stained front door would be like putting rims on a hooptie, anyway.

"You're right." I turned to Chris. "This was silly. Let's not waste our time. We'll just walk around a little more and head home."

Chris's eyes lingered on the price before shifting to me. His hand flattened against my lower back as he gently guided me over the threshold. "Come on. Family tradition, remember? I've never had a fresh evergreen wreath. I'm sure it'll be a delight getting pine sap out of the pristine carpets of the trunk. It'll add a Christmas tree note to the dirt and moss I've recently had the olfactory pleasure of noticing. Two please." He fished his wallet out of his back pocket, and handed a card over to the guy with the swipey thing connected to his phone.

"Chris, you don't need to." The reader flashed and the guy handed back his card. "I... thank you."

Chris nodded to Pat and Eva. "I think your new friends saved you a spot next to them."

If my heart wasn't already three sizes too big, it definitely would have grown after Chris swooped in and saved Christmas for me. I could feel it physically aching under my lungs and ribs. I rubbed my sternum, trying to ease the sensation. There was a pain accompanying this joy that didn't seem fair.

When the workshop began, we collected our materials. There were various evergreen, fir, and cedar boughs to wire to our choice of a frame, materials for bows and ribbons, and boxes of other crafty things to tuck into the greenery.

I chose Scotch pine boughs to lace onto a grapevine frame, topped off with a floppy, red flannel bow. It was historic and homey, like something the March family would place on the front door of Orchard House.

Chris's was minimal. And brutal. The tips of the spruce needles stabbed his fingertips every time he repositioned them. Hisses and curses issued from under his breath with every twist of the pliers. At least he was making Eva giggle.

Eva's wreath, inspired by Taylor Swift, had a mirrored silver ribbon snaking around the circle of evergreens. It was hideous, but she had fun, and more importantly, won against Chris in our little competition.

"It was so nice to get to meet you, Pat. Eva, I think you might have a career in floral design if your singing career doesn't work out." I hugged the ladies goodbye.

"Good luck with your school, dear," Pat said to me before squeezing Chris's arm. "You're a lucky man. Don't let her get away."

He smiled politely. He had every intention of letting me get away.

He just didn't know I wasn't going to let that happen.

Arms laden with evergreens (and face paling as he tried to find a safe place to grasp his iron maiden of a wreath without covering his camel hair coat in sap), Chris was extra quiet as we strolled through the rest of the buildings. Neither of us was in much of a hurry to get on the road. The road meant we had only three hours left of whatever our relationship was.

"The funeral home is from 1920," I gestured to the plaque outside the door of the white clapboard building.

"That's not that old. Gus's family's mortuary has been there since the 1800s."

"And it's still in use?"

"Thriving, from what Decca says."

It seemed to be one of the more popular buildings in the village. In the back was an embalming room, outfitted with a thick slab of an enameled embalming table and thoughtfully curated objects: an antique embalming machine, prep tools, and wooden crates of arterial fluid bottles.

The front room had been for the public. The walls were decorated in Victorian prints, mourning wreaths, and framed hair work florals. A liturgical kneeler was even placed in front of an empty replica coffin. I knelt on the purple velvet cushion.

"I've always been fascinated by the idea that death is something we outsource. I'm not judging. As a society, we're no longer equipped to handle body preparation and home funerals, but I sometimes wonder what good things get lost when we aren't forced to deal with the bad."

He scoffed. "You've been spending too much time with Decca."

"No, that's what connected us. I've always known I'd be involved in deathcare somehow. My dad was a Mortuary Affairs Specialist in the Army. His hope was to do his tours and then live out the rest of his military career as a funeral director at Arlington. His PTSD was so bad after Afghanistan they discharged him. He tried to continue afterward, as a civilian, but he couldn't get past what he'd seen in-country."

"I run a DMORT team with Decca," he said, quietly. "We get called out to mass casualty events like plane crashes or meth lab explosions. It's hands down the worst thing I do. No matter how rare they are, I live in dread over those calls. Only get through them with a morbid sense of humor and a bottle of cheap booze."

He sank onto his knees next to me. "You convince yourself what you're seeing isn't real. That's not an eyeball I'm looking at; surely, it's plastic. That's not a human grease stain on the concrete next to the limbless trunk of a man—that discoloration was probably always there." He blew out a breath and shook his head. "The brain can only handle so much self-deception before you start to think nothing's real. I couldn't imagine doing it for years during a war."

Someone stepped in through the door, looked at Chris and me, kneeling as if we were in prayer, in front of a fake casket, in a fake funeral home, and backed right out through the open door. "My dad gets through it with a lot of cheap booze, that's for sure. His drinking is a little better now, though. His nightmares are better. His medicine is more calibrated too, now, but it took most of my kid years to get him to stop self-medicating and get the treatment he needed, even through the VA. The stigma has lessened, but it's still there."

Chris covered my hands with his and squeezed. I turned from the embroidered Bible verse I'd been staring at. His eyes were soft and far away, but still with me in sympathy. This was what I loved about death care. There was a camaraderie among those who did the work.

His hand stayed on mine, his thumb rubbing across my knuckles. It was no longer a gesture of solidarity, but of longing, of needing to feel my skin under his.

This was hopeless. We'd never be able to stay away from each other. Not for the two years it would take me to graduate. He couldn't *not* give in to me. I couldn't *not* show my vulnerability around him.

"What are your final wishes?" he asked. "Since I know you've already considered it."

His eyes danced with humor, but there was something else there, too. A sincerity that was constant with him.

"Burial? Cremation?"

I shrugged. "Cremation would be cheaper for Dad."

"And if money were no concern?"

"I don't know," I looked into the casket in front of us. "I love old, rich traditions. It's not my culture, but those New Orleans mourning parades with horse-drawn caissons and brass bands? I just find them so reverent, and with reverence comes a sense of letting go, you know? I think funerals need to be sad. You need to deal with the sadness before you move beyond it. People are so quick to celebrate, it stifles the grieving process." I laughed at myself. At what I was saying. "Is it egotistical to want everyone to be really fucking sad at my funeral?"

Chris didn't smile. "I'd give that to you. A sad funeral. Lots of tradition and ritual. Keep 'em all crying."

"I thought you wanted nothing more to do with me after today."

He tucked a strand of hair behind my ear, his fingers lingering on my earlobe. I leaned into him, letting myself feel his comfort and melt at his touch.

"Only for as long as it takes you to graduate. After that, I intend to claim every last piece of you. For as long as we both shall live." He smiled. "So, hurry up and make sure you pass all your classes."

"Yes, Daddy."

He let out a breath that was more like a groan, his eyes floating down to my lips before diving in and capturing them with his.

This kiss was hot and desperate. It didn't matter that we were in public. That we were kneeling on an exhibit in a historic funeral home. That other people were walking in—and straight back out again. He kissed me like I was his *now,* and he didn't have to let me go. Like we didn't have to continue our lives as though we hadn't met.

His tongue was hot against mine, as his hand tangled in my hair. Our breath clouded in the unheated building.

Finally, we drew back. I stared into his eyes, wild with lust but resigned to sadness.

No sadness. We'll find a way, I wanted to tell him, but he was so determined to believe he was a dead man walking. Even if we had to wait—which was a feat I knew we'd never achieve—we'd make it through somehow. We'd find a way.

I stood first. I turned to the room and found myself lost. Our kiss had changed so much I had to reorient myself to the real world.

When I stepped out of the shadows of the mortuary into the light of day, I felt lighter. I was ready to take on the world, or at least however many deans had an issue with my being in love with their beloved professor.

I threaded my fingers through Chris's when he joined me. He didn't pull away like I'd expected him to. He squeezed my hand right back, mourning the loss of the future we'd both been dreaming about.

We visited the other buildings, filling ourselves with cocoa, kettle corn, and cinnamon sugar-roasted almonds that had been scenting the air, calling to me with their sweet spice.

"Let's stop at the gift shop real quick. I want to pick up something to commemorate the occasion," I said, dropping his hand and walking backward with a giant smile plastered across my face.

Inside was a wonderland of kitsch. There were the usual t-shirts and keychains, but there was also a display of items that would make decent Christmas gifts.

"I'd like to get your mom something. Does she like candles?" His mom probably had a standing order of luxury perfumed candles shipped in from Paris, and had no need of a hand-poured gingerbread-scented jar, but I'd spent the whole day in that woman's house, and dammit, I was leaving her a hostess gift if it killed me. Chris could always swap it with something more expensive before he gave it to her.

Turning the corner, the wall opened up to a sea of jarred goods: jellies, jams, salsas, and barbecue sauces.

"Chris, look at this. Cilantro jelly!" I said, reaching deep into the back of the shelf where one last jar lurked. "You know, it sounds kinda gross, but I bet it'd be really good on—ow!"

I yanked my hand toward my body, rubbing the heel and waiting for blood to start pooling.

Nothing. Not even a pinprick.

"You okay?" He laughed.

"There's something sharp back there. Must be a nail or something." I reached back again for the jar, paying more attention this time.

Chris towered above me, which meant he was standing very very close. I smiled up at him, pushing my body closer to his and wrapping my arm around his waist.

"What could that possibly be good on?" He kissed the top of my head.

"Hm?"

"You were saying that would be great on..."

"Oh, cream cheese. Like how you do with hot pepper jelly. Don't tell me you're one of those *cilantro tastes like soap* people. I don't think we could be together if that was the case. I put cilantro on everything—the only thing I can really cook are Chipotle dupe taco bowls—damn, that really hurt."

I shook my hand until Chris caught it, gripping it in his, rubbing his thumb over my fingers.

"I don't see anything."

"It's fine. I'm just surprised. I didn't brush up against the shelf or anything. I must have just gotten the nail point."

He bent his head to look. "Probably a spider. It's dark and cozy back there. You reached in and she thought you wanted to eat her babies."

"Oh, no. I'm sorry, Charlotte," I said to the back of the shelf before turning back to Chris with a big grin. "I love spiders!"

"Doesn't surprise me."

"You don't?"

"I'm indifferent. Let's go."

I purchased my candle and jelly, and a cheesy magnet for my dad and we said our reluctant goodbyes to Fiddler's Grove. *My* reluctant goodbye.

We'd gotten to the car, and he was so busy grumbling about wreath sap gunking up his brand-new trunk, he didn't notice my hand had swollen so much. Good. If he saw, he'd probably make me go to the doctor. I couldn't move my hand to open the car door, but I didn't have health insurance. I couldn't afford the doctor.

He'd started the car and put it in gear. I could barely breathe to say how much it was a shame we were missing the Merry Lights of Christmas.

It was just a spider bite. It couldn't get any worse.

By the time he was merging onto the highway, I could no longer control the way my body slumped down in the seat. I heard someone calling my name from far off. The last thing I remembered was the cold window pressed against my temple and blackness closing around the edges of my vision.

Chapter 11

Chris

"How soon..." Daphne gasped for breath. "After the bite..." *wheeze,* "do you think the radioactivity starts?"

"Shh," I stroked her hair and fought to keep my voice even. "Please try to stop talking. You need your breath to breathe."

She stood—barely—doubled over the hospital bed, the pain too much to take lying down. Too much to take standing up. She'd been changing positions every few minutes for the past hour and a half, trying to find something, anything that would provide the comfort the drugs weren't.

My teeth ground together. The words on my phone blurred together as if I'd removed my glasses. The experience was unique, the chemicals in my body thrashing and surging, blinding me with rage and terror.

"I'm going to try to find the doctor again. I don't know how this is acceptable to them, but—"

"No, stay." She gripped my hand and squeezed weakly. "Talkin g... ohhh, God, this hurts... makes me feel normal. You can always... give them a bad Yelp review later." Even with her pain, nausea, and swollen limbs she was making jokes. My lips tried to find a way to smile, but they seemed to have forgotten the movement. "One star. Did not perform Christmas miracles."

I tried to read more, but it was no use. I'd been poring over articles about black widow, brown recluse, and every other type of monster spider bites in the *New England Journal of Medicine.*

Despite its bad reputation, black widow neurotoxin was no worse than that of any other spider. For most people, the pain ran the gamut anywhere between hardly noticeable to... that grumpy-looking yellow guy on the pain chart under the nurse's board.

Daphne was one of the very few who were heavily affected. And holy shit, she was affected. In the car, she'd slumped, unconscious, into her seat. I'd swerved off the road, shouting her name, rousing her enough to get her to breathe and say a few words.

"Chris, I don't... think... I love spiders anymore."

I'd careened into the ER bay. Her whole arm had swollen to the point the nurses had to cut down the sleeve of her jacket to get it off her. She was puking up her cocoa and kettle corn and moaning in pain. Blacking out when it became unbearable.

They'd immediately hooked her up to an IV with narcotics, muscle relaxers, and anti-nausea meds, but so far nothing seemed to take the edge off.

"Okay then, keep talking."

"I keep waiting for my amazing spidey senses. Climb walls. Can you imagine how easy it would have been to retrieve that skull from below the ravine tracks. I could have just..." She mimed the Spiderman hand gesture. "And it would be like shooom. Ahhh," she winced, gripping her head.

When she looked up, all the blood had drained from her face. "That hurt really bad. Do you think that's the first sign?"

"Of?"

"Of me turning into Spiderwoman?"

I sat, and then immediately got back to my feet. There was nothing else to do but pace, seethe, and rub her back. "If that spider was radioactive, I'm pretty sure we're all contaminated, and we have bigger problems than defeating the Vulture or the fact that we haven't seen a fucking doctor in over ninety minutes."

"Who?"

"The doctor. What is taking them so goddamned long? This entire hospital has twelve parking spaces, and I'm pretty sure one of them was labeled Ambulance Only. What other patients could they possibly be seeing?"

"Other guy. Vulture. Who—?" Daphne asked before dry heaving into the blue plastic emesis bag I held under her face.

"The Vulture." I stroked her hair. I didn't know if I should try to distract her or what. Everyone wanted something different when they were in pain.

Once the nausea subsided, I took her pulse. It was fast, but not terribly so, and that was to be expected in her state. I knew nothing of spider bites other than the journal articles I'd been frantically combing through. I took a deep breath and pushed my glasses higher up on my nose. "The first Spiderman villain. From the comics. He has an electromagnetic anti-graviton generator-powered flying harness that allows him to fly up to ninety-five miles per hour and reach an altitude of over eleven thousand feet."

She blinked at me. Her mouth dropped open.

"I'm a dentist. Does my geekiness come as a shock?"

"I figured you were, I just didn't know your fandom. I took you for a Superman guy. The glasses and all."

"DC Comics doesn't have the moral ambiguity Marvel does. That's what makes it interesting."

"You sound like a sixth grader."

"You wanted to know what kid-me was like. I was a comic book geek."

I carefully lifted her swollen hand again to check out the bite. Nothing in the tiny black and white pictures in the journal articles had given me any insight into why a spider bite would cause this much harm. I wasn't this kind of a doctor, anyway. I was just impotent. There wasn't even a dollar figure I could throw at this problem to get it to go away. It was agony watching her, unable to help.

The sliding door groaned on its track, and a woman in sporty scrubs and a fleece jacket entered the room, her dark hair slicked back into a neat bun. Sneakers splashed garish colors into the anemic space.

"How ya doing, Love?" Her voice was low and calm as she addressed Daphne.

Daphne couldn't talk but gave a thumbs-up.

Liar.

"There's been no change in her pain levels. Why hasn't she been seen before now? There has to be more you can do."

"I'm Kelly. I'm the PA." She addressed Daphne. "Still okay if we talk with him in the room?"

Daphne nodded. "Please." Her face had paled again. She was in the middle of another painful muscle spasm.

"We're going to admit you, sweetie. We've ruled out MRSA, but since the morphine and the baclofen don't seem to be doing much, we're going to go ahead and administer an antivenin." Kelly turned to me. "She has no history of asthma?"

I paused. "I don't know." It felt like I'd known her forever, but the question highlighted how little I actually knew about her. It made my feelings seem... cheap and dishonest. Fuck.

Daphne shook her head once, her face tight with constricted muscles.

"Any other known allergies?"

"I don't know," I shouted. "Why have you waited this long?"

"Antivenin has a higher rate of complications and allergic reaction," she answered calmly, probably used to dealing with people like me. "We have to rule out a number of other things before we give her the hard stuff. It's hard to diagnose a spider bite, unless you see it happen. You didn't, did you?"

"No." I gritted my teeth.

"No one does. Spiders don't bite where you can see them. Until we get your antivenin, we're going to try to make you more comfortable by increasing your morphine. But we need to monitor you more closely, and we need the beds here for an incoming casualty event. I'm sending you to the ICU."

The ICU.

Hearing those words was like stepping onto the ice of a half-frozen lake. Solid footing giving way as the surface shattered underneath me.

Kelly put her hand on my forearm. "It's only temporary. Antivenin works very quickly." She turned to Daphne. "Once we get it in your IV, the pain should be gone in a few minutes. You'll be out of here in a few hours, okay?"

"Hours? I thought you said it works in minutes."

"We don't have any in stock. It's coming from Knoxville."

"There's nothing closer? They can't medevac it?"

The PA glanced at Daphne's tight face and gave a sympathetic smile. "It's not exactly an emergency."

"Not a—look at her!"

"Chris, it's okay." Her voice was weak and thready. "They're going to give me more painkillers."

The PA stood at the workstation in the corner of the room and processed the admissions, her fingernails tapping rapidly on the keys.

I shook my head and sighed. "Cilantro jelly." I crossed my arms and leaned against the wall.

I inhaled slowly, feeling my lungs expand before I let the air go. I didn't realize how long it'd been since I'd taken a deep breath. "Only you would feel bad for the jelly no one else wanted. It's probably been on that shelf since the eighties, and that spider's been using it for a home ever since."

"I don't think..." she licked her lips, "Spiders... live that long." I rooted through her bag for a lip gloss or something to moisten her dry lips. Nothing. I made a mental note to pick up some lip balm to have around for her. Then I canceled that mental note, remembering she wasn't *mine* to have lip balm around for.

How could I care for her, how could I protect her if she wasn't mine?

I trusted that it would be okay. This would be okay because I had no other option. The doctors had a plan. We weren't out of the woods yet, but we were going to the ICU, a situation that filled me with both hope and dread.

At least she'd be out of pain.

TWENTY MINUTES LATER I sat in the recliner next to her bed, holding her hand and watching her face contort with pain, even in her opioid-induced drowsiness.

"Is it any better?"

"Yeah," she winced. "Still worse than getting a migraine and cramps at the same time, but it feels... survivable." Her gray eyes met mine, but she was too drunk on painkillers to communicate much. "I thought I was going to die. Thank you, Chris."

"I thought—never mind. I'll be thankful when you get the right medicine."

She looked down at our interlocked fingers. It didn't seem right to withhold my affection. For what? To keep her locked out of my heart. She was already in my heart. A permanent scar in the tissue. And she needed every bit of affection I could give her while she suffered.

"No, *really*, thank you. You acted so quickly."

My eyes focused on the IV bag behind her as I replayed the imagery of the past few hours. The thud of her head hitting the car window when she passed out. The stillness of everything in my car, even my heart, when I didn't know if I'd make it to the hospital in time. I hadn't thought to call 911 from the road. I just turned around and drove straight back to where I'd noticed the big blue "H" signs on the road. The terror that gripped my guts contrasting the easy glide of the gas pedal under my foot. My arms remembered the weight of her body after she'd lost muscle function; it was a rag doll I carried into the hospital, not the strong, vibrant woman she'd been an hour before. I hadn't even turned off the car or shut my door. A good Samaritan had realized what was happening, parked my car, and followed me in with my keys.

I didn't want to think about why I'd reacted the way I did. It was more than fear. More than humanitarian concern. If it had been anyone else,

I would've kept a cooler head. I wouldn't have felt like it was my own life on the line.

Finally, she'd fallen asleep. I studied her pained face as she slept, grateful for every rise and fall of her chest. I kissed her straight, unlined brow, above eyes that held the wisdom of a life lived with hardship, despite how much she tried to downplay it.

I wanted nothing more than to curl around her and never let her go. I wanted—*I needed*—to make it all better for her. To facilitate her dreams. To make our own family traditions. To be her family.

To do that, I needed to give her up.

Two years was nothing. She didn't realize it. Not at twenty-four. That was the real wisdom that came with age: how quickly life passed. She smiled slightly in her sleep. I smiled back at her. It would hurt to let her go for this little piece of our lives, but she'd be back in my arms in no time.

I felt movement around me. I heard low voices and the buzz of the overhead fluorescent tubes. The IV rack was gone. The bed empty. I reached for my glasses in a panic.

Daphne stood in front of my chair, smiling widely.

"Surprise! I'm all better." She fell into my lap.

I glanced at my watch. I'd been out for hours.

"What? How?"

"That antivenin is great stuff. I could feel my body coming back to life. All the pain fizzled out of me like bubbles in a can of Mountain Thunder." Her fingers wiggled in the air like carbonation.

"Why are you smiling like that?"

"It's dark outside. We can drive through the Merry Lights of Christmas."

It was dark. We'd been here the whole day. "It's late. We need to get home."

"That's exactly what I was thinking. So, here's the plan: we get hot cocoas, we drive through the Christmas lights, pick up some Christmas Eve Chinese for dinner so we can eat lo mein with chopsticks out of the cartons like people in movies, then tomorrow we get an early start back to Knoxville."

"Nice try. Home *is* Knoxville. We have a three-hour drive ahead of us."

"Knoxville?" The ICU nurse was unhooking tubes from the wall, scrunching her nose like something had decomposed in the room. "Ain't going to be no three-hour drive. Ice storm's coming from the mountains."

Daphne quirked her head and gave me pouty face. "Holiday traditions?"

She'd been basically starved for holiday joy her whole life. As much as I hated it, I had to be a Scrooge this time and swipe the proverbial pennies from her eyes.

She looked so hopelessly beautiful, even after her Spiderman poisoning and a stay in the ICU. My fingers itched to untangle the snarls in her hair. To rake those strands silky smooth again until liquid silver streamed through my fingers. To grasp her face close to mine and kiss the smirk off her lips. To give her everything she was ever denied because of lack of money, or opportunity, or attention, or love.

I gritted my teeth. "No."

Her smile didn't even falter.

"We're going home. Real home. Knoxville. There wasn't a cloud in the sky earlier today. We'll beat the weather."

"Cocoa?"

I imagined thick chocolate droplets jostling out from a tiny hole in a to-go cup lid, embedding into the interior of my ten-day-old car, and leaving a stench of rotten milk no car detailer could remove.

"Fine." I gritted my teeth. I couldn't give her what I really wanted to give her—everything, all the time, for the rest of my life. After tonight, this would be it—saying goodnight at her dad's front door, our fingertips touching until the very last minute, a final kiss to her forehead. Goodbye for two years. Goodbye forever was more like it, considering she'd probably meet someone else in the meantime.

At least I'd always have the fetid smell of rotten milk as a memory of these perfect two days together.

The ER was bustling when we made our way out of the hospital. People crammed into the waiting area, quietly crying and staring off into the distance. Doctors and nurses slalomed from room to room as we dodged their paths.

"What's going on?" I asked the only nurse standing still, wrapping the cords around a machine in the hallway.

"Big pile-up on Route 40. We're the closest trauma center, so everyone's coming to us.

"A trauma center who didn't have black widow antivenin," I said under my breath. "Let's go."

"We're not taking 40 are we, Chris?"

"That's the fastest way to Knoxville."

"Not tonight, it won't be," the nurse cut in. "Lanes are closed because of the overturned tractor trailer."

I groaned. "Thanks."

I grabbed Daphne by the sleeve of my coat she was wearing, steering her through the crowded halls.

"Chris, wait. We have to talk."

"The three hours in the car aren't enough?"

"Probably more like four if we can't take Route 40. And no, I want to talk first. I know you want to put this off until you think I've forgotten how much I want to be with you, but I promise I haven't. I won't."

"Daphne. I can't." My words came out so rough they hurt my throat. A middle-aged man in a jumpsuit jerked his head toward us, before looking away again, minding his own business. Between the piped-in pop Christmas music and sounds of an overextended ER, of course *I'd* be the one to draw attention.

I needed to get out of here. Away from the noise and people and the smell of the hospital.

I needed the security of my car, the blare of loud hip hop until we reached Knoxville.

I needed Daphne safe and sound and very far away from me.

Chapter 12

Daphne

"If you take us through the lights, I promise I won't ask for anything else. I'll be a good girl and keep my mouth shut. I won't break out any of the other brochures."

"You're only saying that because all the attractions are off Route 40 and we're taking back roads."

"I'm only saying that because they're all closed. It's Christmas Eve, and it's late."

He looked at the clock on the giant control panel. "That hospital feed you anything while I was getting coffee?"

"In the ten whole minutes you left me alone? No. There was no tray with creamy chicken goop and jello. I couldn't eat anyway. My stomach was convulsing in spasms. I'll never be able to eat kettle corn again." She said sadly.

"What about hot cocoa? That came up first, if my shoes are any witness."

"I'll never give up hot cocoa."

"Are you really all better? Just like that?"

"Just like that. I'm tired from the drugs, but it's nothing cocoa and Christmas lights wouldn't cure."

He said nothing. His jaw clenched, but he said nothing. His hands gripped the steering wheel tighter and his right foot pushed heavier against the gas pedal, but he said nothing.

The next exit had him switching lanes. Then the blinker came on.

"Really? The lights?"

"Food, Daphne. This might be the last exit for a while. You just got out of the hospital where you could very well have died. You need to eat. Even if it is..." he squinted to read the sign, "El Dorado Norte Mexican Fiesta Café." He tried to hide his disdain with a deep inhale. Where were we, anyway? Lebanon at least had a Bob Evans.

This wasn't even a town. It was just an unnamed exit off a back road with a motor lodge that, if it had ever been inhabitable—and I had my doubts—the warped remaining slats of vertical blinds and the abandoned vehicles parked on the weedy concrete pad told me it definitely wasn't any longer. A tenth of a mile past the motel, Chris made a right at a half-lit letter board sign.

Tires crunched over the sparse gravel in the parking lot. Neither of us could disguise our trepidation as he turned off the car. We both stared, wide-eyed, at the restaurant. If you could call it that.

Ahead of us squatted a cinderblock structure that had once been white. Or maybe blue. Or an oddly pretty sunset lavender. It was hard to tell from all the layers of flaking paint.

I was no snob. I'd had some of the best food at truck stops, fast food joints, and food trucks—the kind that catered to day laborers, not art-show attendees. I prided myself on my goat-like stomach of steel and my ability to enjoy just about any cuisine. But this might be my limit. This was... iffy, at best. At least that's what I was telling myself to avoid imagining the diverse strains of molds and bacteria that probably lurked in their walk-in.

I tried to stay positive. "What if the food is really good but they're recent immigrants and this building is all they could afford. We might be about to have the best meal of our lives," I suggested.

A doubtful eyebrow rose high over his tortoiseshell frames. But he unclicked his seatbelt anyway, apparently ready to die on this sword. At least this mishap was *his* doing.

"I've got a good feeling about this place," I said, almost believing it.

"Really? Because I get *front.*"

"Front? Like the mob?"

He still hadn't made a move to open his door. I could tell he was wrestling with the idea of feeding me food, versus potentially feeding me to the mob.

"Mob's a stretch, considering we're in rural Tennessee. Probably more like drugs. At best."

I jumped out of the car and made it all of five steps toward the door before Chris caught me by the elbow.

"Daph, wait. This is a bad idea."

"Probably, but what are the alternatives? We can drive the half hour back to your house and start over tomorrow morning—I already know that's not a real option for you. We can drive ten minutes west and find an Olive Garden or something, or we can continue on these little country roads. But who knows what we'll find the farther we get from civilization?"

Chris swallowed hard, weighing his options.

"If we go back to Lebanon, do you really think you'll be fit to drive three hours at night, after eating unlimited breadsticks? If you're that determined not to end up in bed with me tonight, El Dorado Norte... whatever it's called... is our best option."

"We're not turning around." There was conviction in his eyes as he said it. Turning around meant another night together. Back in bed. We both knew it, even if he had to keep up that pretense of a wall between us, no matter how thoroughly it had been demolished. Every moment, every adversity, had been a wrecking ball to his defenses.

"I guess it's El Dorado, then," I decided.

I avoided touching the rusted railing as I climbed the steps. I didn't feel like taking my fancy new tetanus shot for a test drive tonight. Chris used a handkerchief to open the door, ushering me inside with a hand pressing into my lower back. *Wall indeed.*

It took my eyes a while to adjust to the light. A few men, presumably the truckers, ate alone at old-fashioned laminated booths. It was dark, but it didn't look at all like the source of dysentery it did from outside.

At the hostess stand, an older white woman with black cherry hair and heavy earrings dangling from stretched-out lobes ran her eyes up and down the length of me, over my sliced-up jacket, my thigh high socks, my short skirt. Her eyes turned to Chris and softened. Her entire face was beaming, transformed with a flirtatious smile and knowing eyes.

"The special, hun?" she asked him.

"No... uh... thank you." He turned me back around, using more pressure this time to urge me quickly out the door.

"What's the special?" I threw over my shoulder.

"We don't want the special," he said into my ear.

"Larry," the woman called.

An older man with thin hair and a Titans t-shirt stretched over a big belly came around the corner.

"We're leaving. Now," Chris told me.

"She wants to know what the special is."

"Burgers."

"Oh," I said, relieved, brushing Chris off me and smiling at the man. "I thought for a minute it was going to be—never mind. That doesn't sound very Tex Mex. But yes, two, please."

"Daphne," Chris said through his teeth.

The food certainly looked edible, judging from the plates of the other diners. Besides, it would be rude to leave now.

"Follow me," said the gruff man, leading us away from the other men who hadn't even turned their heads when we'd walked in.

When the man swung open a door that looked like an employee entrance, I felt a small jolt of panic.

It was darker back here. Louder, with music thumping off the walls.

"I hope you brought cash," Chris said under his breath.

Larry heard him anyway. "ATM's over there."

"It's a little... this is an interesting choice of aesthetics."

"Is it, though?" Chris asked rhetorically.

"I—"

"You got any ID on you?" Larry stopped us in front of a set of velvet curtains.

Chris dug out his wallet. "No badges," Chris said through gritted teeth.

Larry looked almost amused for a split second. "Sheriff's our best customer. We got half-price drinks through happy hour."

"What time does your happy hour end?" I asked, knowing it was already past happy hour in most restaurants.

"It don't end."

"What beer do you have in bottles?" Chris asked.

"Heineken alright?"

"Two," Chris said, daring me to refute him.

The man nodded and guided us through the curtains into a small purple room with a few chairs and a very small table. Interesting. There was an elevated platform in the corner.

Chris took a deep breath and shrugged out of his jacket. "Looks relatively clean at least. My feet aren't sticking to the floor like they were in the hallway."

"I don't drink beer."

"I don't trust the taps here. Or the glasses. You've sent us hurtling back through time into the Wild West. I want to take as few risks as possible." Oh, shit. At least Chris knew what was going on. Wait... what *was* going on?

The curtain flicked open and I spun around from where I'd been deciding on what chair to sit in. My breath whooshed out of my lungs. A short, pretty brunette carried two bottles on a tray, talking a mile a minute with a thick East Tennessee accent. "Hi, welcome to the El Dorado. First time?" She handed us our bottles, first to me, then to Chris. Her thick, black lashes lowered as her gaze practically licked over his entire buttoned-up body. Then she turned back to me, biting her lip and giving me the same perusal, like a tiger looking at a thick juicy piece of marbled ribeye—or some choice cut of meat that was way out of my Aldi hamburger budget. "I'm Valentine," she said sweetly. "If you like what you see, I'll be taking care of you tonight." She leaned in close to my ear, giggling. "You're really cute. I'll make it a special night for you both."

"Nice to meet you. I'm Daphne," I said politely, a little confused.

I froze. I didn't know what to do. Didn't know where to look. At her? Was it even okay? Her tiny stretchy red dress. lined with white fur and open down to her navel, exposed a vast expanse of glossy skin and perfect, round cleavage. I assumed she was dressed as some kind of slutty Mrs. Claus. The material looked more like my tights and barely covered her ass or her tits. I could see through to her pierced nipples! Tanned and glowing legs ended in clear plastic platform heels six, seven, no... damn, they must be eight inches high!

I tore my gaze from her feet to question Chris, who was glaring at me under what was becoming a single, perpetually raised eyebrow.

"Crystal's backstage getting ready. We just had a shift change. She'll be taking the floor any moment now." Valentine flicked a switch on the wall and a two-way mirror showed what was behind the dark glass. I gasped audibly. Embarrassingly. From our safe little nook, I could suddenly see a larger room beyond the glass. One with plenty of seating, other tables, and a peninsular stage capped with a silver pole glinting under stage lights. No one was sitting in the chairs.

"Aw, sweetie. You look nervous," she said to me, dropping the overt flirtation from her voice. "Don't be. There are cameras everywhere and I don't solicit. Relax, baby. I'm going to take really good care of you. Unless you prefer Crystal. Let me know. I won't be offended. I'll put your orders in. You sit back... do your thing..." She looked at Chris who was still glaring at me. "Enjoy your food and the show. Then we'll have a little fun, maybe, if you feel comfortable. You like pickles?"

"In what way?" I was almost afraid to ask.

She laughed, her giggle throatier, darker now. "On your burger, sweetie. Oh my God, you're precious."

"Oh. Sure."

The curtain closed. I still couldn't move. Slowly, I rotated my body to Chris.

"What just happened to me?"

"You ordered the Special, annnd... I'm pretty sure that means you're getting a lap dance with your burger."

"How was I supposed to know what that meant? Are we... is this... a strip club?"

"You just pick up on that now?"

"Valentine wasn't just being friendly?"

"Mm," he smirked. "There may have been an element of authenticity there. I'm certain you're exponentially more attractive than the majority of her clientele. Then again, I'm biased."

"You'd think they'd advertise their offerings a little better. How are people supposed to know?"

"People *aren't* supposed to know. It's black market. It's illegal to serve alcohol in strip clubs in Tennessee. So is full nudity. I'm guessing the Special comes with that, too."

Nudity. Was Valentine...? "Do you think it would be rude if we left now?"

"And give Valentine blue balls? You can't skip out on your burger. Besides, this little detour promises to be one hell of a side quest."

"But—"

"You stay here and decide. In the meantime, I'm not tipping Valentine with a black card. We need cash, and probably a lot of it, knowing you and your social mores. This is going to be one expensive meal. Can I trust you not to get in too much trouble before I make it back from the ATM?"

"You can trust me."

The way he did a double-take over his shoulder told me he did not trust me as far as he could spit.

Chapter 13

Chris

When I came back from the ATM, Mrs. Claus was leaning over a seated Daphne, brushing her hair behind her shoulder, lingering too long on those silky strands and whispering into her ear. She'd brought several bottles of water and had Daphne giggling nervously and covering her mouth like a schoolgirl.

I stood in the doorway with my mouth agape. My brain shorted out.

Right. I could trust Daphne. Sure. No trouble at all. Her uncanny ability to fawn in the face of, well... anything, made trying to keep her safe and protected like trying to cushion a minefield.

Now Daphne was biting that plump lower lip. *Fuck me.* What did I ever do to deserve this torture, watching someone else flirt with my... nothing? She was my nothing. Not mine at all.

I checked my watch. I'd give us twenty minutes to scarf down our food, tip the nice lady, and get back on the road. My dick could deal with twenty minutes, as long as Valentine gave us a few minutes alone to eat in peace.

Twenty minutes later, Daphne and I had eaten our burgers, but Valentine was just getting started. I'd drunk both our beers and I'd been minding my business, keeping my eyes off the women and glued to the curtains for so long, I'd started to recognize faces in the stains of the purple velvet.

"The thing people don't understand about sex work is that it's not sex work." Valentine said, grinding her ass into Daphne's lap. "I mean it is, don't get me wrong, but getting naked is the least of it. It's therapy more than anything else. Men come here, my regulars especially, and get help in the work that I'm doing. I'm giving them somewhere they can see themselves the way they want to be seen. They don't come here to get off or just to look at my boobs. They can do that on the internet for free. They aren't here to come. It's not even about being lonely."

"What is it, then? What do they get out of this?"

"They're here to be my savior. For forty dollars a dance, they can protect me from the rest of the scum and be a knight in shining armor for ten minutes."

"But aren't *they* the scum?" Daphne said exactly what I was thinking. Except I was doing everything in my power not to engage. I was purposely trying not to pay attention to anything going on in this room so that we could leave here in a semi-timely fashion and with some of our dignity intact. Scratch that: *her* dignity. Mine was gone.

"Honey, none of them are scum. They're human beings capable of doing scummy things, sure, but isn't everyone? Well, maybe not you. You're a good girl. But we're all also capable of being nice and kind."

I tried not to bristle noticeably when Valentine referred to Daphne as a *good girl*. It was true, and the context was different. But she was *my* good girl.

When I looked at the women, I immediately regretted it. Valentine ran her hands through Daphne's hair again. I crossed and uncrossed my legs, unable to get comfortable with the blood moving, uninvited, into my cock.

"Your hair is so soft. Is it alright that I'm touching you?"

"Sure, if you're comfortable. It feels really nice."

Fucking hell.

Valentine was undoubtedly a skilled professional, adept in the art of making eyes at customers in that way that would make them peel bills off their wads of cash. But it didn't look like Valentine was putting it on for Daphne. Not the way her pupils were blown, nor the way she was pressing herself deeper and deeper into an oblivious Daphne's lap. No one was that good of an actress. This felt uncomfortably voyeuristic.

When I caught Valentine's eye, she raised her eyebrow and gave a subtle glance to my wallet. *Ah,* she was good.

And worth every dime.

I peeled off another stack of crisp twenties and slipped them under the well-used paper coaster. The ATM had a five-hundred-dollar withdrawal limit, but having no idea how much was customary, I'd made three more withdrawals.

This might not be my kind of culture, but parting with my money had never felt so satisfying.

"But you said this place has turned up your Kinsey dial. You now prefer women to men." Daphne was half a second from breaking out a tape recorder, turning it into a full sociological interview.

Valentine, the consummate professional, was able to hold up her end of the discussion while grinding her ass and skimming her fingers over the fluffy fur of her dress, back and forth, so delicately. Teasing Daphne with a soft smile before parting the V just enough to let her nipple peek out.

Daphne's eyes went wide and her mouth parted as she stared at Valentine's boobs. My cock went hard. Jesus, I was not this guy. I *would not* be this neanderthal asshole, turned on by Daphne... exploring her sexuality. Or whatever she was doing. Even if it was right in front of me.

"That's just because men are work. Women don't usually come here because we cater to a select group of teamsters. Sometimes women drive with men, and they'll come along and meet the girls their husbands spend time with when they drive 40, but it's rare. Women truck drivers don't come in alone. And we rarely get anyone who doesn't drive freight. Every few months we get some college boys here on a dare. They're the worst."

"I still don't see how that could drive your sexuality to change."

"I was always into boys and girls. Pretty equal, I guess. The job didn't change me. But do you like to come home from work and do more work?"

Daphne shrugged. "Sort of. Yeah."

"Maybe once I'm in my future career, I will too. This is just a job. If I worked at McDonald's, I doubt I'd be craving a Big Mac on my days off. Besides, a therapist doesn't need to feel seen by her client. She goes elsewhere for that. I go elsewhere, too. I just want different scenery." She touched Daphne's arm and smiled. "Softer, prettier scenery."

"What's your future career?"

"I'm getting my RN. I'm a CNA now. That's my day job. I work in assisted living before I come here at night."

"How do you have time to study?"

"Don't have much choice. I've got bills. Life is expensive. I help my sister, who's disabled."

"I hear that. My dad's disabled. I grew up going without. I'm still without, although in January, I'll have a little bit of a safety net, with a grad school stipend on top of my jobs."

Jobs. Stipend.

The words did something inside me. I leaned forward, resting my elbows on my knees, staring at the colored flecks on the linoleum tiles, keenly attuned to this part of the conversation. Daphne needed that money. I knew it was only a meager stipend. It didn't pay a quarter of what she was worth. But she *needed* it. And I'd almost snatched it away from her. If anyone found out, the circumstances might still snatch it away.

I'd be fired, of course. That, I could handle. I was the one in the position of power. I was single-handedly responsible. But her classmates might not see it that way. No matter how much academics liked to virtue-signal their feminism with lip service, many still acted upon internalized—or overt—misogyny. They'd fault Daphne. Blame her. Find a way to strip her of credibility in other ways, icing her out of authorship, cases, opportunities. She could lose everything.

"Maybe I should have thought of dancing."

My eyes shot to Daphne. My sweet, angelic Daphne.

That was the reality of the cold, hard situation I'd put her in. I imagined her stripping off a stretchy red dress with white fake fur and shaking her pretty tits in some frat douchebag's face while he got rough with her. My stomach lurched, threatening to upset that burger that surprisingly, wasn't the worst thing I'd ever eaten.

Sex work was work. I believed that. I supported that: in theory.

But I didn't shop at that store—*not counting today*—and it hurt to think of my... whatever she was... clocking in for a shift anywhere she didn't absolutely love.

"I have no rhythm, though. I could never do what you do on a pole."

I pinched my lips shut before I said anything that would draw their attention. Despite cycling through various states of arousal ever since Valentine started playing with Daphne's hair, touching her ears, and doing all the things I wanted to be doing to her, I was not a strip club guy. My participation was clearly an afterthought here, and I preferred it to stay that way. No matter how good Daphne really was at working a pole.

"You're a smart girl. You could learn that, easy. What you can't learn is confidence. That's what makes money here. It's not your body, it's not your act. It's whether or not you believe it."

"Well, there goes that. I don't believe it."

"Girl, I get it. The most beautiful women... and men never seem to know they're beautiful. But look at the two of you. You're like magazine beautiful. Book cover beautiful. But you don't need *work the room* confidence. You already won."

"I haven't though. He won't be with me."

"Oh, honey." Valentine sat straighter and removed her fingers from where they'd been twirling Daphne's hair. She looked at me and then whispered something in Daphne's ear that made her eyes go wide again.

"Are you... Can I ask you a personal question?"

"I don't usually do extras, but you're like, so pretty. If you want to fool around a bit, I don't mind."

"No, that's not what—*Extras*?"

I looked up from my phone, where I'd been doing a backlist of old Wordle puzzles. What now? *We're doing extras?*

Valentine stood and pranced around Daphne's chair in her skyscraper heels that looked like medieval torture devices. She circled once as Daphne looked over at me with her eyes wide, then returned to the front again, slipped her fingers under the neckline of her dress again, edging the material back.

Surely it was just a tease. She'd know her audience and wouldn't actually... Oh shit. She did. She definitely did.

In a single beat, Valentine burst out of her dress like a can of biscuits, rocked her hips to the music, and straddled Daphne's lap wearing nothing but a tiny sparkly thong.

Daphne blinked and her cheeks turned red. "Actually, I was wondering if you have breast implants."

I slid down in my seat, cradling the back of my head on the cushion. I stared up at the coffee-colored stains on the acoustic ceiling tiles.

"Baby Girl, are you kidding?"

"Is that offensive? I'm so sorry. Sometimes I can't tell if I've gone too far."

"Of course I have implants. You ever see real tits as tight as these?"

"I've never really seen another woman's boobs. Naked and in person. I've never had sisters or roommates or..."

"You've never fooled around with a girl?" I turned my head to watch. So much for minding my own business.

"No." Daphne's cheeks were red.

"Are you even into women? I assume everyone's bi these days. Not to mention—"

"You're naked in my lap. Maybe I'm like a... Kinsey Two, I guess? I think women are beautiful—you're beautiful, Valentine—but I n ever... I'd rather..." She shrugged and sort of nodded uncomfortably in my direction. I didn't know why I was so relieved. Daphne wasn't mine. She couldn't be mine. Which meant she was free to be with anyone. But I didn't want to watch the fallout of my own love life start right now.

"What about him? He's definitely into dudes. He's got that look about him."

"Nope," I rolled my head on the back of the chair.

"He's a nerd with nice clothes." Daphne explained. Accurately.

"Sorry to refute your theory," I said.

"You want to feel them?" Valentine asked Daphne, matter-of-factly, but her eyes were trained on me. And my wallet.

Well played, Valentine.

"Oh my gosh, do you mind? I didn't think I was supposed to touch you."

I slipped a few more twenties into the stack. Fuck. Might as well lean in.

Valentine looked quickly at the camera in the corner. "You can touch me if I allow it. Go ahead. They're silicone, so they feel softer than they look."

Slowly, Daphne raised a hand to Valentine's under boob, lifting it with a flat hand, as if weighing it. I stifled a groan and tried to adjust myself in a way that didn't make me look... like I belonged here. But there was the rub. I *was* here. And I was getting hard as fuck watching two women touch. It didn't matter if it was partially against my will. Maybe strip clubs were the great social leveler. No matter your ethics or your education or how your parents raised you, your dick could still get hard watching beautiful women.

"Don't be afraid, it's totally cool. Here." Valentine grabbed both of Daphne's hands and placed them on her tits, showing how hard to squeeze.

"They're not what I expected."

"It's nice, right?" Valentine shrugged. Was she blushing? "Feels really good when you do that."

Valentine leaned closer and whispered something to make Daphne gasp and look over at me. As hard as it was keeping my eyes to myself, the women were so close, whispering and nodding and giggling—there might have been kissing—it was an exercise in futility. Valentine stopped the grinding and did more of a slow, rocking motion on the edge of Daphne's knees, arching her back and thrusting her breasts forward as Daphne's index fingers moved closer to the apex, circling her areolas gently, slowly, ever closer to Valentine's pierced nipples.

"I love your piercings," Daphne said. "I've always wanted mine done. Did it hurt?"

My cock pulsed. I could feel the pre-cum dribbling out, moistening my boxers.

"The first one was okay, but for some reason, the left one hurt like fuck. And it took for-fucking-ever to heal. But it makes my nipples stand out more. And it feels really good to have them sucked. Your mileage may vary, though. I've heard some horror stories."

Daphne twisted the little silver barbells.

I groaned. I tried to look away. Lord help me, I tried. But this was too much. My cock was so hard it hurt. My abs clenched. I breathed out a slow breath. Then it got even worse. "Why wouldn't you be with her? She's sweet as pie, gorgeous, sexy, smart. You don't put a ring on that, I might."

She gave Daphne a flirtatious smile before standing up and pulling Daphne by the hand. Both women slunk closer to me. Oh. Shit.

"Have we been ignoring you, mister?"

"I've been enjoying the show just fine from here." I crossed my legs.

Valentine squeezed her boobs. "For a little more of Daddy's money, I'll let you play with them, too."

I gritted my teeth at the wrongness of the word coming from Valentine's mouth. It sounded so seedy, so repugnant. I bit back my disdain and tried to keep it professional. "I think we're good."

"Maybe Baby Girl wants to have a little fun." Valentine turned to Daphne before circling my chair. "Go on, baby. Just like I did with you."

Daphne smiled a real smile. Not coy or flirtatious. But like this was just a joke.

But when she bent down and uncrossed my legs before sliding my knees apart, I'd lost the punchline. She wasn't dressed in a nylon sock like Valentine, but she was still provocative in her short, flirty skirt and thigh-high socks that flashed the thinnest strip of naked thigh.

Throwing her hair over her shoulder, Daphne spun around and bent her knees. She held the arms of my chair and pushed her ass back into me, not so much grinding on my lap, but hovering lightly. Only occasionally would she get too low and brush against my dick. I let out a hiss as I tried not to lose all control.

"You really would have been good at this. Now turn around, slowly."

Daphne followed Valentine's order, keeping her eyes on mine. Her pupils were huge. I bet if I reached between her thighs, she'd be dripping after all of Valentine's flirting and teasing.

My mouth watered for her.

Valentine lurked somewhere behind me, trailing her fingernails down my cheek before I jerked away. I didn't want to be touched by anyone else. I didn't want anything sexual from anyone but Daphne. And I was currently getting too much from Daphne.

My hands tightened into fists. I wanted to reach out and run the tips of my fingers over that line of skin between her socks and her skirt. I wanted to follow it with my tongue. But not here. Instead, I licked my dry lips and held her tightly by the waist to still her, which made Daphne think I wanted her to sit fully on my lap. I groaned when she came down hard on my unadjusted balls. "Uh. Okay. Darling." She ground against my dick. "Sweetheart. That's enough. That's... I can't... please, stop."

"Awww, that is so sweet, you two."

Daphne nodded to Valentine and started undoing the buttons on her sweater. Then she started undoing the buttons down the front of her dress.

"He's gotta pay for his show, Baby Girl. Don't forget. She deserves some of Daddy's money, doesn't she, mister?"

Oh, Right. I was salivating, practically hyperventilating, over getting to see Daphne's tits again. It was all new, like I'd never seen them before and couldn't wait to see what she'd unveiled when the last button slipped through its hole.

I unfolded more bills off my stack, but instead of putting them on the table, I held them out for her.

"Use your teeth," Valentine instructed.

Daphne clenched the money in her teeth before peeling open the front of her dress. To me, and to Valentine. She hadn't worn a bra. Her nipples were hard as rocks and I knew they'd be sensitive. She'd want my tongue but not my teeth. Fuck I wanted to give it to her.

She dropped the bills and tucked them into the top of her sock (also hot) before playing with her nipples, circling the ripe peaks with the tips of her middle fingers.

"I knew you'd have the prettiest tits," Valentine said. "I definitely think you should get them pierced. A little metal bar through those perfect nipples would be so cute." My cock surged. "Daddy thinks so, too."

The word didn't even faze me anymore. Somehow, in front of Valentine, we could be ourselves. It felt like a little reprieve of the tragedy of being pulled apart. A Christmas miracle.

Daphne's eyes drifted closed and she started to rock herself in my lap. Her hands came down, and through my pants, she started to give me... extras.

Shit.

I pulled her dress closed and buttoned her as fast as I could. Her sweater, too.

I stood, catching Daphne as she fell off my lap. I took a deep breath. "We really have to be going. Valentine, it's been a pleasure."

I opened my wallet and gave her the rest of what was inside.

"Oh, shit. Thank you. It was nice meeting you two. Come back anytime," Valentine called out to Daphne, as I dragged her out of the room.

"Hopefully by now we've been here so long, they've cleared up 40," I said once we were back in the restaurant—which felt like another dimension to that private room.

A man wearing only a Slipknot t-shirt and beanie passed us, coming in the door from the freezing outside. "40 east or west?" he asked.

"East," I said.

The man shook his head. "Still shut down, man. Last time I saw a mixed chemical spill that bad, it took them eight hours to neutralize everything and open the lanes. Weather's coming in, too. Best bet's to bunk down for the night. The last thing you want is to be caught driving these mountains in ice."

"I appreciate it," I nodded. Of course it was still shut down.

"Stay safe."

"Thank you, sir," she told the man.

I grabbed Daphne's hand. I'd literally drag her out of the club if I had to. We had to be on our way. We'd wasted enough time. It was seven o'clock. It was dark and freezing. My cock was still hard as a rock, and my underwear were squishy with pre-cum from the Daphne and Valentine show.

"Who'd have thought for forty dollars we'd walk out of there with burgers and a new friend?"

"Forty?"

"That's how much Valentine said the dances were."

I stared at her sweet, innocent expression, watching it change with the realization.

"You spent more than forty, didn't you?"

"A little."

By the time I pulled her to the car, I couldn't wait anymore. I spun her around and pressed her against the passenger side door, holding her face between my hands.

"What the fuck, Daphne?"

"Wha—?"

"What was that about? You think it's fun getting me turned on like that?"

"Like what?"

I grabbed her hand and pressed it against the front of my pants. "Like this."

Her fingers closed around my cock and I couldn't help but rock into her hand.

My hands laced into her hair and tightened into fists, pulling her face up, closer to mine.

Her lips quivered.

"Chris, I—"

"Who was that for? For you, or all for me? How much more are you going to put me though? I can't fucking have you, Daphne. I will not do anything that will jeopardize your future."

"Chris, please..." She squirmed against me, standing on tiptoe to feel my cock between her legs. Goddamnit, I was pressing my whole body against hers, but I didn't pull away.

Oh, God, I should back away. I should, I should, but I couldn't.

Her eyes were black, her pupils had overtaken the gray. There was fire in her face.

I cupped her chin with my other hand, running my thumb along her lower lip until she sucked it into her mouth, holding it still with her teeth, stroking it with her tongue until I groaned, thinking about those lips opening as I forced my cock between them, that tongue swirling around my head.

I pulled my thumb away, trailed her wetness down her throat, her collarbones, her chest, plunging my hand into her dress and pinching her hard nipple. It wasn't gentle, the way she liked.

"Oh, God, yes," she said as she exhaled.

I rolled my hips against her. Just once. A mistake. I didn't know how good it would feel. How fleeting. The ache in my cock flooded back in, worse than before, needing more and more relief.

Fuck the cold, I opened her dress and sweater. The negative temps made her nipples hard as rocks.

She was gorgeous, writhing wantonly against my car with her tits spilling out for anyone to see. *Anyone* could see us, driving past this shithole club, walking to and from their trucks.

She raised a leg, as desperate as I was for relief. I rocked against her again before running my hands down over her thighs, lifting her, wrapping both legs around my waist so she fit right where we both needed.

I moved my cock against her core and leaned forward to suck her nipple the way she'd been teasing Valentine's just a few minutes ago. She smelled of Valentine's cheap perfume and her own musky arousal. The sacred scent of her that had driven me insane in the club.

"Yes," she whispered. "Right here. Don't stop."

"Shh, baby. I'm going to take care of you. Come for me. Use me."

My cock rubbed against her pussy as I pinned her to the car. Slowly. So slowly. The layers of fabric dragging painfully against my skin, needing to get her off.

"Kiss me, Chris."

I devoured her mouth, drugged by her tongue and the feel of her thighs, bare above her high socks. She hadn't put her tights back on after the hospital and her skin was freezing, but she didn't seem to mind.

I couldn't get enough of her. I needed to breathe her in, needed to be inside her, but it was impossible. I couldn't do it. Couldn't have her. Not here in this nasty parking lot. Not even at home, tucked safely between my own sanitized sheets.

But I could let her come. We both knew she needed it after the club.

Her legs squeezed around mine while I held her by the neck, pushing her away from me so I could look down her body, at her, working herself on me, writhing without a concern in the world for anything happening around us. I felt the warmth of her pussy grinding painfully, perfectly against my cock that was so achingly hard, it felt like it was trying to push itself through the fabric,

"Daphne, fuck," I growled. "How do you do this to me? How is it possible that you turn me into such a..." I shook my head.

"Slut?" she said, almost out of breath.

"I was going to say... yeah." I laughed. "I guess so."

"I'm a slut for you, too. I can't get enough of your cock—oh, God. There. Don'tmove don'tmove—and your... mouth. I love the way you look so sweet and boyish, and then eat my pussy.. . like—ohhhh—like a starving—Daddy."

Her breaths grew thicker. She gripped harder with her legs, pulling me closer with her arms. I covered her mouth just as her scream broke free. Fuck, she was bringing me right with her. Even through layers of clothes I was coming so hard I was seeing stars that weren't in the night sky.

My hands clawed against the car roof, almost dropping her as she started her boneless slide. My orgasm had come out of nowhere. No buildup. No tension, just a sudden explosion of searing pleasure that...

oh, shit it wasn't stopping. Warmth flooded my pants as I fought to come back to reality, but I didn't care, I didn't care, I didn't fucking care.

My body was moving without the will of my brain. Scrambling to reach her even though she was right there.

So close.

Here.

My hand was running through her hair, cupping her jaw, pulling her toward me as I moaned against her mouth, not quite kissing her, but existing with her.

Tears leaked down her face, pooling against the web of my thumb. Cold as soon as they hit the frigid night.

"I'm not—This isn't... I don't know why I'm crying. I'm okay. I'm not sad. I'm just... so much. I feel so much."

My pants were sodden with cum, but it barely registered. Daphne's back and shoulders relaxed against the car, her legs still wrapped around me with a sleepy smile on her swollen lips, tear-streaked face, and pink nipples standing out in the dim light from the club entrance. Vapor clouds puffing out of our mouths as we panted and watched each other come down.

"Don't let me go, Chris."

Doom washed over me with her words. Replacing the bliss of sharing another orgasm with her. We'd had a moment of unicorns and rainbows and now, rightfully, she'd landed us back in reality. Unpaved parking lots. Burgers with lap dances. Dry humping my student until I was a soggy mess of shame and guilt.

I unpinned her from the car, easing her legs down.

"You are, aren't you? You're still going to let me go?" She asked. "After that? After everything?"

I said nothing. I buttoned her dress and sweater and zipped her coat, adjusting myself the best I could as I walked around the car.

I had no choice but to let her go.

I TURNED OFF THE overzealous spray of water at the rest stop sink, brushing errant drops of water off my shirt. I looked in the mirror, lengthening my torso to tuck in my shirt. It felt oddly free, now that my soggy boxers were in the bottom of a trash can and not glued to my balls.

Outside at the vending machines, I bought a few bottles of water before something acid-green caught my eye.

At Walmart, where I usually shop, it's Mountain Thunder, and it's best in cans. At the Save-A-Lot, it's called Mountain Holler, and I still haven't decided if it's Holler as in yelling, or Holler as in a hollow, like "Butcher Holler," from the Loretta Lynn song. It makes me laugh. It's the best of all the cheapo Mountain Dews, but I don't shop at Save-A-Lot very often because Walmart's produce is better. I've never actually had Mountain Dew. Not the real stuff, anyway. Name brand soda's a luxury.

The memory made me smile. I could see her telling me this. She'd been sitting on the counter of my parents' house in my boxers and t-shirt and wool socks, feet kicking the cabinets underneath, fingers dipping into the tiny bowl to take pinches of red and green sugar to sprinkle on the gingerbread men I was smearing with icing.

That was *before*, when I could gaze up at her adoringly, kiss her and touch her whenever I wanted, thinking we'd have all the time in the world to learn each other's quirks.

Now that our time was just about up, I could leave her with one final offering.

"I was worried you fell in," she said as I opened the car door.

I handed her both water bottles and she tucked them in the cupholders.

"One more," I said.

I passed her the real, honest-to-goodness Mountain Dew.

"For me?" Her eyes got all big and round in that sexy pitiful way that made my chest feel heavy.

"Have at it."

She practically cradled the bottle in her lap.

"I'm too cold right now. Do you mind if I save it?"

"What you should do is toss it in the garbage, but it's yours now. Do what you want with it."

She smiled and tucked her hands back under her legs where they'd been when I'd left. I had turned off the car and taken the keys into the bathroom with me by habit. Now, she was freezing.

I started the car and blasted the heat before placing my palms on the wheel. I didn't shift into gear. Didn't make a move to leave the parking lot.

"Here's what we're going to do. And, Daphne, I need you to accept this without argument," I said to the windshield. "Please."

I felt her curious eyes on me.

"I'm going back west. I'm getting off at the Lebanon exit and we're going to see the Christmas lights. If you still want to see them."

"Yes!"

"It shouldn't take us longer than a half hour. After that, we're going to find the quickest alternative route to Knoxville and I will not stop this car until I've delivered you to your father's doorstep."

I turned to watch her face melt into a heartbreaking resigned sadness.

"I'm not going to kiss you goodbye. I'm not going to listen to your proposed solutions. I'm going to drive back to my apartment and my cat, send Jeanette an email with a confession and a detailed timeline of my actions—maybe I'll leave out the strip club—and start praying that'll be enough to keep you safe and maybe keep my job."

Daphne pinched her lips together, holding back a response.

"Then I'm going to spend the next two years avoiding you at all costs. And so help me God, I will be strong enough to do it. I will drown out every mention of your name. I'll turn tail and run with every wisp of blonde hair I see around every corner. I'll find someone else to teach your classes, even if I have to cover their six-figure salary myself. Every email with your name attached will be automatically forwarded to my assistant."

Her hand came up to cover her mouth.

"For the next two years, you will date whomever you like. Fuck whomever you like." My voice was rougher as those syllables passed my vocal cords. "You will form incredible friendships, business contacts, and forge a network with your cohorts. You'll volunteer for any and every assignment that gives you field experience, no matter how far away it takes you. Most importantly, you'll finish your master's, if not your doctorate."

"But I don't—"

"I'm not finished. At the end of those two years, or longer, if you decide to get your PhD, after you've walked across the stage to receive your diploma. If you aren't partnered, dating, fucking, or in a romantic relationship with someone. If you still remember I exist, and you want to try again..."

I took a deep breath and looked into her eyes.

"I'll find you."

She was silent for a minute. Looking at me with an unreadable expression. Her face was quizzical in the best of times. Now that she was trying to maintain a sense of mystery, it was impossible.

A slow, cold smile spread across her mouth. Something sinister. Bitter. She reminded me of Anubis when she sauntered across my desk to lie across my keyboard while I was working.

"Yes, Daddy."

Chapter 14

Daphne

THE WAY CHRIS'S FACE closed up, shuttering those looks of desperate longing from me—desperation and longing, but also sadness—I knew. He yearned for me the way I yearned for him. With a force that couldn't be stopped.

But he hated himself for it, whereas I gave in.

It was stupid to try to stop feelings this strong, though he was desperate for that, too. To stop this more-than-attraction. This... *whatever this was* between us.

It wasn't love. It couldn't be.

No way. Nobody fell in love after two days. Love took months, maybe even years. Love took overcoming hardships and putting the other person first again and again. Love was a long haul up a mountain road with switchbacks and steep grades. Not an easy drive in a luxury car.

But what we had wasn't lust either. It wasn't as cheap as that. It wasn't about the sex. I thought it would be when I suggested it, but our sex immediately became more of the embodiment of our connection.

Lust and sex I could part with. Even as good as it was with Chris. I could go without for two years. I'd be busy anyway. I didn't have a sexual need.

My need was for him.

My desire was to be his counterpart, to take care of him in ways that complemented the ways he took care of me. In just our short time together, I'd never felt more nurtured, respected... loved. He'd grabbed me and wrapped me up in his world with a vulnerability and honesty I'd never experienced.

He made me believe in fate, destiny, reincarnation.

Or none of those, really. We were just very, very compatible, and very, very into each other, and there was no way I was letting him go.

I didn't need the distraction.

And *not being with him* would be the ultimate distraction.

I wanted to wake up to him every morning, sharing bagels and coffee like we were in a nineties romcom—were there any nineties romcoms that showed couples waking up with bagels and coffee? I couldn't remember, but it seemed like a very Nora Ephron thing to do with someone you fell for after two days.

I wanted to read in bed together and curl up in his arms every night. I wanted to analyze bones with him. I wanted to feel the kisses he'd plant on the top of my head when he brought me a steaming mug of hot cocoa while I took over his desk to study.

Chris took the exit for the Merry Lights and I wiggled in my seat.

"I have a good feeling about this."

"That makes one of us." He took a deep audible breath.

"Oh, grumble, grumble. Why are you so down about this?"

"Considering this is our fourth detour in twenty miles, we're still half an hour away from where we started..." he looked at his watch, "twelve hours ago. And we should have delivered you and this skull to your respective destinations four times over, I'm a little anxious to know what's lurking around the next river bend."

"I'm sure this is the last time. The final waypoint. No more stops after this. If I have to pee, I'll hold it."

"Somehow, that makes me even less sure we'll make it home tonight."

"It's only eight. Plenty of time."

He grumbled again, wordlessly, and punched his turn signal.

"Oh, it says we have to tune in to AM 780."

"Why?"

"The lights are synched with the music. That's the point of the Merry experience."

"I see."

"This car is so high-tech, I don't even know which buttons to push."

"I'm not sure if I even know." The touchscreen lit up as his hand hovered over the commands. "I turned on the bluetooth and never expected to turn it off."

I swatted his hand away. "I can do this. You drive. So we can be done faster." I stuck my tongue out at him.

"We're waiting in line."

"Here it is."

Disco music screamed into the car, jarring us out of our cozy ride.

"Are you sure this is the right station?" he asked.

"Umm... yeah." *No.* And honestly, I was disappointed, too. I listened for a few more bars. "They replaced the words *macho man* with *Santa Claus*, so I'm assuming this is accurate. Maybe there'll be a dancing Santa in leather somewhere."

"One can only hope there'll be some wildly inappropriate element for our amusement."

I turned my evil smile on him. "I can come up with some wildly inappropriate amusement in this very seat." I let my dress slide a little higher on my thighs and spread my legs.

He groaned. "My poor trousers can't take any more amusement this evening."

As we drove through the Merry Lights—they were indeed merry, if slightly underwhelming because of their choice of music—I started squirming in my seat. I couldn't help it. He'd ruined my last pair of panties, and the seat warmer felt good on my bare bottom. Plus, the lights allowed me to watch him behind the wheel, where he was competent, sexy, and maybe even enjoying the Christmas spirit a little bit.

He knew I was aroused. I could see the war in his eyes behind the bursts of color dancing in his glasses. He bit his lip. His eyes could barely stay off my legs.

"This is fun. It would be even more fun if your fingers were in my pussy."

"Haven't you had enough?"

"Of you? Stupid question."

He ignored me. "I didn't think Christmas could get worse than Wham!, but the Village People managed to top it. Or bottom it?"

"I hate to hear where you stand on Mariah." I slipped my fingers under my skirt. "I'm already leaking on your seat. You might as well finish me off."

He groaned and reached over like he was doing some kind of vile chore. When he flipped my skirt up, there was a hiss. "Where the fuck are your panties, Daphne?"

"As trashed as yours after that last episode."

"Spread your legs, sweetheart. Wider." I did as I was told. He licked his middle finger before sliding it down through my slit and around my throbbing clit before his ring finger joined. A throaty sigh escaped the back of his throat. I loved the way his elegant hands looked, rubbing through my pussy. His hands made me melt, made me come, made me... I gasped and arched my back as his fingers pushed into my vagina.

"Retrofitting any and all words associated with Santa Claus, elves, reindeer, and/or the North Pole into non-holiday lyrics will always be worse than a legitimately talented musician singing a well-composed pop song—even if I don't personally enjoy the song, it's a problem with oversaturation, not Mariah."

"Oh, shit. Chris. Speaking of oversaturation, you better stop, before..."

"You got me into this." He pulled his hand away and reached behind the seat, searching for something. "You're not getting out of this car without coming." He threw me his cashmere scarf.

"Seriously? This?"

"It's all I could reach. Better that than turning the seat into a sitz bath."

"Make it fast. There's a hot cocoa stand up ahead."

"And you're telling me because?"

"Oh, come on." I twisted in the seat and got up on all fours. The position was better for him. Better for me. I watched the lights as I rocked myself on his long, perfect fingers. The feeling was coming. My belly felt full and heavy, needing release. "Fuck. Daddy." My head fell forward.

"Just... try not to spill."

I looked up. He was smirking.

The car was filling with my scent. I'd be embarrassed if I had any shame left. But Chris had already robbed me of that.

"The irony of that statement is bananas, you know that, right? I'm over here, ruining your butter leather seats" I clutched his wrist while I fucked myself harder on his hand, his thumb circling my clit, avoiding the pressure I needed. "Oh, fuck. Daddy… You're hauling a skull we found in the woods, and two pine wreaths that are probably leaking sap. What's a little hot cocoa spill? Brigitte can take it."

"Oh no." He groaned, but didn't miss a beat as he curled his fingers against my G-spot. "Oh, no, no, no. You did not name my car." His thumb pressed hard against my clit.

"Of course… I did. Fuck, fuck, fuck. I'm gonna." I wadded the cashmere scarf against my pussy just as the orgasm crashed through my body. I kneeled upright and let it go, soaking the soft fabric as my body convulsed. "Oh, shit," I mumbled. "Oh, shit, oh, shit. It's— I'm…"

I held the back of the seat before slumping back down. The cashmere hadn't caught everything. It wasn't exactly an absorbent material. There were droplets everywhere. His cuff was soaked. I'd splashed on the center console. But the way he looked up at me, with pride and affection, made it okay.

He'd wanted this. He'd wanted my cum all over his expensive car.

His fingers slid out of me. Looking in my eyes, he licked them clean, slowly, thoroughly, before going back to our conversation. "It's a machine. It has neither name nor gender."

"I knew you'd say that," I said breathlessly, still feeling the pulse of my pelvic muscles. "That's why I didn't consult with you before naming our firstborn."

His mouth opened. Then closed. Then opened again. The car inched forward. With both hands back on the steering wheel, he made his way toward the hot cocoa stand.

"Thank you."

A slow smile spread across his mouth. "If you spill chocolate on my seats, I'm picking the music for the rest of the trip."

"Your music will put us both to sleep and wreck my baby, Brigitte."

"She's not your baby. She's an *it*, and if we're going to anthropomorphize a machine, it's *my baby*."

Suddenly, our baby lurched forward with a jolt and an audible crunch. My neck snapped down before jerking up again. "What—?" Chris's hands flew off the wheel. His foot plunged down on the brake, making sure the car who'd hit us from behind didn't ram us into the car in front.

"Are you okay?" he asked.

I nodded, too stunned to talk. Chris maneuvered the car to the side of the lighted path and the minivan behind us followed. Once he got it in park and shut off the engine, he blew out a breath with closed eyes.

"Fuck."

"Maybe it didn't leave a mark. They didn't hit us very hard. My neck doesn't even hurt."

"Yet." He looked up over the rim of his glasses.

We both stepped out of the car slowly, not wanting to see whatever carnage the back end had been dealt, but having no choice.

I glanced at a flurry of movement through the rear windshield. I knew exactly what was going through their heads, and I was flooded with empathy. They'd just hit a Mercedes. A fancy one. The damage would be covered by their insurance, but whatever it was—I was afraid to look—would cost a hell of a lot more to repair than a Toyota.

Chris wore a look of calm serenity as he stared at the cracked bumper and dented rear fender.

"Oh, poor Brigitte," I said, patting her wounds.

"It's just a car," Chris said quietly.

"Really? Because you look like you're tearing up."

"Just a car. Just a car. Just a car."

Okay, so the serene expression was shock. The anger would hit him soon. Once his mantra inevitably failed him and he learned this wouldn't be fixable without sending it to some very fancy repair shop. Possibly even out of state. This car was shipped here ten days ago from Germany. I doubted there was anywhere closer than New York that could repair it.

I kept that information to myself.

The driver side door of the minivan opened. Voices hollered from inside. An old man in a ball cap and suspenders hobbled down from his seat, zipping up his coat while he limped toward us.

I tugged Chris's sleeve and he turned.

"Real sorry about that, son. I was looking at that dumb dancing Santa over there, and realized too late you'd stopped. Wife tells me I shouldn't be driving at night." He scratched his chin. "Never let me live this down."

Chris's jaw clenched.

"I reckon you need my insurance card." He reached into his back pocket and hauled out a fat wallet, searching through it for his cards. "You like the German cars? Never ridden in one. My kids finally settled me on this Chrysler. Always been a Buick man, and never thought I'd be driving a minivan, but they don't make those big ole cars for old men like me anymore." He handed Chris his card, but Chris just looked at it. As if he couldn't figure out what he wasn't supposed to do with it. He didn't lift his hand to take it. He didn't even look at the old man.

I stepped in. "I'll just take a picture of that. We can call tomorrow morning. At least it's just a little ding."

I said it for Chris's sake more than the old man's. To snap him out of whatever plane he'd drifted into.

The old man chuckled, "That's going to be one expensive ding, young lady. No wonder he looks shell shocked. Don't worry, though. I've got good insurance."

I looked at the card. I had the same insurance, and I knew it was good. Walter Gallagher was the man's name. "Can I get your phone number, Mr. Gallagher?" I asked, typing it into my phone.

There was a kind shrewdness in his plump, lined face. He looked like someone you couldn't get anything past, but he'd look the other way just the same. He seemed like someone born to be a grandpa.

Under the bill of his ball cap, his eyes were still startlingly clear, ice blue, reminding me of something from earlier today. The wreath-making workshop. Lord almighty, had that just been this morning? I feel like I'd lived a lifetime since then.

My eyes moved to the top of his head. *"All gave some. 58,479 gave all"* was embroidered over service ribbons. Vietnam. I recognized the ribbons because I used to ask people about them whenever I'd gone to the VA hospital with Dad. A Purple Heart. A commendation medal. He was a hero.

"Chris, I—" I whispered.

"Daphne?"

I turned around. A girl was jumping out of the minivan and helping her grandmother with her footing. Older woman. Puffy blue coat. My friends from the wreath-making workshop.

"Eva! Patty. It's so nice seeing you again." Eva had the same ice blue eyes as her grandfather. That was where I'd recognized them. I loved these moments when the world felt so small and full of love.

"You were supposed to be on the road hours ago. Decide to stick around for the Lights?"

"I... no, it's a long story, actually."

"Walter, of all the people to rear-end. It's our friends from this morning! Remember I told you about that sweet young couple that sat next to Eva and me? This is them. Daphne and..."

"Chris," I reminded her.

"Chris. Handsome devil. And he cares so much about you, you'd have to be blind not to see it. As blind as Walter, here. Don't you let him get away."

"I don't intend to." I smiled conspiratorially.

"I keep telling him the doctor doesn't want him driving at night, but he insists. See, Walter, this is what happens."

"I flew choppers on blind missions in 'Nam and lived to come home to you. I think I can handle driving an automatic van through some Christmas lights."

Patty rolled her eyes. "You just proved you can't. You ran right into the back of this nice fella's pretty car."

"Well, I wouldn't have if you weren't shouting for me to look over here, and look at that. That dancing Santa worth it?"

"Eva, you want to take a walk with me to get some hot cocoas?" Daphne asked, taking care of situation perfectly, as usual.

"Yeah, let's go!"

Chapter 15

Chris

I WAS FUCKING DONE for.

My life was spiraling out of control.

I sat in my car alone, my eyes aimed at my phone screen, focusing and unfocusing on the tiny words. I cradled my forehead in my hand as I read and reread the misconduct page of the UT faculty handbook. The page that informed me that, without a doubt, I would be fired for having an "amorous affiliation" with a student. It was exactly what I'd thought. But seeing it on the screen was even worse. It had turned this beautiful and real relationship I'd begun with Daphne into something gross and shameful.

The letters blurred from disbelief—not in the consequences themselves, but that it had been me. *Me. I'd* been the one to break this rule, a rule I would have upheld honorably if I had known. Disbelief that *I'd* now receive their sanctions, that *I'd* have this stain on my permanent record. This stigma of predation would follow my career.

My eyes stung with the dry heat blasting directly at my face, but I wasn't capable of lifting my arm to turn it down. The car radio was still tuned to the Merry Lights station and the Burmester surround sound was running through the same sloppy Christmas songs that had been playing on repeat throughout the lightshow and our accident. My life was crumbling into bits while men sang the words *Santa Santa Claus*, to the tune of "Macho Man."

The phone buzzed. I was so startled to be caught reading this incriminating information—like they could see what I'd been looking at—I knocked the phone directly under the seat instead of reading the text.

This is the start of it, Chris. Better learn to face that stigma now. Just like when I was twelve, and Dad walked in on me just as I'd unbuttoned my pants, and I had to convince him I wasn't about to jack off to the porno magazine I'd gotten from Jake. Even though the box of tissues was right there. And I may have been fourteen. Or fifteen.

I'd only been checking the official rules. Checking to see exactly how right I'd been when I told Daphne I'd committed a violation and we'd need to stop all further contact.

Some small part of me had held out a slice of hope that I'd been wrong. That there'd be a contingency for the *real* relationships. That those rumors I'd heard about a tenured professor losing everything had been a response to something truly heinous. His situation had been nothing like mine; it couldn't have been.

In Fiddler's Grove, when she'd reached out for my hand while strolling through the historic buildings, I couldn't help but thread our fingers together. I knew I was skating on thin ice, but part of me could still dismiss it. Willful ignorance. It had physically hurt my heart too much to deny her that connection.

My right hand had burned with the need to clasp our fingers together and pull her close to my side. I'd delighted in the scratch of her calluses on my palm, the corners of her fingertips, the softness of the backs of her hands. Before I could think, I was turning to face her, reaching up to cradle her neck, and pulling her in for a promising kiss in the middle of the busy simulated street.

In the hospital, I still hadn't looked at the handbook. What did I care about the rules then? I only cared about her staying alive and out of pain. I cared about the way she'd clutched her stomach and dry heaved over a bag and the way her body shook from head-to-toe torment no narcotic seemed to touch. I'd watched her right hand swell up to twice its normal size, trying to grasp onto some hope, say the right prayer, or think the right positive thought that would make her well again.

Her pain had left me exhausted, wrung out from my inability to stop it.

The way my heart lurched when her body had gone quiet after receiving the larger dose of morphine... no rulebook could drive as much fear into my soul as her momentary stillness had.

In the strip club—*outside the strip club*—I didn't need to look to know what I was doing was wrong.

My fingers still smelled like her. This whole fucking car still smelled like her.

Now, she was on the mend. Her hand had almost shrunk back to its normal size and color. The drugs had mostly left her system, and she had no residual pain. I'd given in to her plea to see the Christmas lights because it was easier to give in than fight her. I'd given her another orgasm because it was easier to give in than to fight *myself.*

But this was it.

There were no more tourist attractions. No more stops. I didn't relish driving through the mountains at night or in the cold, but after reading the rules in black and white, there was nothing gray about our situation. All I'd needed was for my car to be wrecked to stop denying it.

I was wrong, wrong, wrong.

It didn't matter that I hadn't known about her status when we'd met. It didn't matter how I'd felt about her or how I continued to feel now—for the record, like my heart was breaking. She and I could have no further association. At least not until she graduated, which was two years—maybe longer. Maybe never.

I contorted my body to dig around under my seat, searching for my phone. No luck.

"Fuck," I muttered to myself as I opened the car door to step out. Cold shocked my face and shoulders through my thin shirt as I knelt on the gravel. The temperature had plummeted even further. Colder than the sun just going down. This was a bona fide polar vortex. Wonderful.

Finally, my fingers lit on smooth glass and I flicked the phone out from under the seat. I stood, shivering in my shirtsleeves before I remembered I'd given my sweater and coat to Daphne, since her insubstantial leather jacket was even less substantial after the hospital had sliced up her sleeve. I rummaged through my bag for a fleece and slipped it over my head while checking my texts. The wind ripped right through it, but it was better than nothing. And the agonizing bite of the cold felt good, in a way. Like penance for my sin.

It was Decca. **Did you get the skull to the lab okay?**

Fuck. Decca was the last person I wanted to talk to. Actually, anyone but Daphne was the last person I wanted to talk to, and I couldn't fucking talk to her.

I thought back to the smirk that had been on Decca's face when she introduced me to Daphne. The insinuation of naughtiness when she suggested I bring Daphne to my parents' home rather than drive all the way back to Spring Hill to pick her up the next morning.

Fuck it. Decca was the reason I was in this mess to begin with. She'd known Daph was a student. She'd known we couldn't be together, and yet she encouraged it.

She could play coy all she wanted, but she was a party to my downfall, and I wasn't going to let her off the hook easily. She deserved to be in this mess with me.

I skipped a courtesy text and went straight to a phone call, my stomach tightening with every ring. I paced the gravel parking lot at the end of the Merry Lights, where Daphne had insisted on waiting in a line as long as the Nile, at the hot cocoa truck. I looked up at Daphne, who was laughing with Eva and some other people she'd met in line. The twinkle lights from the awning of the food truck illuminated her white hair and gave her a halo. She looked up and smiled at me. No, not at me; it wasn't meant for me. It was about me. She was talking to someone about me. And smiling. I raked my hand down my face, scratching at the stubble.

She still had nothing but confidence that we'd walk through this unscathed. That tomorrow we'd be boyfriend and girlfriend, and no one would have a problem with it because we hadn't known what we'd gotten ourselves into, and whoops, now it's just a funny origin story that everyone would accept because she was so damn adorable, they'd take pity on me and cheer for us.

God, I hated this. Hated this situation. Hated that I couldn't really share it, now that I knew what we couldn't be. I couldn't be in this with her. She was all smiles and hope, and I had to be the one throwing rocks at her to get her to leave. When all I wanted was to protect her and care for her.

"Hey!" Decca answered finally. She sounded like she was smiling. "How'd it go yesterday? You get the skull to the lab okay?"

I fully intended to use words, but ended up huffing out a laugh at how not okay everything was. Where did I even start? My indignation had overtaken.

"We're not... there. At the lab. And... I'd appreciate it if you wouldn't call the lab to let them know our ETA just yet."

"Ooookay. What's the matter? Where are you?"

"Lebanon."

"The country?"

"The city."

She was quiet. "Lebanon's a suburb of Nashville, which you were supposed to leave two days ago. You could have walked farther by now."

"We couldn't have walked through the Merry Lights of Christmas now, could we? It's drive-through only."

"Funny. You sound like my friend, Chris Carter, but it's almost like someone's gotten hold of him and turned him into a man who participates in spirited holiday extravaganzas. Care to elaborate?"

I blew out a long breath. "Daphne and I... um... hit it off, and we ended up staying at my house an extra night." My words tripped out slowly at first, before the rest of it came out all in one slurred sentence. "When we finally got on the road, we stopped at a rest stop. Daph had picked up this brochure for Fiddler's Grove Historic Village, and she told me about her dad and about how she'd never been able to take a real road trip and stop at all the dumb little places along the way, and I fell for it. So we stopped."

"Okay..."

"How much of this do you want to hear, before I make a complete jackass of myself?"

"Oh, full jackassery. I want it all."

I'd assumed as much. "When we were in the gift shop at Fiddler's Grove, she reached into a back corner for a jar of cilantro jelly—"

"What's cilantro jelly?"

"Not the point. She got bitten by a spider and had a bad reaction. By the time we got the proper antivenin and... ate some food, it was dark, and she really wanted to see the Merry Lights of Christmas, so we're there. Here. She's getting cocoa."

"Is she okay now? How were the Merry Lights of Christmas? I've always lowkey wanted to—"

"Why didn't you tell me she was a student?"

"She's not a student. Yet. She'll start in January."

"Right. So... student."

"Oh." The line was dead for several seconds while she worked it out in her head. "Wait, by 'hit it off,' you mean you..."

"Precisely what you're imagining. What the hell else do you think we were doing alone in my house all day?" A mother yanked her child away from me, scolding me with a deservedly nasty look.

"*All day*? Good for her." I could hear the smirk in her voice.

Here I was at the finish line of my career. Telling Decca made it official that I'd violated the ethics of my office.

"Do you have anything to say for yourself?"

"Technically, I told you to give her a ride to Knoxville."

"Bullshit. I shouldn't have even been at the site. You set this whole thing up. And... *and*... I specifically remember the words *don't let her get away* coming out of your mouth."

"I love your faith in my omnipotence, but... alright fine. I said that. I set you guys up. I love you two together. I don't see what the problem is."

"There are rules about faculty and students."

"Yeah, but..." She laughed. "Come on... You're not even going to be her teacher. You work mostly in the dental school. Besides, it happens all the time. We all know at least one professor whose spouse was once their grad student."

"Not here we don't. At least not recently. More than my job is now on the line, Decca. My expertise as a witness."

She was silent for a long time. "I'm sure they have contingencies for this. The semester hasn't started yet. You're a star. They'll grant leniency. You really think Jeanette's going to let you go?"

I was silent for a while. Staring at the woman in line. The blonde in the oversized camel car coat, playing hand clap games with the kids in line next to her.

"This is real, isn't it, Chris? She's it for you."

Just then, Daphne locked eyes with me and gave me a wave so silly and cute, my eyes stung with unshed tears. "Yeah," my voice broke. "That's the problem." Wind whipped through my insubstantial layers. I cleared my throat. "But I'll wait for her. I've told her that already. I know it's going to be hard, but there's no other way."

"Want me to talk to Jeanette?"

"No. I've read the rules. They're not going to break them for me. God, if this were any other university, it wouldn't be as big of a deal."

"They must've had issues in the past."

"No kidding. And I wouldn't do that to her, anyway. I know how it would look if she came in dating someone from the department. Like she'd slept her way in. Or onto a team or a paper."

"That's how I felt as soon as I met Gus. I just knew he was for me. How's Daphne, anyway? What kind of spider sent her to a hospital?"

"Black widow, we think. That's what they gave her antivenin for. She's fine now. Like it never even happened."

"No superpowers?"

I laughed. "She wishes."

"Chris? If you want me to help you hide this, I will. No matter what the rules say, I *do not* consider love a breach of ethics. Just tell me how I can support you both. I'm going to tell her the same when I call her. In the meantime, I'll ask the cards."

I felt strangely lighter after talking to Decca. Maybe it was the confession, or maybe it was just nice that she understood, she had my back, and didn't think less of me. I leaned back against the driver's side door when Daphne returned, bearing two steaming cups of hot cocoa.

I stared at her hopeful face for several impotent seconds before taking the cup from her.

"Aren't you freezing?"

"Yes."

"I'm sorry. I should've—"

"Nope. Keep it." I was in that weird, almost drunken, half-manic headspace where nothing made a difference. I was floating in a daze of surrealism. The wind blew and cold hit my face like razor blades. Somehow, I was able to simultaneously recognize the feeling while disconnecting from the ability to do anything about it.

She handed me a cup. "It's probably still too hot to..."

I grabbed it and gulped down the viscous chocolate. It wasn't too hot. No commercial beverage was ever hot enough. But it was... bad. Revolting, actually. And that wasn't me being a snob.

"What is this?"

"It's anise. They had different flavors."

"What, in God's name, would make you order a licorice-flavored hot chocolate? What's wrong with just chocolate-flavored hot chocolate?"

"No! That's not what this is. It's—" She took the cup back and sipped. "Oh, ugh. That's really gross."

"No kidding."

"I'm sorry! I didn't know anise meant licorice. I ordered you something that sounded fancy, thinking you'd like it. Anise is such a pretty word. It's a floating, lacy word. They ought to just call it licorice. Except that's a pretty word, too. Not at all like something that tastes like demon piss. Here. Have my salted caramel."

"No thanks."

"Come on. Don't go all Scroogey on me." I couldn't meet her teasing smile. Couldn't even meet her eyes. "Chris." She placed her hand on my cheek and turned my face to hers. But she said nothing. She only looked deeply at me, as though looking alone could tell her what she needed to know. Yet somehow it did.

She swallowed and nodded. "Dance with me?"

Frank Sinatra was singing the opening lines of "Have Yourself a Merry Little Christmas." It wasn't Judy, but it was worlds better than Christmas at the disco. And despite everything, it made me want to wrap my arms around her and embrace the joy of the season. Even if it was a melancholy joy and we were dancing to a melancholy song.

I could deny her nothing. As wrong as it was, everything felt right when she was in my arms.

Taking both cups from her hands and placing them on the roof of the car, I held my arms open. When she clasped my right hand, we were both too cold for there to be much sensation, but every time I touched her meant something.

She laid her head on my chest as I led us over the gravel lot. She followed my lead with ease, our legs a compatible length. Further proof that our bodies had been made for each other. I inhaled deeply and let my breath out slowly.

Other couples started dancing around us. Even Walter and Patty. We were no longer the only attraction. We were just another couple, dancing outside our cars under the strings of glowing Christmas lights.

So anonymous it felt safe enough to lift her chin, lower my mouth to hers, and brush her lips with mine.

She didn't let the kiss end there. Daphne never settled for a little when she could have it all. It was something I loved about her. Her body moved closer, as if she'd been waiting for my invitation. Her icy hand slid behind my neck, sending shivers up my scalp. My mouth pressed more firmly against hers, parting her lips and breathing me in.

We'd stopped dancing. The world fell away. As long as we were together everything felt perfect, even when it couldn't get worse.

"We'd better go." She was the first one to say it after pulling back. Finally, she must have realized the direness of our situation.

Why was I reluctant to go now?

Chapter 16

Daphne

"I'LL DRIVE THIS SHIFT."

"Very funny." He nodded his head to get me to step away from the driver's side door.

"You said I could. If I don't drive now, I might not get another opportunity."

"I received new information. All bets are off, and there's no way you're driving this car. Not for the first time at night."

"We should really go back to your house. Everyone keeps talking about the storm."

"I told you after the club, we're doing the Lights and then we'd be on our way. There's still plenty of time before it's expected to hit."

A few miles down the road, I was squirming in my seat from the effort of trying not to talk. I knew he was keeping his emotional distance, since we couldn't keep physically distant in this tiny car, breathing the same air, and feeling the warmth radiating off each other's bodies. I was trying to respect that. But I couldn't bear his very ducal playlist of sleepy time Christmas choirs.

The GPS wasn't just counting down the miles, but the time left on our relationship. In three hours and forty-eight minutes, I'd be home, and Chris would be driving away from me.

I was desperate to keep him. To tell him how it really made me feel for him to cast me aside like this. But after the strip club... and the car, afterward... I had nothing left. He wanted to shut down, closing off access to parts of himself he'd shown me freely before.

Maybe I was wrong not to make it easier on him.

"Tell me things you know," his voice cut into the silence. He'd flicked on his blinker to merge onto a road heading north. We were only a few miles outside Lebanon, which was no booming metropolis, but it boasted nationally recognizable chains and the comfort of humanity. Suddenly, we were on a black road to nowhere, the lights of the car cutting a path through the black night and encroaching forest.

"Like what?"

"Anything. I'm not asking you *not to talk* for the next three hours."

"Um. I know your mother's chinoiserie is probably Ming dynasty, won at some New York auction house and not a reproduction bought from an online catalog."

"Ah... you'd be correct about that assumption."

"Which part?"

"All of it. The piece I think you're talking about is called the Hundred Crane Ginger Jar. There's a matching pair of garlic-necked jars in the main entrance. All Ming. Sixteenth century. Bought from Christie's, who acquired it from Marchant, for an ungodly amount of money."

"Ooh! I hadn't even seen the others."

Ever since I was a kid, I'd been bougie. I'd always swiped back copies of Southern Living and Architectural Digest when the library left them for the taking, dreaming about what it might be like to live in a house where you could choose your decor, rather than picking up castoffs from the side of a road.

"How much? Ten thousand?"

"No..."

"Fifty?"

He stayed quiet and looked at the GPS. Ignoring me, essentially.

"Come on. I want to know how the other half lives. And how much they pay for pottery."

"Let's just say that damn jar was the reason I wasn't allowed in the solarium until I'd graduated college. I think my mom expected me to throw a football into it, or skateboard into the table. Absolutely ridiculous."

"Would you have?"

"Probably."

"Smart woman. I still can't imagine you as a child. I refuse to believe you weren't born thirty, except..."

"Except what?"

"Except when you dry hump me in the parking lot of a strip club and fingerfuck me until I'm squirting in your precious—"

"Okay."

"You hypocrite." I smiled at him, even if he couldn't see. "You did the things. You're just too gentlemanly to hear about them?"

"Fair enough." He laughed. "For an only child of a wealthy family, I was a fairly normal kid. I built rickety forts in the woods behind my house. I cut myself trying to whittle when I discovered knives. Burned the fort down when I discovered fire and thought I could upgrade it with a fireplace. I played baseball and soccer and football."

"No. You did not play football."

"Kicker. Honestly, that's all my parents would let me play. The ironic part was I was the player injured the worst, senior year. Blew out my knee. But that's what made me get serious about school. And music. I had nothing else to do while I recovered."

"I was never a kid. We have this one photo album where I must have been four or five and I looked like I was happy. Doing little kid stuff. But I don't remember any of it. A few years after that, my parents divorced, and I went back and forth between Mom and Dad's. One day Mom took me to Dairy Queen for Blizzards and told me she was getting remarried. Greg, her boyfriend, had a two-year old, and I'd finally have a brother—not that it mattered much to me. She was so nervous to tell me. Couldn't stop messing with her rings. But she was happy and excited, so I acted excited, too. Even by eight, I knew I had to give people the reactions they wanted. It was easier for everyone when I pretended.

"Then they had the twins. They lived halfway across the state and my dad was rarely concerned about driving me back and forth. Whenever I went there, I was always a visitor. I had my own room, but more and more, Mom used it to store her craft stuff.

"Dad's felt more like home, so I'd stayed with him when my mom moved to Franklin with Greg. But that wasn't what I needed either. I'm what they call a parentified child. I know that now. Back then, I was praised for being an old-soul, or mature for my age, because I was quiet. But I wasn't those things at all. I was quiet and observant because I was stunned into muteness when other kids talked to me. I didn't know the right things to say or how to move my body like they moved theirs. I was desperate to be like them, loud and uncaring. I just didn't know how to be. I didn't know how to play. I didn't know how not to be ashamed if I accidentally did step out of line and get too loud or happy. I always felt like I was offending somebody for just being me. Every time I stopped being hypervigilant, something would happen to prove that I wasn't worthy of the same love or consideration everyone else seemed to get so easily."

I chewed my ragged cuticle. Chris remained silent, allowing me to continue when I was ready.

"Everything I did had greater consequences than anyone else. Even now. I finally meet the man I want to be with, and it's supposed to be so easy. But he won't keep me, because it's too hard."

"Daphne, keeping you would be the easiest thing I've ever done."

"You know why I just recently graduated? Because my mom transferred my college savings to my sisters and my dad didn't fight it. I lost my academic scholarship because I couldn't keep full-time enrollment with my full-time job. And it took me six years to graduate. I should have my master's already."

"Timing," he said. "Always timing."

"None of this should be an issue right now." I took a deep breath. "I know why we can't be together. I'm not trying to make you feel guilty. I'm just trying to add texture to the portrait. To be open and show you who I am. I don't want to hide with you, or pretend and be polite."

He squeezed my hands before returning them to the steering wheel. Something was happening with the fog outside. "Have you ever talked to someone about this? A professional?"

"You mean TikTok videos don't cut it?"

He chuckled a little, but I knew he didn't want to. My words hurt him. My self-deprecation hurt him. That was one of those things I loved about him.

"No, sweetheart. An actual therapist."

"Therapy costs money. Dad has TRICARE, which is really good insurance, but I got kicked off that too, when I was no longer enrolled full-time. Work didn't have insurance, and I didn't get any through the school, because it was too expensive. I'm hoping, once I'm at UT, I can talk to one of the school counselors. I know I shouldn't feel like this, but it's so hard not to be resentful. For falling through the cracks the way I did. For the way my brain works, filling up every nook and cranny with random junk thoughts. In the meantime, I'm making up for it by being a brat."

"You're not a brat. Even if you were, you'd have every right to be."

"Are you giving me permission to keep pushing you?"

"Technically, you don't need my permission to do anything."

"Except what I want to do with you."

"Which is?" He straightened the wheel.

"Start twining our lives together."

He groaned.

"I know. Don't say it. I can't hear another *no* right now."

We rode in silence for a few more miles.

"But, do you think it's wrong that I like to call you Daddy, now that you know I kind of need a father figure?"

"Daph, we can't—"

"I'm not trying to start something, but can we talk seriously about us for a minute? Because even if you make us wait two years, we'll be right back here, and I'll be asking the same thing."

He exhaled loudly. "I don't know a whole lot about the subject, but I was under the impression kinks aren't born from trauma. They're just kinks. This is new to me, and I never thought it would be something that I'd respond to so... viscerally. But I obviously do. Does that mean there's something wrong with me? I don't think there is. And you don't need a father figure. You need someone to nurture you, let you grow in your own ways, hold you accountable... cherish you. Isn't that what any partner should do? It doesn't matter what kinky name it has. That's love." He smirked. "What you call me is just the cherry on top. Sweet in a raunchy, toothsome way."

"Are you saying you love me?"

"That wouldn't be fair, would it? Telling you. Then having to hide it."

"Not fair at all." He hadn't really said it, so I wouldn't really say it back. But I smiled in the dark, letting his half-spoken words sink in and letting myself feel loved—maybe for the first time.

"Toothsome," I repeated, echoing his word from earlier.

He laughed. "You can bite into it. Gnaw on it. It has meat."

"It feels good in my mouth. The word. *Daddy.* It makes me feel like Marilyn Monroe in Gentlemen Prefer Blondes."

"I've always had a thing for Marilyn. Your voice is like hers. A little. Darker. But you both have that breathless quality. Like you just woke up from..."

His words trailed off. He pushed his glasses higher up on his nose and squinted into the mist, flicking the windshield wipers in vain to clear the thickening fog.

He drove several more miles, or maybe it was only one more mile the way he slowed and shifted gears to a lower speed.

The tires were slipping like they were bald and we were driving on a greased track.

"Uh, Chris?" I gripped the door handle and glanced over at him, even though it was too dark to make anything out beside his profile in the dim cabin lights.

"Fuck." Chris slowed the car almost to a crawl, then downshifted once more. The car slipped again.

The brake lights up ahead told me we weren't the only ones in trouble.

"Tell me that's not—"

"Black ice. For the last five miles, we haven't been driving. We've been skating. And it's getting worse. That's not rain you hear hitting the windshield."

"Drive slower."

"My foot's barely on the gas as it is. We can't make it to Knoxville like this."

The car skidded again. German-engineered, electromagnetic steering or not, even Mercedes-Benz couldn't save us from this. The only bit of luck we'd had so far was the light traffic.

Chris tried to downshift and gritted his teeth. He was already in the lowest gear.

He steered into yet another skid when the tires lost their grip on the sheet of glass that had been pavement all but fifteen minutes ago.

Blood rushed through my body, as if every beat of my heart might be its last.

We were sliding across the lanes to nowhere. The car began to spin. It was the same floaty feeling I'd had in the hospital when they'd given me all those drugs.

I didn't know what was real. What sensations my body was feeling. *Not like this*, I thought. *Not like this.* My brain slowed down, trying to capture each flashing image as a still shot. Maybe it was easier to process trauma one frame at a time, rather than as a whole movie.

I scrabbled frantically to grip something: the console, the seat, the door handle. Grasping for anything to help brace myself for impact. However it would inevitably come.

Comically soft, it turned out, or it would have been funny, if I'd been my usual self. We'd hit the guardrail with a slow, agonizing crunch. The sudden stop of momentum wasn't even jarring. I'd barely noticed we weren't moving.

Then I opened my eyes.

From our diagonal position, the headlights shone into nothingness. Blackness. We were inches away from a steep drop. Whether it was into a ditch, or off the side of a mountain, I couldn't be sure, but it would have hurt a lot. And not just Brigitte.

My heartbeat pounded in my neck and ears as I stared ahead into the blackness ahead.

"It's okay. Sweetheart, it's okay," Chris was saying softly. His warm hand was on my cheek, turning my head to him. "Look at me, Daphne. Breathe. We're okay."

I gasped and sucked in a lungful of oxygen.

The car had gone into a skid and rotated one-hundred-eighty degrees. We were on the shoulder, facing the wrong direction on a one-lane road. No headlights shone in our direction, but there would be soon enough.

"Slower, sweetheart. With me. Inhale for four counts. Ready? One, two, three, four. Exhale, two, three, four. Keep that pace, okay? I need to get us out of here."

Chris had done everything right. He'd steered into the direction the car had swerved. He'd already been in the lowest gear when he engaged the clutch and hit the gas as lightly as possible, to flatten out the tires. But even perfect driving and four-wheel suspension were no match for Mother Nature at her cruelest.

Once we were going in the right direction, we inched along as slow as possible.

"Careful," I said. Not because he wasn't being careful, but because I didn't know what else to do.

He was quiet for a while, gritting his teeth in concentration. "We've got to get off this road."

"I agree. There was..." I shook out my hands, willing them to stop shaking, "a sign. A while back. I wasn't paying attention, but maybe there'll be something up ahead."

"I read it. Something tells me you're not going to like it very much."

"Anything's better than spending the night in a ditch."

"See that?" He pointed to the neon sign glowing in the woods on the side of the road.

"O-EL," I read. "Noel?"

"I'm pretty sure there's supposed to be an M and a T in that sign."

"An M and a... No, Chris, you can't be thinking—"

"I'm thinking staying the night there might save our lives."

"Shit." My voice trembled. My body was still shaking.

"Talk to me, sweetheart. Let me hear your voice."

"Okay, um... what does this button do? Do you think maybe the traction could—"

"Not about the car. Tell me something you know. Something you've always wanted to do. If you could take a road trip anywhere, where would you go?"

Okay, I could do this. I could distract us. I'd been training for this event my whole life. I had a mind built for distractions. "I've always wanted to go to the Smithsonian. Especially, the one with the jewels."

"I've been there. It's the Natural History one. It's impressive, although I always preferred American History." His breathing was steady, as if we weren't in mortal peril. It calmed me as well.

"Of course you've been there." I laughed, already recovering from my panic and starting to feel pretty silly about it.

I loved that he'd been there. He could take me and tell me things. He could probably even navigate Washington D.C. traffic the way he drove, and from everything I've read, the roundabouts were a nightmare.

"Still have that Mountain Dew? The sugar would be good for you right now."

"It's somewhere behind me. I'll get it later. Tell me about D.C."

"My parents took me there every few years. We rarely had vacations that weren't educational. D.C. was always great, but some of them were so boring I wanted to claw my eyes out. One time, they sent me to a ranch in Montana."

"That sounds fun."

"It wasn't. It was also the worst time to find out I'm allergic to horses. Plus, it ended up being one of those scared straight places. It was me: privileged rich kid, and four teenage gang members who'd been granted leniency from juvie."

"Were you bullied?"

"At first, yeah. But then they realized I was in it with them. And maybe I even had it worse since my horse changed gait every time I sneezed. They took pity on me, and we all made it out together. I'm still good friends with José; he's a social worker now. I went to his wedding a few years ago in Scottsdale. Two kids. Just took his kids to the ranch. It's a lot nicer now. They loved it."

Even in the dim moonlight, I could tell he was smiling.

"You want kids, Chris?"

His smile faltered. "Maybe. But..." He flicked on his blinker, even though there were no other cars around us.

"But what?"

"I'm... I don't know if..."

I understood. "If I told you I want children? Does that make it easier to answer?"

He paused for a moment, then looked at me, at my flat belly, which he clearly longed to unflatten. "Yes. Unequivocally yes." He turned off the road into the motel driveway that sliced through the woods. "I want a family."

"Me too. With you."

He didn't look at me. It was still too dangerous to take his eyes off the road, even driving... I looked at the gauge... six miles per hour.

"I've always loved kids. Always thought I'd be a great mom, but I guess I never thought it would actually happen. I expected to end up sad and alone. Like how I've always been. It's hard to manifest what you've never seen before."

"Daph—"

"I know, Chris. I know you don't want to hear this for two years, but I have to say it. If I don't, I might explode. You make me want things I've never seen for myself. I look at you, and I..." Shit. He wasn't going to like this. "I see a more full life than I'd allowed myself to imagine before. I always thought I'd end up like Jeanette. Married to my work. I love the work, don't mistake that. But before I met you, there was a big part of my future that felt like a shadow. Now you've shown me the full, colorful, rainbow spectrum of what it could be like. I want the dude ranch and the Smithsonian and the loud annoying road trips to boring, hot, educational historic sites with kids fighting in the backseat. I want it all. As long as you're driving."

He said nothing. I knew why. He couldn't say what he really thought about any of that. It was fine. But I still wasn't going to give him up, even if that only meant fighting with him for the next two years. It was something.

There was barely an audible rumble as we drove over the cracked and broken off bits of pavement. The long driveway to the top of a hill. The parking lot looked an apocalyptic wasteland. I half expected zombies with unnaturally bent limbs and dangling eyeballs to start swarming the car in their slow, brainless way. Not even the tight harmonies of the Andrews Sisters singing through the speakers could counteract the uneasy feeling I had. In fact, I might never be able to listen to "Santa Claus is Coming to Town" again without thinking of impending doom.

Great. Now I was picturing Zombie Santa. Jitterbugging with Mrs. Claus.

On the bright side, these potholes were no match for the AMG suspension, which still functioned beautifully after two fender benders. When would I get a better opportunity to experience this?

Chris parked in front of the flickering vacancy sign. The "no" wasn't illuminated, but the rest of the sign didn't seem to be in excellent working order, which wasn't exactly encouraging.

Without speaking, he reached into my lap and squeezed my hand, holding it until I flipped it over and laced my fingers with his. Then I raised our joined hands and kissed each of the knuckles of his trembling hand. He'd been so calm on the road, but now he needed to let all that adrenaline out.

"This is going to be fine. It's gonna be fine," he repeated. "We're okay. We'll be okay."

I didn't know if he meant tonight, or for the long haul, and I didn't want to ask. There were other cars pulling in, the parking lot wasn't empty, and we still didn't know if they actually had any vacancies. We weren't out of the woods yet. Not tonight. And as far as our relationship went, according to Chris, we were so deep in the damp underbrush of some dark forest, it was hopeless to think we'd ever see the sun again.

Chris's eyes closed and he rested his head on the seat back, finally letting on that he might have been just as panicked as I was.

"You drove perfectly. You steered into every skid, took it slow. No one could have done it better."

I kissed his hand again and let it go.

Then we both looked up at the rental office.

Jagged shadows of cracked and torn shades swayed in the green light of the windows. A faded arrow pointed right, toward a pool, and when I turned my head, curious to see the sorry state of it, it was even worse than I thought. The "pool" was a gaping wound in the ground, not only drained, but un-barricaded. Not even a dusty ribbon of caution tape flapped in the breeze.

"Chris, I think this is a murder motel."

"It's... probably not." His eyes were now trained on the flaking paint on the sign.

"No, seriously. We're about to walk right into a true crime podcast. The couple are so relieved that they escaped the first problem, they don't even realize they walked right into the lair of a killer."

"The ice was nowhere near our first problem today. On the bright side, if I get murdered, we don't have to wait two years to see each other. I can haunt you. You'll just have to check in the same room every Christmas Eve, when my spirit turns corporeal for a few hours." He did a spooky hand gesture. "How's that for a Christmas tradition?"

"Suddenly that ditch on the side of the road is looking pretty good."

He laughed. "Stay in the car. I'll see if they have some rooms."

I nodded and did as I was told. I wasn't about to be the damsel who inserted herself into where she didn't belong and mucked up the works.

I breathed deeply when he locked the doors behind him and ice skated into the rental office. We'd made it safely to the motel without incident. Without further incident, anyway. It had been a long day of incidents. I hadn't realized I'd been holding my breath for quite a while. When I let out a long, slow exhale, his last words hit me.

Some rooms?

Headlights shone in my eyes as another car parked next to us.

I unclicked my seatbelt, clicked off the car, and grabbed the keys. I hustled to catch up with Chris before he made a huge mistake.

"Chris," I shouted. There was a woman in line behind him.

"Good news," he said cheerfully. "There's room at the inn. We won't have to find a manger."

"Yeah, about that. Rooms? Don't you dare get us two rooms." I turned to the motel manager, a pale, stringy-limbed twenty-something-year-old man, desperate for some green veggies and a retinoid lotion, and told him the same thing. "We don't need two rooms. We'll make do with one."

"Daphne," Chris said with a tone.

"Chris," I used his same tone. "This isn't the time for ethics. There are cars streaming into the parking lot, all needing a place to stay."

He looked around like I was playing a dirty trick on him. "Fine. Get back in the car."

"Fine." I wasn't about to fight him on that. Not after pulling my elbow through some kind of gelatinous puddle that had been drying on the check-in counter.

I just hoped the water ran clear. I didn't expect a hot shower, but I wanted to at least wash my hands after using the toilet.

In the time it took him to complete his transaction, two more cars had driven up behind us. The NO flickered to life above the VACANCY and Chris and I exchanged a look of gratitude at our timing. Finally, a bit of luck.

Then he turned the car around and parked in the farthest space at the end of the low, cinderblock building that looked like it hadn't been painted since... well, I couldn't say when, but it needed painting.

A rusted gutter hung off the corner of the roof.

Tennessee was one of the most beautiful places on earth. Why was the universe so determined to highlight the ugliest parts of her tonight?

"You still don't think this is a murder motel?" I raised my eyebrows, looking at big 13 on the door. Good thing I wasn't superstitious.

"Nah. If I had to guess, it's more of a... suicide motel."

Fucking death care workers and their morbid sense of humor.

He shrugged. "Want me to check it out first?"

"No point. No matter what lies inside the room, it's safer than out here." He gave me side-eye. "Isn't it?"

"Let's leave this part out of our future Christmas traditions."

Chapter 17

Chris

THE RUSTY, DILAPIDATED SIGN simply read "MOTEL."

The slip I'd signed elaborated that it was the Hickory Hills Motel, located in Weans Hollow, Tennessee. That someone had bothered to give it such a bucolic name struck me as odd.

Ordinarily, I wouldn't have paid much attention. I'd have handed the man my credit card without thinking about the affectation the name gave the place. But the carbon paper credit card sales slip made me take note. As did the diamond-shaped plastic key ring I'd been handed. It was almost quaint in its midcentury design, except it wasn't the kind of midcentury that had ever been cute to begin with.

This was purely utilitarian, and always had been. More like a bomb shelter that no one had remembered to bury. The kind of place where you took notice of every detail. Cementing every stain, cigarette burn, and belly-up bug into your memory, in case you'd be called to testify after witnessing the kind of heinous crimes that happened in places like this.

Shit. This might win the prize for the sketchiest place I'd ever set foot in, and that included real life crime scenes. How this business remained in operation was beyond my comprehension.

"Now or never," I said, more to myself than to Daphne. I'd been trying to put up a brave front, and I had no intention of dropping it at any point before we checked out, but on the inside, my bones were rattling like a cartoon. I couldn't help but think of the bodily fluids I'd find painted on the walls. The state of the toilet. The clarity of the water.

I shivered and forced myself out of the car after Daphne had already girded her loins to do the same.

I grabbed our bags from the back.

"Oh, Chris. Look." She pointed to the sky. "The stars are so bright here."

I looked up, my eyes immediately drawn to the Pleiades, the Big Dipper, Orion. No Star of Bethlehem, but Polaris was particularly bright.

Daphne held my naked hand in her gloved one and together, we both looked and looked. Maybe it wouldn't be so bad after all. As much as I needed to get away from Daphne as fast as possible, this detour meant a few more precious hours with her. In my heart, I was grateful for more than just a safe place to hunker down through the icy weather.

"Thank you, Chris." She turned to me with a plaintive look. "I know this is my fault. It's all my fault that we have to stay here in this shithole. If we hadn't gone to Fiddler's Grove, or made the wreaths. If I'd picked grape instead of cilantro jelly. If I hadn't been allergic—or whatever I was—to that spider. If I hadn't spent so long talking to Valentine, or pouted about missing the Merry Lights of Christmas—oh, God, I really fucked everything up, haven't I?"

"Daphne, no." I pulled my hand out of hers and cupped her cheek, rubbing my thumb across the top. I needed to touch her, to reassure her. "The fault is mine. We should be sleeping at my parent's house tonight. I was the one who put us both in danger, because... I was afraid."

"Of what?"

"That after one more night with you, I'd fall too hard to let you go."

"You already have," she said sweetly. "You're just pretending it's not true."

I chuckled. There'd been a Cold War conflict between my head and my heart, but hostilities were heating up. I looked at her and all I could see was that she wasn't mine to touch. Or reassure. While my fingers burned to pull her close and never let go.

But I did pull her close. Tonight, we were alive, and we were here, and she was mine. And she'd be mine for the rest of the trip.

"I wish you'd told me before all this."

"That I'm going to be a student?"

"Yes."

"I'm glad you didn't know. We wouldn't be here. Even if we get murdered in this motel tonight, I couldn't think of a better way to spend Christmas Eve."

I dropped my hand. "That's the sweetest and dumbest thing you've ever said."

Somehow, we made it to the door, gliding more than walking.

"Oh my God, look at the key! I wonder if they'd let me buy one."

"Stay here. Let me take a look inside."

"Oh, come on. We're having an adventure."

Daphne nudged me aside and flicked on the lights as we braced ourselves for what we were about to see.

The bulbs flickered a bit while they warmed up with a vaguely orange glow, but nothing scurried across the floors or up the walls. That alone let me start breathing more regularly. On a night as unseasonably cold as this, any number of critters could be building nests in the empty rooms. So far, so good.

The room was unsurprisingly outdated, but almost warm. Even better, it was clean. The bedspreads were tucked carefully over the pillows. There were no bits and pieces of trash on the floor. A quick look in the bathroom told me the minimal stains on the tub were a natural result of age and rust rather than lack of cleaning. The overhead tube lights were unappealing, but there were towels and plenty of toilet paper. It wasn't a spa, but it was functional, and… I tested the water in the tub faucet… scaldingly hot.

"I wouldn't recommend a soak in the tub, but I think it's safe to say you won't come out of the shower with a bacterial plague. Although, now that I know you and your propensity for sudden almost-death, maybe we should knock on wood."

Daphne had already turned on the TV and was bouncing on her bed while she flipped through the channels.

"How are you feeling, by the way?"

She took a deep breath and ascertained. "Tired."

"It's been a long day." I leaned against the doorframe of the toilet and shower room, and crossed my arms. "Especially for you."

"Not long enough. You're going to leave me tomorrow."

I studied her face. I had only hours left to capture it, sending it deep into my hippocampus. I already knew I'd get no sleep tonight. I'd be lying awake in bed, holding on to every twitch and smile.

She came over and wrapped her arms around me. Her eyelids fluttered closed. She was close enough I could feel her soft breath on my neck.

"Do you think he'll be okay out there?" Her eyes shot open as she pulled back, having practically shouted into my face.

"Who? Did you see an animal?"

"Winston."

"Who?"

"You know..." she jutted her bottom jaw out. "Winston. That's what I named him, anyway. His underbite reminded me of a bulldog, but it seemed disrespectful to call him Bulldog, so I gave him a human name. After Churchill."

"Yes, thank you. I made that connection. Just not why you're asking about the skull. Nor why you've chosen to give him a name at all."

"We're spending so much time with him—"

"Unfortunately."

"He's the reason we're together—"

"We're not together."

She made a face like she didn't believe me.

"I needed a name to call him when I thought about him."

"Like my car?"

"Yes! Did you feel the way Brigitte handled that rough driveway?"

Now I couldn't help but smile. I knew exactly what she was talking about. The smoothness of the ride almost halted my hesitation about the motel stay.

"Well? Do you think he's okay out there? Should we bring him inside?"

"I think Winston's used to being exposed to much higher an d... well, maybe not lower temperatures, but every other possible weather element in the hundred years or more he's been dead."

"But..." She glanced out the window wistfully and bit her cuticle, a gesture I was starting to recognize as one of real concern. "I feel bad."

"Alright. I'll bring him in. If that'll make you feel better."

"Thank you, Chris."

I stole my coat back from her. When I turned the handle, the wind blew the door open. Fuck, it was freezing. I'd already forgotten the bite of the cold after a few minutes of being in the warmth."

The ground was so slippery, I had to swish my feet back and forth to keep from falling.

Suddenly my feet weren't under my legs. My hand shot out and Brigitte caught my fall. I was able to grab on to the rear bumper to keep my ass from hitting the ice.

That's when I noticed the music. I'd absently assumed it was someone's car radio, but now that I was actively listening, I recognized human voices.

A fire burned in a metal trash can in the parking lot, just a few doors down.

"The Holly and the Ivy." It was one of my favorite traditional carols, only this was sung to a different tune. Dark, lush, and beautiful.

I slid back into the room and tore off my coat, grabbing all our clothing and telling Daphne to put on every warm thing she had, which now included every warm thing I had.

"Chris, wh—?"

"Just come with me."

"Anywhere." She rushed to get dressed.

I locked the door behind us and made our way closer to the singers. Four men and four women were bundled in thick parkas and hats, singing together with perfect intonation. Vapor clouds puffed in the air around them, adding to the fog and making the night even more ethereal.

I closed my eyes as their next carol, which had started in C, took a turn into a darker key. Not A minor, though. Something more atonal and haunting.

"Oh, wow." Daphne gasped. "They're really good. Aren't they?"

I knew this piece, too. But I'd never heard it arranged like this. The melody was sad and lilting, more felt than heard, as the fog created an acoustic shell around their voices. The choir's pristine tones, dissonant harmonies, and the facility of their voices told me they weren't just good. They were a professional ensemble. Stuck here just like us. Making the most of this murder motel by offering an impromptu Christmas Eve concert.

"Yeah." I laughed. "They're good."

Daphne lifted my arm and put it around her shoulders as she hugged me. It was so frigid, her body temperature barely registered against mine, but somehow, I was impervious to the swirl of cold wet air around us.

More and more people began coming out of their rooms. Singles, couples, and families all silently joined us around the fire. We looked into each other's faces, acknowledging our situation, our shared humanity, our gratitude.

All in this together. Listening—*worshiping*—together with quiet reverence. Giving thanks that our lives were spared tonight. That we'd had shelter. That we were here to experience this pristine beauty together.

My parents were "diet Episcopalian" and had occasionally dragged me to church for midnight services on Christmas Eve. It was okay, but church had never felt like this. Standing here in the cracked parking lot of a dilapidated roadside motel, the woman I loved under my arm, strangers coming together in fellowship, was maybe the most perfect, pure spiritual experience I'd ever felt.

The choir sang a few more songs, easy ones, gesturing for everyone to sing with them. When I looked down, Daphne was staring into the fire rather than singing. "You okay?"

She nodded, but I didn't believe her. Everyone clapped and began to part ways, too cold to stay outdoors any longer.

"That's twice you got to sing carols—no thanks to your mom." I said, when we were back in the room.

"I wasn't even thinking about that. I'm just... overwhelmed with it all. I'm happy, but I know you don't want me to show you how much. It's just hard to hide it from you when you're the one person who's going through this with me. It's happening to both of us. I just wish you'd let go a little."

"I can't." I couldn't disguise the pain in my voice. Our time left was too short.

"I know."

"There's no just a little with you. If I give in, I'm off a cliff."

She nodded. "I've been off the cliff. Jump with me. We'll figure it out."

I laughed and tucked a strand of hair behind her ear.

"Do you always get what you want?"

"I rarely get anything I want. Just my job with Decca, and school. The only things I wanted, I fought tooth and nail for. And they're the best things in my life. Now you. And I'm going to fight for you, too."

Part of me wanted her to fight for me. Maybe all of me wanted that. I shouldn't let her, but I was too tired tonight to stop it.

We'd been through too much today. She'd faced death twice. Tonight, I just wanted to hold her, settle into the shitty, lumpy mattress and pretend that I didn't have to leave her tomorrow.

"Stay here." I went back out to the car and returned with a bottle of wine and some food I'd packed us. I always swiped a couple bottles from Mom and Dad's cellar whenever I visited them, and this time, I'd taken a few extra. Celebratory bottles of wine and whisky I'd wanted to share with Daphne. Most could wait two years. But it was Christmas

Eve. We'd survived the night. We deserved something special to help us celebrate instead of sulk.

Daphne flipped through the channels until she finally landed on *It's a Wonderful Life*. It had just started. Little Mary was whispering into George's trick ear over the ice cream counter.

I unwrapped the paper cups from the bathroom counter. Lord, help me, but I was pouring a 2000 Chateau Lafleur into paper cups. I almost cried at the injustice. When the cork creaked its way out of the bottle and the scent wafted into the air, there was no mistaking why this was such a good vintage.

"You brought wine?" Daphne smiled as I handed her a cup.

"I'd intended to save it for your birthday," I smiled. "Whenever that is."

"March thirtieth."

"Or another special occasion. But, seeing as how I won't be around for your birthday, it's Christmas Eve, and we're making our own Christmas traditions..." I poured the wine into my own cup, "Uncorking a special bottle of wine, and watching *It's a Wonderful Life* is one I wouldn't mind repeating every year."

"What's special about this wine?"

"It's from your birth year. I happened to notice it on my way out. It's one of the few good bottles from the region that are ready to drink now."

She held up her glass. "To fancy wine and George Bailey."

"And us surviving this night."

Chapter 18

Daphne

WE TAPPED OUR CUPS and sipped, staring into each other's eyes. I thought it smelled vaguely like chlorine from the bleached paper, but the wine was good enough it didn't matter.

"Oh! This is... something."

"Good? Bad?" He put his nose over the cup. Even now, without the fancy glass or an elaborate swirl and sip routine, he looked like a connoisseur.

"I don't know anything about wine. You know that. But good doesn't seem like a good enough word. I just don't know how else to describe it. If this is wine, I could get used to this."

"Please, don't. Even I can't afford a Lafleur habit."

"What am I supposed to be tasting?"

He took a sip and savored it, staring at the orange floral bedspread as he thought. "Medium-bodied with silky tannins. Berries and currants with hints of truffle and cracked stone."

"Cracked stone? You can really pick out all those flavors?"

"No. That's what *Wine Spectator* wrote when I looked it up to see if it was any good. I don't know much about wine, besides whether or not I enjoy drinking it. It's why I raid my parents' stock whenever I go back. I trust whatever they have is good. I do know that it should not be served in paper cups, and at the very least, it should breathe a bit first."

"While it's doing its thing, then, I'm going to take a shower. Send me your thoughts and prayers that I don't run out of hot water, and that it stays clear."

"I'll see what's under the bedspread. We've been operating under the assumption the sheets are clean."

It felt wrong not to kiss him before turning away, but I was trying hard to be on my best behavior. He was in enough turmoil.

The water wasn't as hot as Chris's house, but I couldn't complain. I wasn't even under the stream long enough for my hair to become saturated before I felt a breeze and whipped around.

Chris nodded toward the bottles of shampoo and conditioner he'd placed on the bathtub ledge. The ones I'd used in his guest shower. I mentioned several times how much I loved them because they smelled like Earl Grey tea.

"Thank you," I said, shielding my body from him. Not because I wanted to. Because I was trying to make it easier on him.

Chris opened the curtain wider and leaned against the wall. His arms folded across his chest as he watched me with an expression of placidity. No smile. No scowl. He was just there. Taking me in.

If he wasn't going to make this easier for himself, neither was I.

I turned to face him, raising my arms up to my hair, separating the strands and showing my body to him. I was his to see, even if he didn't want it to be true.

The way he was looking at me, like he was trying to unnerve me...

He didn't though.

"Join me?"

"I can't."

"But you can watch me shower like I'm putting on a private show for you?"

"I can't do this either."

"Take off your clothes or I'm pulling you in, cashmere and all."

He scratched his nose and let his gaze slither between my legs. It was predatory in a way he got sometimes, like he was done with the pretense of being a gentleman, and couldn't take it a second longer.

Slowly, with his gaze locked on the water trailing off my hard nipples, he kicked off the wall, and pulled his glasses off his face, carefully folding the arms before placing them on the sink counter. His movements were deliberate and precise. This was calculated. The thrill of seeing him like this rushed through me and I shivered under the water.

He grabbed a fistful of his sweater by the back of the neck and tugged it over his head, bringing his button-down with it.

Chris wore clothes exceptionally well. I loved men in clothes, how they draped and hung in long, clean lines when they were tailored to the right frame. Chris was exactly the right frame. A body built for slouchy library tweeds and slim tuxedos. He even moved well in clothes, with an easy, languid gait that was sexy without trying to be.

I'd never really looked at his body without the clothes. He didn't try to hide himself, it just always happened that he got me naked, and couldn't be bothered removing his own clothes until after we'd both come. By then, I was too delirious to really notice the details.

Now that I could, I found his naked body equally impressive. He was thin, but not scrawny. He had the lean muscles that spoke of a childhood playing sports and semi-regular enjoyment of physical activity in adulthood.

He unbuckled the side of his pants and they slipped down. He hadn't been wearing anything underneath them, since he'd creamed in his boxers after the strip club.

His cock was hard. It was always hard. That was the only way I'd ever seen it. His refractory period was like a nanosecond. I was pretty sure it was a superpower. An annoyingly pointless one, since it meant his balls must be constantly aching around me.

Probably similar to how I was constantly aching around him. Every minute his thick, uncut, perfect cock wasn't filling me up was time lost. And shit, the way it swung low and heavy, already leaking threads of pre-cum as he stepped over the tub, had me dying for it.

"Don't bother touching. No use looking either. This is my problem, not yours. Turn around."

He wet my hair under the stream of water and pulled me back out again, while all I could do was squeeze my legs together and brace myself against the wall. I loved how he controlled me. Something about him made me surrender to his every whim. Finally, I'd found my safe person and I could relinquish every bit of exhausting control.

I heard the cap of the shampoo bottle flip closed. Seconds later, his hands were in my hair, massaging my scalp slowly and firmly with his fingertips as he worked the tea-scented shampoo down my long stands. When he felt my hair was sufficiently clean, he moved me back under the water and massaged the shampoo out. Then he repeated the process with the conditioner. Never had anyone treated me so gently before.

When I turned to face him, he looked like he was in agony. Not because of the state of his arousal, but because this, *us,* was torture for him.

"Chris, please. Let me touch you. Tell me it's okay. I want to make you feel good."

He groaned and reached for the soap. But he didn't lather up his hands.

"I think you better do this part."

I took the bitty bar and rubbed it in my hands before soaping up my tits, spending way more time there than was necessary. "That's what you said to me about my rock-climbing harness."

"I was right." He started shampooing his own hair after I'd finally moved on to my arms. "I knew you were going to be trouble."

After he rinsed his hair, I cleaned between my legs with plain water. Then I turned around, bending over farther than strictly necessary, and used my soapy fingers over my ass, first my cheeks, circling smaller and smaller until I was sliding down the slick center. I stayed there, rubbing my tight hole and moaning from how good it felt, not just the nerve endings there, but giving him his sordid show.

I looked back. His gaze was right there. He was no longer cool and controlled.

Garbled syllables escaped from behind me before he cleared his throat.

"Clean me here, Daddy. Please?"

He groaned. "Oh, fuck." His hand gripped my hips.

"I want you to have me here. I've never had anyone there before. I don't want it with anyone but you. Do you want me there, Daddy?"

I turned around and—fuck the no touching rule; he was the one who joined me in the shower. I placed my arms on his shoulders. It would have been chaste, sweet, if his cock wasn't bobbing against my belly.

"You think there's a place I haven't wanted to fuck you, darling? I can't wait to feel your ass clenching around me, sucking me in." He smiled deviously. "In two years."

Disappointing, but not unexpected.

"I don't believe you. Not even you have the willpower to wait. You need to come before then. I need to come before then. I need to come now."

I grabbed his cock and lifted it up. Not toward my entrance, just up. Between us.

He let me. He even went further, lifting my leg and wrapping it around his waist. His dick was positioned in a way where he could rut against my belly while his balls hit my clit. Just that alone made me want to die of happiness, but he took it further.

He reached behind me, sliding his slippery, soapy fingers through my slit. Back, back to where I'd been massaging my asshole, getting it ready... for what, I didn't even know. We weren't prepared. I knew water was no good as lube. I knew he wouldn't cave, but now this.

His fingers were stroking over and over my entrance. It felt so filthy, even though I told myself it wasn't. It was beautiful because it was what I wanted and what he wanted and there was nothing dirty about my body, or our desires, or us exploring it all together.

He circled and circled, rubbing his cock absentmindedly against me.

"Let me in, sweetheart. Let me feel you on my fingers." The way he kissed my temple was so sweet and tender, it was easy to relax further, breathe into what I expected to be pain.

When he pushed in so slowly with his fingertip, we both moaned.

"Fuck." He shook his head and exhaled. "Tight. So fucking... yeah."

"More, Chris."

"Does it—" he breathed. "How does it feel?"

Honestly, it felt amazing when he was rubbing the outside. The moment he entered me it'd stopped feeling like anything sexual, and it was just fine. But the pleasure came anyway, because he was inside me in a place no one else had been before. I hadn't even put my own fingers inside my asshole. Of course, there was the issue of Dad's terribly tiny water tank and shower sprints, but also, I'd never really been curious.

I couldn't give enough of myself to Chris and giving him this made our situation… better somehow. Or maybe worse. I had no idea what I was doing anymore. I suspected he didn't either.

He went in further, moving so slowly it almost didn't register as movement, but his cock was stroking my belly in rhythm. I pressed my hand flat against it, increasing the pressure.

"Stop, sweetheart. I'm going to come."

"I need you to come. Come for me? Please, Daddy."

"Oh, Jesus… fuck." He was spurting up onto my tits from below. "Oh, fuck, you're so good. How am I supposed to…?" There was a noise like a whine, attached to a moan and then more words. "Shit, I wasn't go nna… your ass is so perfect. My darling. Your fucking… and your sweet tits."

It was nonsense. Nonsense! But I loved that he got this way when he came. Spilling verbal gobbledygook because he was so blissed out from me. From my body. I gave him this. It gave me so much power I could float out of this murder motel bathroom and live for years on just this feeling. I fucking loved rendering this intelligent, educated man incoherent; like calling me sweet, old-fashioned names like *sweetheart* and *darling* while he did the most depraved things to my body.

"I'm hanging by a thread, here, Daphne."

"Break it, Chris. Don't wait for someone to throw you a line. Break that thread. With me. Say the word and I'll cut it so fast you'll be free falling."

"I already am."

"I am too."

He looked so much younger without his glasses. Not age wise. There was no difference there. He probably looked thirty-six ten years ago, and he'd look it twenty years from now. But there was a vulnerability in his eyes that was hidden behind his tortoiseshell frames. There was hope. And mischief.

Then again, he did still have his finger in my ass.

THAT NIGHT, AFTER WE'D settled into a happy sort of delirium from the wine, and held each other during that perfect final scene of It's a Wonderful Life, we lay in bed, side-by-side.

We should have been sleeping. It was well after midnight on what had been the longest, most eventful day of both our lives.

But I couldn't keep my eyes closed.

Chris was there, he was right there across the pillows. Glasses off, face composed, even if it wasn't quite at peace. His eyes were closed but he wasn't asleep.

Ice pelted against the windows and rooftop as my desire overpowered my will to be good.

I didn't come in the shower. Now the need was building up again, and I didn't even know my own body anymore. Only that it was made for fucking him. Being licked and sucked by him.

I turned onto my other side. I wasn't wearing underwear. I hadn't worn them since the strip club and I wouldn't wear them tomorrow. I didn't have any that were clean. It was easy enough to touch myself in just his extra t-shirt.

My fingers slipped between my pussy lips. I was already wet. I canted my pelvis forward just enough and opened my legs. Reaching farther down, I easily slid inside my vagina with two fingers, but it wasn't great. I wasn't thick like his fingers or his cock. I couldn't reach my G-spot that made penetration feel good like it did with Chris—achy, like I wanted to crawl out of my skin with pleasure before everything inside me built up and up and up, swelling with need until it burst, sending a million little fragments of my soul shooting out.

This wasn't doing it for me, but I kept going. Maybe it would do something for him.

He groaned behind me, reaching around my waist and dragging me back to him.

"Are you trying to drive me crazy, sweetheart?" His warm breath bloomed on my neck, under my ear. "Do you know how hard it's been, lying next to you, knowing you don't have any panties on? Now this?"

"No. How hard is it, Daddy?"

He moved his hips forward, pressing his hard cock against my ass. I whimpered with need for him. "Please, Chris."

"You need me to touch you, baby?" His hand came down between my legs. "God, you're soaked already."

I parted my legs further as he played. His touch felt so much better than mine. "Your little clit is all hard. Filled with blood. I want to taste you, want to feel it dragging across my tongue."

"Yes, Chris."

He rolled onto his back and smiled up at me. "Come up here. I'm already a dead man, you might as well finish me off and make it good."

I knew I had the biggest, goofiest smile on my face. It was a triumph of sorts. It conquered my doubts and quelled my fears.

"Um... how?"

He scooted down the bed and adjusted his pillow vertically. "Hands against the wall. Use my mouth and take what you need. Use me up, because I'm not going to get another chance at this for a long time."

Shit. I was already leaking down my thighs.

"I'm going to get a towel."

His chuckle came from low in his belly and turned on the faucet inside me.

I ran to the bathroom in my socks and t-shirt, catching a glimpse of my red cheeks and wild eyes in the mirror as I passed. I looked hot and needy, every bit of my greed for him showing on my face, in the tangles of my hair and the rock-hard peaks of my nipples.

When I came back to the bed, I peeled off my shirt and socks and straddled his face. His handsome, distinguished face that looked way too smart and aristocratic for this.

But he was a secret freak. So was I. We brought it out in each other.

"Spread your knees. Lower. Lower. That's it. Fuck, you smell good." He groaned as he moved his head back and forth, brushing his lips across my swollen pussy. "Nothing makes me harder than the way you come."

When he spoke, it was quiet and serious, thinking through every one of his filthy words. It wasn't dirty talk. It was a love letter, written with yearning and fire.

The first lick was slow and intentional. He grabbed my ass and opened me from behind, moving me on his face, using me like this was for his pleasure, rather than mine.

He groaned and swirled his tongue around my clit, moving his head back and forth until his entire face was slick and wet.

My orgasm built heavily in my pelvis. Sex had never felt like this with anyone else. Chris was the only one who'd wanted my vulnerability, and didn't use my kindness against me, but upheld it as a strength. Not because he wanted dominion over me, but because *he* was kind. And vulnerable. I could lose my inhibitions with him, and the more I lost, the more he gave.

He ripped himself away from me with a choked moan. "Come in my mouth, Daphne. Even if you squirt. It's okay. I want every last drop."

His face was so raw and pleading when he'd said it, asking for me to come like I was doing him a favor. He stared into my eyes and sucked my clit between his lips, his fingers working inside me. The pressure built so suddenly I had no warning.

"I'm coming, Daddy. Oh, God, it's... coming." I shrieked and I shot a stream of fluid onto his face and into his waiting mouth, spilling out onto his chest and the pillow under him. It was so wrong. So filthy. So perfect.

We were so fucking perfect together.

My hands slid down the wall and gripped his hair, dragging my pussy over his tongue to lick up the last drops. I was thoroughly spent, but I needed more. I needed to feel him stretching me and filling me up. "I need your cock, Daddy. Please."

I sat on his shoulders and leaned back until I could reach to wrap my hand around his hard cock.

His eyes squeezed shut and he pushed my hand away. "You have no idea what I want to do to you right now."

"Tell me." I rose up and inched my way down his body, kneeling over him, reaching for him again, but he jerked away. His jaw tightened as he looked away.

"I want to tear you to pieces. Pull you apart and fuck you so deep you're screaming."

"Yes." I wrapped my hand around his cock, rubbing the wet tip on my lips, licking the thick beads of pre-cum as more and more eased out of him with each stroke. I closed my eyes, I took him in my mouth as deep as I could while circling my tongue around his head. I was a lolling, drooling mess as I made love to his cock, caressing and sucking to prove myself to him, to prove my worthiness.

He groaned, a deep gravelly sound that made my eyes roll back in my head and suck him harder. "Fuck. What are you doing to me, you sweet... how do you... oh, fuck. Fuck, yes."

He held his head in his hands like he was in agony. The wet, choking noises coming out of me as I bobbed on him, trying to take as much as I could. Was I even doing this right? Who knew? Who cared. Chris was leaking more and more salty bitterness into the back of my mouth and the sighing, breathless, tortured sounds of his impending pleasure matched my own until he was gripping me by the neck and pulling me off of him. I didn't even have time to swallow the trail of spit and pre-cum that had been pooling in my mouth, it just came drooling out after me.

"Fuck. I can't. Get off me."

I scrambled back like I'd done something wrong. Oh, shit. I really had this time. I had done... something.

He was up and on his feet, grabbing my duffel bag and throwing it onto the bed.

"Chris, no. What are y—" The words stuck in my throat as panic set in.

He rifled through the bag and produced the box of condoms. "You need to be fucked? You need Daddy's cock?"

"Yes." Everything was moving slowly, like I was drugged. I was almost afraid of what he was going to do to me, but more afraid I wasn't going to find out.

He threw a condom onto the bed in front me. "One more night. I can't fucking take another moment of not being inside you."

I grabbed the tiny foil package and ripped it open. Immediately, he was around the bed, his eyes boring into me with each step until he was gripping the back of my head and pulling me up and into his ravenous kiss. He kissed me like he was a man dying and I held the spark of life in my lungs. He breathed me in and consumed me. My body was on fire. But there was a promise that it would soon be quenched.

I rolled on the condom with shaky fingers. I was more nervous this time than our first. Or our second, or third, or tenth.

He broke the kiss and picked me up, turning me away from him and pushing my torso down onto the bed. “Hands and knees.”

I scrambled to follow his order.

The bed shifted behind me, and I crawled up to accommodate him.

“No, you don’t. Come back here.” He yanked my hips so hard, my arms shot out in front of me and I landed on my face. His hand was immediately on the back of my neck, squeezing hard and pushing my face into the bed. "That's better."

Fuck. I didn’t know he was capable of *rough*. I didn’t know I was capable of liking it.

“I know you can’t see your pretty little cunt, Daphne, but it’s fucking gorgeous. Lips so puffy and proud, like she knows she’s my undoing. Making me her slut.” I bit into my lip as his fingers slid through my lips. I knew I looked obscene, the way my ass was sticking up into the cold air, fluid already building inside me, leaking down my legs.

I heard the slap before I felt it. A current of shock ran up my spine. The sweet sting sent a gush of fluid pouring out of me.

I whimpered when I felt his tongue there, on my pussy, soothing the sting and cooing sweet words so low, I couldn’t discern them.

He slapped again, and I sucked in a breath. Now he licked lower, catching trails of my wetness on his thirsty tongue. “I don’t want any going to waste.”

Then he was pushing me down again, into the mattress. His cock was there, his head replacing his tongue and hands... oh, God... rubbing through my slit, teasing before... oh. Fuck, he was deep. All at once, and so deep. "Oh my god." All of his cock was rammed inside me and it so thick he was going to rip me in half. It was too much. It wasn't enough.

With a grunt, he fisted the flesh at my hips and dragged my body closer to him, sliding his cock so far in my knees lifted off the bed.

"Daddy."

He held me there, using me, fucking me like it was nothing. Like *I* was nothing, pounding into me fast and hard, with a brutality I wouldn't have thought him capable of. Punishing me for our predicament. For his betrayal to himself and his damned ethics. For giving in.

And I wanted to take it. God, it felt good taking it. His cock and his punishment and his pleasure. All his anger and resentment and the ironic unfairness of the situation.

His fingers were bruising my hips. He was pulling my cheeks apart wider and wider, as if he could somehow crawl inside me.

Each thrust split me open, slamming into my cervix so hard I could feel it in my throat.

"Oh, god, Chris. Yes, that feels... it feels..." and it did feel. It felt more. Painful. Degrading. Glorious. Being used by Chris was a pleasure beyond pleasure. "Yes, Daddy, I love how you're fucking me. Use me. I'm yours."

"Fuck. Don't talk," he ordered. He slowed his pace.

"Yes. Chris, yes," I begged him through clenched teeth. "Fucking use me. Take it all out on me."

This was good. This was so good. This was exactly what we needed.

"Please," he begged. His voice, his will, his conscience all on the edge of breaking. "Don't, baby. Don't talk."

It was happening already. In spite of his order, or maybe because of it, my body was skyrocketing off a cliff before I'd even realized I'd climbed the mountain. "Oh, Fuck, Daddy, I'm coming. You're making me come." A wail escaped from somewhere deep in my lungs. Like an animal in heat. I had no consciousness, no humanity. My body was made to be pleasured by this man. It didn't matter how he fucked me, I was always going to come with him. "Oh, God, your cock feels so good."

But he wasn't letting me feel it. He was pulling out. No. No. Come back, I wanted to say, but I was still coming and my pussy was gushing cum all over… his face. Holy shit, he was there, under me, catching as much of it as he could in his mouth while it rained all over his face and chest. He massaged my clit and I kept coming. I didn't know if it was another orgasm entirely, or if my body decided not to stop the first one.

Then he was inside me again. Plunging into me without relief. I looked back and saw he was still wearing his glasses, only they were fogged up and covered with droplets of where I'd squirted on him yet again. His hair was soaked, slicked back from his forehead with my fluid. "Remember it, sweetheart. Remember how much of a slut you are for Daddy's cock. Remember exactly how it feels. How well you take it. What you reduce me to." He gripped me hard by the back of the neck, giving me nowhere to go. "Remember what you fucking do to me."

He didn't slow again. He didn't even give me time to recover. Somehow, some way he went deeper, harder, fucking me ruthlessly as his fingers clawed into my skin and sinew. I bit the pillow to stop from screaming and waking the poor traumatized neighbors, but my orgasm was building again. He grunted with each stroke. The sound of pain and self-loathing mixed with bliss. He grabbed a fistful of hair and jerked my head back. My scalp burned and my eyes teared up, but he fucked harder and it was the best feeling in the world. I could feel the stream running down my inner thighs, not as wet as before, but the orgasm just as powerful. The tears streaming down my face from his tight grip in my hair and the acute angle of my immobile neck.

"Fuck. This is wrong. It's wrong. I can't do this," he chanted as he shallowly thrust inside me, losing the edge of roughness.

"No, Chris. I need you. Stay with me."

"Stop it. Stop. I can't, I—fuck." He slid out, his cock still rock hard. I looked over my shoulder to find him sitting back on his heels, breathing hard.

I rose onto my knees and kissed him, tentatively at first, not knowing if he was so disgusted with himself he'd pull away, but he kissed me back, communicating all the feelings he couldn't verbalize.

I gripped his cock. Hard. Hard enough that when I stroked him, the condom slid off into my hand. His eyes flared open and I nodded.

"No," he pleaded, cradling my face in his hands. "Baby, no. Don't do this to me."

"I want to feel you. Just once."

"It won't make a difference. You won't be able to feel it."

"Can you feel a difference?"

"I've never done it without a condom."

"Me either. Please." I begged. "If I can't have you for two years, I want you tonight. All of you. Fill me up, Daddy. Make me yours, so I can't forget."

He lost.

He collapsed on top of me, his chest falling onto my back, still pressing me down onto the mattress. Lining himself up, he slowly pushed himself back into me, groaning as he felt every inch of my bare cunt. "Oh, Jesus, you feel... I was wrong. There's a difference. There's a fucking difference. Oh, fuck, I was wrong, I was wrong. Oh darling. My darling girl... so fucking good. So..."

He fucked me slower now, his hands spanning my waist and pressing me down into the mattress while he knelt behind me. My legs splayed in a frog-like position. It felt fucking amazing—the way the sheets rubbed my clit on the outside and he massaged it from inside me. It always felt amazing when he was deep, whether he was going nuts, or blathering sweet, incoherent words of pleasure and praise.

His pre-cum, my ejaculate, and our moisture all mixing with wet, slurping sounds, making it fucking filthy and hot, turning me on even more.

Every time his cock dragged against my G-spot, it felt like the one. This one. This was going to be the stroke that sent me over the edge. But the next one came, and the next and the next. I grew more and more slippery with every bead of moisture that slid out from between us. From both of us. More frantic as every stroke felt like it was going to kill me. The pleasure was going to actually explode and I was going to die of bliss and dehydration.

The slow slide of his cock, filling me up, then the rush of heat pouring down as he eased himself back out. The way he moved his hips so that his balls massaged my clit when he was bottoming-out inside me made me lose sense of the room around us.

I heard myself moaning and panting from outside my body. I felt the orgasm from somewhere else, too. I'd slipped off into a different plane of existence where nothing existed in the same way anymore. He'd coaxed so much pleasure from my body, my soul was likely floating somewhere above us. When he flipped me over and wiped the hair from my face, he had to position my legs, to splay them open for him.

"Willing. Eager. Enthusiastic," I said. "Just can't move."

He let out a single hoarse choke of a laugh and leaned back on his knees. For a moment he didn't move. He just looked in my eyes with his sleepy, curious expression and smiled, catching his breath. "One more?"

I shook my head. "I have nothing left."

"We'll see." He wrapped my legs around his waist as he held me up, pressing into my clit with his thumb.

"Chris... how?"

"What, baby?" He hissed as his hips pumped. He was close. I didn't know how he'd held out so long.

"How do you know my body so well?" His face melted as he struggled to keep it together. I wanted to come again. For him. Wanted to let him have more.

And it was. It was coming. The muscles were tightening around him.

"I don't. I try things and watch your reaction. If you like it, I do it again." He started to shudder his hip against me, uncontrolled and spazzy. "Sweetheart, please," he begged. "Come for me."

I reached down and circled my clit as his hips shook against me, and a sob broke from his chest. He was coming. He couldn't help himself, he was coming. Fuck he looked good like this.

"Oh, fuuuck, this is..." he slowed the roll of his hips to watch, open mouthed and panting, as his cum poured into me. The first time. I felt the warmth slickening my pussy and it brought me with him. Only a little less overwhelming this time, only a little gush, dribbling onto his cock. "Oh, Daphne, yes, look at this. You're so fucking... everything. You're..." he stopped talking and pulled out, but rather than flopping onto the bed with me, he lifted my hips up and up and up to his mouth, draping my legs over his shoulder. And licked.

He was caring for me, cleaning me the way he always did, unconcerned that it was his own cum he was eating out of my pussy.

Or maybe that was part of the appeal. A source of pride that he'd marked me, and I was still his to consume.

I was owned. And when he looked down into my eyes, with his tongue deep in my cunt, we both knew he wasn't going to let me go.

Part Three

Chapter 19

Chris

THE SHEETS SLIPPED DOWN her body, exposing one nipple as she stretched her arms up. Her body was all smears of color and soft edges without my glasses, but my already hard dick jerked with arousal. There was no better way to greet the morning than waking up with a naked woman in my bed.

Unless it was the woman I'd lost my fucking mind with last night, and now I had to tell her, yet again, that we couldn't be together.

Daphne rolled to her side and I fixed my gaze on the cracks in the ceiling plaster.

"Merry Christmas, Chris."

"Merry Christmas, Daphne." It came out hollow and thin.

"I'm going to shower, if that's okay. I'm sticky. Do you want—"

"I'll go after you," I said without looking at her.

After what I did to her last night, I couldn't stand myself. Couldn't stand to face her disappointment and there was no getting away from it in this tiny room. How often was I going to keep giving in and lying to myself about it? Denying her needs and wants only to succumb to my own when they grew overwhelming? I hadn't been fair.

I'd proven to myself that I couldn't handle seeing her, knowing her. I'd have to block her out completely and that felt like torture. And at this point, it felt like the wrong decision. I just didn't know how to make it right.

I started folding up our things. Laying out what we'd need to get home. Home, to an empty apartment. No historical facts blurted out whenever they popped into her head or silly destinations to divert my attention.

"Where are you, Chris?" she asked from the bathroom door.

"Nowhere good."

"Obviously. Do you regret last night?"

I laughed. "No. I should. But I don't. Unless..." I looked up at her. Her arms were folded protectively across her chest. "Did I hurt you?"

"No. You're hurting me now. And *you're* hurting."

"I know. I know I'm shutting you out, and I hate that I don't have the answers. All I want to do is protect you and I'm doing the opposite. I'm causing your pain."

"You want to protect me?"

"Darling," I wrapped her in my arms and folded my body around her. "Yes. I want to do everything in my power to shield you from every unhappiness, every pain, every hint of discomfort."

"Nobody has ever done that for me."

"I know."

"I don't *need* anyone to do that for me."

"We all need that. All your life, people should have been protecting you, loving you, and they failed." I held her out. "But you can't let me do it either. You can't give me that. I haven't earned it yet. You have to get through a little more by yourself, sweetheart. Because I can't protect you if we're together. If we're caught—and we will be caught—it's not a matter of me losing my job. As unfair as it is, it'll discredit your career before you've even established it."

"I can't allow myself to think love can possibly be that cruel." She searched my eyes. "Unless… it's not love."

"I don't know." I shook my head. More willful ignorance. I fucking knew what it was. "Anthropologically, I think… men need to take care of someone. To protect them. We use it to trick women into making it feel like love, but it's just oxytocin and dopamine. It's selfish, egotistical. We do it to make ourselves heroes or knights. Just like Valentine said."

"I know you're wrong, Chris. But I can't be the one to convince you you're wrong. You have to do it on your own."

"CAN YOU BELIEVE WE'VE been on the road for a full day, and we haven't stopped for gas once?" she asked.

Once we'd gotten on the road, Daphne had easily slipped back into her holly jolly persona, but I knew it was a lie. A coping mechanism.

All I could do was let her maintain that shield. Pretend I didn't notice what she was doing. How hurt she was.

I'd pretend, too. "At this point, I'll only be shocked if we make it to Knoxville today. I'm grateful for every time I don't have to get out of the car and look at the damage done to Brigitte. I'm full up on heartbreak at the moment."

She grinned. A real grin. "You called her Brigitte." Maybe we'd be okay.

"After two accidents in one night, I figure she's earned her name."

"I know. She was so pretty. I'm sure someone can fix her. Or you can send her back to Germany."

"No. This was proof that I shouldn't have spent money I should have donated."

"Are you going straight to the lab? Can I come?"

"Yes. And No."

"Come on, please? No one will be there. It's Christmas. I just want to see the facility. Bask in its hallowed halls."

"It's just a normal bio lab."

"I'm coming."

"I'm dropping you off at your father's first."

"Hasn't this trip taught you that you can't control anything? We're just going to get thrown together again and again until you stop fighting it."

I said nothing. We managed to make it through a whole verse of Dean Martin singing "White Christmas" in silence. It had to be a record. Not that I enjoyed her silence. I just enjoyed that she wasn't saying or doing anything that was making me fall even harder for her.

"Oh!" She screamed. "Pull over."

My heart seized. I jerked the wheel to the right, careening off the road onto the shoulder before throwing the brake. "Fuck. What's wrong? Daph—"

Adrenaline coursed through my body as I whipped off my seatbelt and scrambled over her, two fingers at her pulse, looking at her pupils for signs of unequal dilation and reactivity. All I could think about was the black widow bite from yesterday. We were a lot farther from a hospital now. If there was another in the car, maybe from the wreaths, she wouldn't stand a chance.

She stared at me with wide eyes. Blinking once. Twice. "I saw a sign for a cemetery."

My head dropped as I let out a long-held breath. I rested my forehead on her chest as I gripped her arms. "Jesus, Daphne, I almost had a heart attack. I thought..." I slunk back into my seat. It was amazing how quickly I'd stopped the car and scrambled over the console–as if I could have done anything, anyway. But now, it felt like I was moving, thinking, feeling in slow motion. "You're... okay though?"

"I'm fine." She nodded. "But... can we visit? Please?" Her voice was so tiny.

"The cemetery?" My brain was still interpreting slowly as it settled itself into its pre-panic state.

She scrunched her eyebrows together like I was the crazy one. "You don't like cemeteries?"

"They're fine. I just don't like almost crashing the car after hearing you shout like you're dying, only for it to end up being nothing."

"Not nothing. I love cemeteries. The historic ones. If I don't have a direct cremation, I hope my family lays me to rest in a beautiful old cemetery. I want strangers to see my headstone–the flowers or the hourglass or whatever image is carved into the stone. They'll see my name, and maybe it hasn't been spoken for a hundred years, but they'll see *Daphne McKinnon* and wonder what kind of woman she was."

I grunted and restarted the car, my heart still racing.

"You don't like thinking about your final resting place?"

"Not mine, sweetheart. I don't like thinking about yours." Her only physical existence reduced to a few dusty bones like the ones in the back of the car. It was impossible. She was too vibrant for death. And yesterday, she'd come entirely too close.

"I don't particularly care."

"If I had your money, I'd want a whole mausoleum. Fluted columns, brass plaques on the crypts. I'd want my great-grandchildren to be able to walk inside that iron gate to put flowers in my little flower urn thing and know that one day, that's where their bones will rest, too."

"Crypt vase."

"Huh?"

"The little flower urn thing that sticks to the wall. It's called a crypt vase." I checked the rearview mirror. No one was on the road. No one had been on the road most of the morning. It was Christmas. They were home with their families and gifts and cookies.

Moments like this reminded me why it felt like it was Daphne and me against the world. The joke was, we weren't allowed to fight on the same side.

"Your family has a mausoleum, don't they? Exactly the kind I want?"

I was quiet for a beat before answering. "Yes."

"Figures. I'll just have to marry you for your mausoleum, then."

My brain spasmed at the word. I stopped breathing. But it wasn't altogether unpleasant. Instead of feeling like an anchor had dropped, jerking me into the dark depths of a tormenting sea, I felt... lighter. Buoyant.

I'll just have to marry you.

Whatever her reason, those words sounded good. It sounded exactly right.

"Chris? Did you hear me?"

Wait. She'd kept talking. She'd been saying things. Other things. My mind had stopped on what it wanted to hear. I shook myself out of my reverie and put on my blinker. What was one more stop?

"Um... no, I didn't, but let's take a walk. Burn off this adrenaline rush."

"We're really stopping? Chris, I... You really are the best, you know that?"

I shook my head. "You can say it. Doesn't make it true."

"You don't want to hear what I *really* want to say. But it doesn't make it *untrue.*"

I drove through the gates and followed the winding drive around the graveyard, looking for a place to pull over. Not that it mattered. There was only one other car here.

"Go up there, where those trees are." Daphne pointed. "It looks like the oldest part."

I parked on the road and we got out. We hadn't been driving long this morning but it felt good to stretch and move.

"Oh, no. I think she needs help." Daphne took off through the gravestones before I had a chance to turn around.

The car had its hood up. That hadn't been the case when we'd pulled in. It could be a ploy. They could have seen us coming in the fancy car and decided to tug on our hearts. Or Daphne's heart that was way too big for her own good.

"Daph, wait."

"Excuse me!" She was hollering to the person under the hood. "Do you need help?"

An older white woman with frizzy brown hair looked around the hood with surprise. "Nothing you can do."

She went back to the engine.

Daphne walked closer, saying, "I can take a look. I don't mind. I know engines."

The woman glanced at Brigitte and raised her eyebrows at Daphne. With Daphne's lustrous blonde hair pulled back in a low ponytail, and wearing my coat, she looked posh and expensive. Not that Daphne wasn't expensive—two car crashes, an ER visit, and a two-thousand-dollar lap dance burger, this road trip was costing me a fortune—but she was so much more than that. This stranger had no idea.

I was the useless one.

"No offense, but you don't look like you know a thing about cars, except for calling a service, which might not be a bad thing, except they'll tow it to a mechanic I can't afford."

"What happened to it?" Daphne casually ignored the woman's lack of confidence in her ability, and glanced at the filthy engine.

The woman sighed. "I turned it on, went to leave. By the time I got around the loop, it was running so hot, I turned it back off. Scared to drive it any further. I know Rob used to do something to it to keep it from getting too hot, but I don't know what."

Daphne nodded.

"Never thought I needed to know what to do. I'm not as willful as I look, I just never thought there'd be a time so soon when Rob weren't here. It was always his job, worrying about the cars and fixing up the house."

The woman bent into the driver's seat and pulled out a pack of long, slim cigarettes. She lit one up, holding the pack to Daphne, who shook her head.

"Won't hurt nothing to look, I guess. Don't know how you can do much of anything out here. Rob kept some tools in the back."

Daphne walked to the front of the car, slid her arms out of my coat, and handed it to me. "I'm Daphne, by the way."

"Carol."

"Like a yuletide Carol!" Daphne's eyes lit up. Carol's did not. "Any way..."

She ducked behind the piece of lumber holding up the hood of the old Plymouth, where the sun had scorched the burgundy paint into a splotchy raspberry shade.

Daphne pulled out the dipstick and the woman craned her neck over her shoulder.

"Rag?"

The woman nodded and rummaged through the truck before giving an old flannel shirt to Daphne. "It's okay to mess this up?"

"I'd rather have a car that runs than another one of Rob's old shirts."

Daphne wiped the stick and dipped it back in again. When she pulled it out, she frowned. "Oil's low. You change it?"

"Last month. I know I have to do that much. Think they messed something up?"

"Probably not." Daphne said. She touched the blackened engine cover with the back of her hand before laying the shirt down and leaning across it. "Chris, can you turn on your flashlight?"

I handed her my phone, and she shone it into the engine. I had no idea what she was doing, or what she was looking for, but she was on the hunt for something.

"It's my first holiday alone," Carol said. "Rob's been gone since August. Feels like we just buried him."

"No leaking under the oil cap. Seal still looks okay." Daphne replaced the thing she'd unscrewed and looked at Carol. "I'm sorry for your loss. You have any kids?"

"Rob did. But they were partly mine, too. And three grandkids. But they're spending the holidays with their mom's side. Rob and I weren't married. Never got around to it."

"You've got a lot of caked-on gunk around the valve cover, but I don't see any pooling or wetness. Could be you just need a new gasket, but that doesn't usually cause a thermal event like what happened today. And I can't tell you where it's coming from without removing the cover." She shifted her weight, practically hopping onto her belly. Legs dangling, over-the-knee socks slipping down her thighs.

Was it rude to get an erection while she was lending a helping hand? Yes, of course. But trying to avoid being turned on by anything she did was useless. Her kindness and competence was my kink. Watching her diagnose this faulty engine while her ass was in the air with her corduroy skirt hiked up around the tops of her thighs was damn near pornographic.

Carol narrowed her eyes at me like she knew what was going on inside my head. And in my pants.

Daphne was now wedging herself under the car.

"Parking brake on?" I asked.

Carol nodded.

I gestured for her to come closer and handed her my business card. "Have the car towed to a shop. Fix whatever needs to be fixed. I'll take care of it."

Carol took the card and nodded to Brigitte. "Looks like you got your own mess to take care of."

"Yesterday was not her finest."

"I appreciate this," she said, with a weight in her voice that was too complicated to parse.

Daphne scooched herself out from under the car with her legs clamped shut, trying to keep her skirt down. "There's a lot going on under here. You've got a leak for sure, but I can't tell where it is without running diagnostics. You carry any oil with you? Maybe we can add enough to get it to a shop."

"Rob used to take care of this," Carol repeated.

Daphne and I locked eyes. "I know it must be tough. Especially today."

Carol nodded and sniffed. "I'll get you that oil."

"What did you and Rob do on Christmas?"

"Do?"

"Any favorite movies? Family recipes? You know, holiday traditions." Daphne smiled at me.

"He liked *National Lampoon*. I never did. I didn't watch it this year, but now I kind of miss it. Rob had that kind of Christmas spirit. He was like a kid, he got so excited at the presents. Every year, he wanted a real tree. I told him the fake ones look good now and they're cheap. But he'd rather have a real tree than fancy presents, so we always got a real tree. That's what I was doing here today. I got one of them mini Christmas trees for him. Not real, though."

Daphne slipped my coat back on as Carol talked and talked about Rob and his kids and how she'd see them sometime this week to give them their presents, and she didn't know what she was going to do about this car the way it kept leaking oil. Daphne listened without judgment or impatience, knowing the woman needed a friend.

"I sold my car three days ago for the same reason. There was nothing I could do to keep it from leaking. It had grooves in the engine block. A new one would have cost more than the car was worth. I loved that car, though."

I wished she'd told me that three days ago. I would have bought her a new engine if she wanted to keep the car.

"You live far from here?" Daphne asked.

"Ten minutes."

"Start her up. Let's see if the temperature's gone down enough to get home. It won't last. You'll need more oil. You'll need to take it in and find that leak, too. Or sell it for something more reliable. I'm sorry I couldn't do more."

"Dishwasher door's busted, too. Feel like swinging by my house?" she laughed. "You've done enough. Thank you. Your husband's coat's got a grease stain now."

Daphne smiled. "We have to be on our way, but good luck."

"Well... guess I'll go home and watch *Christmas Vacation*. Maybe even make the peanut butter cookies Rob loved. The ones with the forks pressed into them. Thank y'all. That was really sweet of you to stop and help the way you did. Most people would'a drove on by without looking."

"Merry Christmas, Carol," I said.

When she'd turned out of the cemetery, I grabbed Daphne's hand.

"Take a walk with me." The weather had broken and it was in the forties, but the sky was still painted like a film noir. Daphne was the only color in the cemetery.

I kissed her knuckles.

"Don't. I'm greasy."

"You're perfect. I don't know how you do it."

"Do what? The car stuff? My dad taught me. And I went through a program in high school when my academic classes weren't hands-on enough to keep my attention."

"No. That was fun to watch. But I'm talking about your empathy. You're so compassionate with everyone. You never leave a place without making a new friend."

"You're compassionate. I saw what you did for Yuletide Carol. I pretended not to notice to give you your privacy, but I noticed."

"Throwing money at a problem is the least I can do. It doesn't put me out. You put yourself out for people."

"Sometimes too much."

"Mm." I tilted my head. "I saw that with some of the people who worked for my parents' charities, giving one hundred percent and burning out. You're different, though; you light up when you give."

We sat on a memorial bench at the top of the hill, under a stand of sentinel oaks, their final, clinging leaves shivered in the wind. It was still cold, but it felt tropical compared with the negative temps of last night.

I picked up a stick and twiddled it between my fingers while she basked in the silence of the historic cemetery.

"That's an interesting one." Daphne pointed to a headstone carved with a woman's hand holding a rose. She was somber and quiet. She knew—we both knew. This was it. Our hours were counting down. Today wouldn't be like yesterday, with a hundred detours and catastrophes that made the day feel like it was a year long.

"Very nice." She could say anything, and I'd agree with her.

She knocked into my side. "You really don't care what you want when you die? Even if you already know your final resting place, you still have options."

I shook my head again, concentrating on de-barking the twig. Now that we were alone again, I kept thinking about *that thing* she'd said before. It meant nothing. It was just a thing you say, but I liked hearing it.

"You could be donated to science or something. My first guess for you would be The Body Farm, but obviously that might affect the students' ability to remain objective—measuring and analyzing data about their former professor's state of lividity.

"How would it work?" I said abruptly.

"Oh, I don't know. You'd have to talk to the person who handles donations. I know there's a long waitlist. Everyone wants to be a part of forensic history. Maybe since you're affiliated—"

"Not body donation. What you said before, about the... mausoleum."

"I just think they're so stately and regal—"

"About marrying me."

She froze. "Marrying you?"

"So that you can be buried in my family tomb."

"Oh. That. I was just—"

"I know what you meant. Let's pretend it's not entirely out of the question. As a solution to our other problem."

"Other problem?"

"Waiting."

She swiveled to face me. "Are you considering—"

"Not considering. Curious. I doubt it'll actually work, or if you'd want to, or... What..." I swallowed thickly, "would it look like, you think?"

She smiled that smile that showed all her perfectly imperfect teeth. "Probably the same as the day we spent in your parents' mansion."

"House. It's a house."

She grabbed a twig and followed my lead, picking the bark off, flake by flake. "My legs dangling off the counter, while I watch you cook."

"My neighbor, Gita, would love you. She brings me so much food I can hardly finish it all."

"I can't wait to meet her." She scooted closer to me. "Let's see. It would look like me, sneaking scoops of cookie dough whenever your back is turned–"

"I knew there should have been more cookies."

"...you, frowning at your computer and pinching the bridge of your nose under your glasses, until I forced you out of the house to go to some ridiculous performance art show."

"Sounds awful." I stroked her thigh, needing to touch her in the worst way.

She leaned in closer. "You'll hate it. My taste in art is the worst."

"It would be getting to feel your cock inside me every night when we go to bed together. Falling asleep with you slowly softening inside me. Waking up to your toothpasty fresh mouth on my clit. Getting fucked until I can't move and then feeling your cum slip down my thighs."

She straddled the bench. "You, lifting my skirt and fingering me in the diner after you found out I'd forgotten my panties."

With her legs parted wide and short skirt stretched across her thighs, I could clearly see what was not underneath. Bare pussy. Just another pair of thigh high socks today.

I fisted my hands, though I didn't remove them from that stripe of bare skin between her skirt and her socks. I rubbed, but as much as I wanted to shove my fingers inside her and finger fuck her until she was christening the cemetery ground with her gushing cum, I was going to be respectful of the dead.

I sighed and shook my head at her. "I meant academically."

I reclined on the bench and laid my head in her lap. Immediately, her incredible fingers were in my hair, scratching and stroking, looking down on me like an angel. My Christmas angel with the golden hair.

"I don't know. It might gain me enough respect going into the program as... your wife." I knew it was hard for her to say the word. It was hard to hear it. It was too much of a fragile dream, the idea that she could be mine today, tomorrow. For the rest of our lives.

"I'd spend the day working at the lab, or in class. Studying in the evenings, or working on papers until you came home from your classes, or fieldwork, and decided to distract me."

"I can't wait to be your distraction." I smiled. Truly smiled. It was the first time all day.

"What does this mean?"

"I don't know, sweetheart. I don't know what to do about any of this. It doesn't make it any more right. I'm clearly still in the wrong, as far as the handbook goes."

"Oh my God, Chris. Enough with the fucking handbook."

"I don't know if marrying you would be enough, or—or if you even want to..."

"I would want to marry you, Chris. For more than your family crypt. But it won't be enough, and you're not really asking. This is just another thing that'll get my hopes up."

We were quiet most of the ride home. The hope that had sprung up in the cemetery had dissipated more and more, the closer we got to Knoxville. It was as if our speaking the word *marriage* had been too loud to sustain the idea. Or maybe it was the UT Campus, that all-knowing being that could see into our souls and cast our actions in a shameful dirty shadow.

By the time we got to Daphne's house on the outskirts of town, the only one talking was the GPS.

"Is anyone home?"

There was a string of lights on the small blue house. Old bulbs. Big ones, half of them burnt out or missing.

"Dad's home, he doesn't go anywhere. Do you want to come in and meet him?"

I looked at the door and shook my head. I didn't want to introduce myself as just a colleague or professor.

The thought of leaving her here turned my stomach, but I had too much to think through, and my prefrontal cortex stopped functioning whenever Daphne was near.

"If you think there's no such thing as love," she said, "that it's all hormones, then what do you think disillusions anyone into imagining they love each other?

"Who said there's no such thing as love?"

"You did. This morning at the hotel."

Another carol started and she let me ignore the question through most of it.

"Are you going to answer?"

"I don't know what I think. You make me realize a lot of what I don't know. My whole foundation is crumbling. I'd always thought real love was a decision; borne from all the small things you do for each other. Eventually, lust mixes with care and a desire to see only good things happen for the other person. I'd thought I loved women in the past, but it didn't feel like this. Like I can't catch my breath when I look away from you. Because I only have seconds left to see your face, and smell your skin, and hear your laugh."

I took off my glasses and scrubbed my hand down my face, as if it was a reset button. "This feels unbearable, parting from you. I don't *want* to bear it. I'm trying—"

The world was quiet again. A mist had descended, shrouding the heavily forested road near her house in gloom.

"I don't know how I was living before you."

"It took you three days to realize that?" she asked.

"It took me twelve fucking minutes to realize that."

I turned off the car. We sat in silence, neither one of us making the move to open our doors. In the rear view mirror, I saw a man walking a dog down the road. He passed the driveway, staring at my car, puffing on an electric box. I wondered if he was a neighbor. If he knew Daphne or her dad. It didn't matter either way. I was just jealous that he lived close to her and I didn't.

"Don't make me into your manic pixie dream girl."

"I don't know what that means."

"Like in movies, when the cool, free-spirited woman comes into the life of a solid, staid man, and shakes him up a bit before he drops her for being too crazy."

"I don't think that fits you at all."

"No?"

I shook my head. "You have opinions on Ming Dynasty porcelain and early twentieth century telephone etiquette. I love that, but I don't know that those characteristics would be considered *cool* by many people. You can fix cars without consulting Google. That takes a tremendous amount of self-discipline. Too much to be free-spirited. So what if you wanted to see some of the sights on a road trip? That doesn't make you manic or elf or whatever you called it. You're just you. And if it wouldn't cause the ruination of both our careers, I'd keep you. But right now, you have to use that self-discipline to get through this grad program as fast as you can, so I can be yours."

"So that's it then."

"I don't know, Daphne. I need time."

The sound of her door opening gutted me. It was really happening.

She gathered her things from the front seat. Her unopened Mountain Dew bottle, her backpack, her hot cocoa trash and our empty water bottles. Tidying up behind her as I stared, unseeing, out the windshield.

Then she took off my coat, folded it, and placed it in her seat. "Sorry about the grease."

I carried her overnight bag and wreath to the back door, watching every microdroplet of mist glint in her hair.

Her key crunched in the lock. Just when I thought she wasn't going to say goodbye—maybe that was for the better—she whipped back, grabbed me around the neck, and kissed me hard. My lips moved with hers, opening her mouth and tasting her for the last time, taking everything I could from these final seconds.

"Listen to me," she said, after she pulled back. Her eyes were still wild and she hadn't let go.

"I know you're the one, Chris. I've never cried in your arms, but I don't have to to know you'd hold me until my tears dried on your shirt. We haven't seen each other through loss or hard times, but I know I'll always hold space for you. I don't know your greatest shame—besides me—or your greatest fears. I don't know if you believe in a higher power, or how you vote, or what made you go into odontology, how many kids you want, or where you even buy eight-hundred-dollar pants, but I know you're the one."

"Daphne." I lowered my forehead against hers.

"Somehow, I love you. And..." she took a deep breath. "This isn't goodbye. It doesn't matter how much you try to keep me away from you because I'll keep coming back. I'm your home now. And you're mine. Don't ruin this because you think you have to get on some honorable high horse. Love is just as powerful as honor."

Chapter 20

Chris

As soon as I opened the door to my apartment, I knew something was wrong. It was the same old apartment. Clean yet stuffy from being shut down for a few days. Cozy enough because of the exposed brick and wide-plank floors.

Just quiet. Too quiet.

A large antique Agra rug and rich jewel tones balanced the clean, mid-century lines of the furniture. I was informed of this by previous girlfriends who'd been shocked not to find a bachelor pad dominated by a video gaming system. Mom had done it all. I neither knew nor cared about home furnishings. Considering I spent most of my waking hours in a dental office or a stainless-steel lab, I was just happy to come home to a place where the color palette wasn't white and silver, and the lighting wasn't emitted from thousand-watt LEDs.

Without Daphne, the apartment seemed just as cold and sterile.

I dropped the skull box on the kitchen island. I'd bring it to the lab in a few days. There was no rush. The students would document their findings once they returned from break. I'd make sure Daphne would be assigned to this case. It was nice to be able to see a project through to completion, especially your first.

Anubis was unsurprisingly vocal in her greeting, serpentining through my feet and scenting my ankles with near-constant trills and moans.

"Okay, okay. I missed you too." I reassured her with long, firm strokes, the way she loved to be pet. Her bowl was empty. "It's not time for dinner yet. And I think we can forget about that salmon in the fridge. You might like stinky rotten fish, but I'm not going to stink up my apartment by unwrapping it."

Last week, Nubi and I had decorated the little Christmas tree in the window. I stared at it now but was uncompelled to turn it on. I was uncompelled to do anything but wallow.

Instead, I did something I rarely did. I reclined on the couch with my feet up, poured myself a Laga 16, and melted in front of the TV, settling on a replay of Friday's terrible Mississippi State/UTEP bowl game.

I wanted to avoid anything that hinted at Christmas. This fog of self-pity and loathing was decidedly *not* a holiday tradition I was keen to repeat. With any luck, I'd avoid the next two Christmases altogether. Maybe I'd travel. Somewhere in the Caribbean where it wouldn't remind me of Daphne and her holiday traditions.

Except I couldn't imagine going anywhere without Daphne, so never mind.

Work. That's what I'd do. Once Nourishing Nashville re-opened, I'd throw myself in. I'd wash dishes. I'd prep. I'd sous. Whatever needed to be done, I'd do it.

My phone buzzed in my pocket. My heart jumped.

Her. It was her.

FaceTime from Unknown. I sat up.

"Daphne?"

"Frohe Weinachten!" Mom said.

"Who's Daphne?" Dad said in unison.

"Merry Christmas, Mom. Dad," I said, breathing to slow my racing heart. "It's late there, isn't it?"

"We had to talk to you on Christmas! Oh, Christopher, we met the most wonderful family who invited us to their home to celebrate Christmas. It was lovely. You would have had a wonderful time."

I laughed. "How much have you had to drink, Mom?" We both knew being invited to a stranger's house for a holiday celebration would never be my idea of a good time. Daphne, however... she'd leave with plans to see them again next year.

"A lot of glühwein! And it was better than at the markets."

"Who's Daphne?" Dad shouted from off screen.

"We're going to go back to Reiner and Heike's for New Year's Eve. Heike's going to teach me how to make lewwerkneedl, which tasted a lot like grandma's meatloaf—remember the one with the liver?—except Heike's was delicious!"

"—Köstlich!" Dad shouted from the back.

"Köstlich!" Mom reiterated. "That's German for delicious. And she served the most köstlich cherry sauce with her apple pie—oh, Brian, remind me to ask her for that recipe, too. Reiner and Dad hit it off talking politics. Reiner's a representative in the Bundestag—that's like our House of Representatives. They have a very lovely home," she repeated.

"That's nice, Mom. I'm glad you had a good time."

"We're coming to visit next summer. I've simply got to see her garden in bloom. The pictures looked gorgeous. You should come with us, honey."

"Has he told you who Daphne is?"

"No. And hush, Brian. Let Christopher talk."

"It's okay, Mom."

"Is she a new girlfriend, dear? Daphne's a lovely name. Oh! Why don't you bring her—when we visit this summer? It'll be perfect! What a lovely way to get to know your new friend! Although, I'm sure I'll get to know her before then, anyway. I'm getting ahead of myself."

"Okay, Mom. I'm sure you're tired. Glad you had fun with your new friends."

"Wait. One more thing, before we let you go. Are you ready Brian? *O*— Ready? One, two, three. *O Tannenbaum, O Tannenbaum, wie treu sind deine Blätter.*"

My parents continued to serenade me in German with "O Christmas Tree," which they must have learned over the past two days.

I smiled into the camera, but inside I was dying, thinking about Daphne.

It was her favorite carol. *The Peanuts one, not the Nat King Cole one,* she'd said. I'd played it for her on Christmas Eve Eve. Then I'd fucked her on the piano bench.

Once I'd hung up with my parents, I refilled my scotch and sat at the piano, immediately playing the Vince Guaraldi song.

It was easy and melancholy, and exactly suited the mood of the room—the mood I was giving it.

I was riffing on the chorus when someone pounded on the door.

"It's open," I shouted.

I glanced over my shoulder to see Gita unloading bags on my kitchen island, giving me a snarky head bob when she noticed me notice her. "I heard the piano." She crossed her arms and leaned against the counter.

"Sorry. I'll close the lid." I got up, but she stopped me.

"No, no. I like it." She wobbled her head.

I sat and tinkered with another that matched my mood. Not really a tune, even. I didn't know what it was yet, or if it was going to be anything. Chords. Arpeggios. D minor.

"That's how I knew you were home." She opened her containers of food. Gita's family had moved into the apartment next door a little over four years ago and I'd ordered them fried chicken from the downstairs restaurant in welcome, not realizing they were Hindi and didn't eat meat. They appreciated my gesture anyway, and invited me in to share their potato and cauliflower curry. Harish was a pathology resident and we'd quickly bonded over atypical cells in the few spare moments he wasn't in the hospital. Gita and I had a shared a sense of social justice and a love of her cooking.

"Priti said you were staying in Nashville for Christmas."

"We were supposed to be home yesterday. There were some... complications."

"We?"

My fingers stilled over the keyboard. *Shit.* Gita was a bloodhound. She didn't do vagary and she didn't do small talk. As a tax lawyer who worked exclusively with nonprofits, she believed in focused presence and attunement with community. At that first dinner, she'd asked me how I was giving back to the world that had given me such privilege.

She liked my answer, and I liked that she cut through the bullshit. I hired her firm to take over my charitable giving, and she was so good at making my money go where it was most effective, my parents had her manage their whole Nourishing Nashville network.

Now, though? No way. I wasn't ready for that Ginsu knife of hers that cut through bullshit like it was a tin can. Daphne was a hope, a whisper of a hope. Thinking that whisper threatened to turn it into a dreaded finality: a brick wall of separation.

I gave Gita no response, except to resume playing.

"Come eat with us. Priti's been watching Christmas movies on cable for the past month and begged us to get her a tree. We did." She shrugged. "It's not good to be alone on the holidays, Christopher. You need people around you. Good food. Laughter." She gestured to the containers. "I made this just in case. Hoping I *wouldn't* hear you playing sad music through the walls."

"Is it sad?"

Gita narrowed her eyes and brought over a tray of something that looked like hush puppies. "Muthia. Your favorite."

I shook my head. "I'm not eating at the Bösendorfer."

"Priti said she heard a girl's voice when you called. Was that her?"

"No. I mean, yes, but... it's not going to happen."

She nodded impatiently, not letting me change the subject. "I'd like to call her something besides *her*. What's her name?"

"Daphne."

Gita held the container closer. "One bite won't get crumbs in your precious piano. Don't wait or it'll get soggy. It just came out of the fryer. You need food to heal a broken heart."

I popped an entire crispy, aromatic garam cake into my mouth and wiped my hands on my pants before returning them to the keys. "'S'good," I said around a mouthful of spice and steam.

She knew my kitchen as well as I did, opening the cabinets and getting down a bowl and a fork. When she opened the other containers, the spices fragranced the air. Ginger and cardamom and too many others I couldn't place. "Kala turkey. I made it special for you. You eat turkey on Christmas?"

"My family usually does. Thanks, Gita. This means a lot."

"This doesn't mean you get off without telling me the story. You know how it is: I feed you. You tell me what it's like to be a young person in the dating scene."

"I'm older than you."

"Biologically, yes. But I have a career and two and a half children. Once you have kids, you start aging in dog years. Now spill before I eat all your muthia." She pinched off a bite of something else fried and delicious looking. "What the hell are you playing, anyway?"

A Slavic-sounding left-hand stride. A dark right-hand melody in a minor with a heavy emphasis on trichords.

"Oh, uh… I think it might be… 'Jingle Bells.'"

"That's not 'Jingle Bells.' I know that one. 'Jingle Bells' is *Oh, what fun*. You're playing *Shit, my life is over*."

"We can't be together. Daphne's a grad student. That's the story. Nothing else matters until she graduates."

"Do you teach her?"

"No. Maybe. A few one-off seminars. She might be assigned to my supervision for her field hours, but that's only if there's a backlog with caseloads."

"*If*." She raised her eyebrows. "*If* doesn't sound like a good enough reason to keep you apart."

"It's good enough for the university."

"The university is unreasonable."

I shrugged.

"What is she doing this Christmas? You can't at least spend the holidays together?"

"She's with her dad."

"She doesn't have a big family either?"

"No."

She took a deep breath and wobbled her head again in disapproval. "There's nothing I can say, then."

"Really?" Gita was very insistent with her opinions. Usually steamrolling over my own until I agreed. If she thought my actions were asinine—like she clearly did now—there was no stopping her.

"If you don't have the balls to go out on a limb for her, you don't deserve her."

"I'll lose my job."

"So? Mr. Rich Man. Form a company and enter the private sector. Or live off your savings and take a break. You could use one. You've been working three jobs for ten years."

"I'll lose my credibility. I don't know how it might affect previous cases I've testified for or against."

"How young is she?" Her face was controlled, braced to hear the worst.

"Twenty-four."

"Psh, I'd already married Harish, immigrated to this country, and was pregnant with my second child at twenty-four. And I was in law school. That's plenty old to know your own mind."

"I agree. It's only the student thing. I'd be marrying her tomorrow if I could write my own ethical code. But I can't. I have to abide by the rules I agreed to follow."

"Ethics schmethics." The gleam in her eye was fierce, but her sing-song British-Indian accent was too melodic to take seriously when she pulled out her Americanisms. "You won't be able to wait if she's already making you play music this sad. You're already old, Christopher."

"I can wait. I will."

"You can't and you won't. You'll do something stupid and reckless because you'll get so desperate to be with her."

"That's what she said."

"I like this Daphne already."

"Only because she agrees with you."

"Of course. Why else would I like someone? Listen, Christopher. You're a rich white man."

"What does that have to do with it?"

"Rich white men have ways of making problems disappear."

I lowered the fallboard and swiveled around to face her. "Do you know how hard I've worked to avoid my rich white man privilege? How long I've been trying to make up for it? My whole life, Gita. I'm not going to lean into it now."

"Yes, I do know; I'm your lawyer. You pay me to help you make up for your privilege. But—assuming Daphne feels the same way about you... does she?" I nodded. "Your situation is hardly unethical. She's not in your department. At a different university, this wouldn't be an issue. Someone else grades her exams."

Maybe she was right and my situation was just not-wrong-enough to make me a total ass. "I'm not going to sneak around."

"I'm not telling you to sneak. What are the options here?"

"It's her or my job. Or we wait two years, but now three out of the four people who know us don't think we'll wait. So... it's her or my job." Putting it in black and white like that made me see there *was* no option.

"Jobs don't keep you warm at night, jobs make you play this Christmas bullshit that sounds like a horror movie."

I laughed. My tune was indeed growing darker and darker the longer we talked.

I stood and popped another piece of muthia into my mouth.

"You busy, Gita?"

"Harish has an eighteen-hour shift. Deep is with his friends, and Priti's monopolized the TV with bad Christmas movies. As long as I can stay off my swollen feet, I'm not busy."

"Want to help me draft my letter of resignation?"

"Let's go."

My goal was to slip the letter into Jeanette's mailbox like the bomb I knew it was, and run away as fast as possible.

I hadn't expected her office light to be on and her door ajar when I passed her room. I hadn't expected her to be packing up the decades of books and decor and all the academic shit that often built up like barnacles in professors' offices. She was retiring, but this looked like she was running off in the middle of the night.

Once again, my timing was great.

Unless it was Decca, whoever would be taking her spot would be even less amenable to my predicament. I wouldn't have the shared history with them that I had with Jeanette.

All the more reason for me to leave.

I knocked on her door. She looked up from wrapping up a cat skeleton that had been on the same shelf since I was in grad school.

"You too, huh? Come on in."

I stepped through. "This is how you're spending your Christmas?"

"How else should I spend it? I've spent decades building this career. This place. I'm leaving the only family I have at the end of spring semester."

I wanted to say something to contradict her, but it would only be empty words. "Work life balance has never been our strong suit in this program, has it?"

She looked at me pointedly. "That needs to change."

"Okay." But I wouldn't be here to change it.

"Have a seat. Wait. Let me clear off the chair." She gathered a stack of papers and journals and made another pile on the floor. "Drink?"

It wasn't Lagavulin, but I accepted a plastic cup of bourbon and we toasted each other a Merry Christmas. It scratched and clawed its way down my throat, but it reminded me of the wine Daphne and I had drunk from the paper motel cups, and I quickly finished my cup.

Jeanette followed suit and refilled our cups. "What's your story? You have family. What are you doing here on Christmas?"

"Logging in some remains Decca found a few days ago."

"Why didn't Decca take them to her lab?"

"She had to make cheese straws." I smiled.

Jeanette shook her head. "God love her. She found balance."

"Also..." I blew out a long slow breath and handed her a thick white envelope from my jacket pocket.

"What's this?"

"My resignation."

"You've got to be fucking kidding me." She said, not quite under her breath.

"I'm trying to balance my scale. I've worked hard. Now I need a life."

She looked at the envelope like it offended her. "I'm not taking that."

"You will when you hear the next part." I swallowed and looked her dead in the eye.

Her breathing slowed as she braced against news she could probably imagine.

"This is a courtesy. Advance warning." I nodded to the envelope. "I violated a regulation."

"*What regulation?*" Her voice was cold with rage.

I smiled bitterly. "You know which one."

"No."

"Sexual misconduct."

"No." She sighed and closed her eyes, shutting me out like she didn't want to even see my face anymore. "Not you. Why did it have to be you?"

She leaned back in her chair, clasping her hands across her belly. "Don't tell me that. I don't want to fucking hear about your indiscretion. Who was she? He?"

"I won't tell you the student's name."

"At least tell me they're over 18."

"Yes."

She was quiet for a long time, her blue eyes boring into my skull. "Consensual?"

"Of course, but that doesn't matter."

"Grad student?"

"Yes."

She let out a long, slow breath. "I know you. I know you'd never coerce anyone. Don't come at me with this. I don't give a shit."

"The dean will."

"For fuck's sake, don't go to the dean. Look, I don't know the circumstances, but you've always kept your dick in your pants before. You're quiet. You're wholesome. You're the person least capable of being flippant about this." She threw a hand up in resignation. "I don't know what's going on. I know you'd only do something like this if you were serious. But don't do this to me. I need you."

"For?"

She looked around her office. "This."

"What do you mean?"

"You're connected. Don't tell me connected people don't have ways of making allegations go away."

"I won't do that to her. It's not an allegation; I'm admitting it. She's not a problem to make go away."

"You can't stay away from her until she's finished?"

"No." God, it felt good admitting that. I'd been pinning it all on Daphne. *She* wouldn't be able to stay away. *She* would find ways to sneak. But the truth was, I was the one who, like Jeanette said, couldn't keep it in my pants.

"I've never had connections. I don't know exactly—"

She leaned forward, placing her elbows on the desk. I could smell her whisky breath from several feet away. She must have done a number on that bottle before I'd gotten here. "Think carefully about my next question. Are you trying to sabotage yourself... or do you want a solution? I can't help you if it's sabotage."

"There is no help." She raised her eyebrow, waiting. "No, I'm not trying to sabotage myself."

She smiled. "Christopher Carter, only son of Marcia Galvin Carter, L&C Railroad fortune heiress. Surely someone like you knows solutions always exist for those with enough money."

It was the same thing Gita had said. But wealthy or not, I was new to the world of corruption and naïve enough not to know how these things worked.

"How do you know about my family?"

"Everyone who fundraises in Tennessee knows your parents."

"I always thought I flew under the radar."

"Not under enough." Jeanette slapped a copy of the Vanderbilt Alumnus magazine on her desk. On the cover was an old white man in a bow tie and blue blazer (of course), a promise about football championships (in my dreams), and an interview with Marcia and Brian Carter, about Nourishing Nashville and their other philanthropic endeavors.

"They went on and on about how proud they were of their son."

"What's this have to do with me?"

"Money."

"I already give."

"*Their* money. Foundation money. I want the building to scream *Made possible by an endowment from the Marcia and Brian Carter Phil-*

anthropic Foundation when you walk into the marble lobby, like you're turning on a PBS show.

"Why?"

"We're expanding. We need more land. Bigger facilities. More faculty."

"And that's why you're stepping down?"

"Smart man."

"I'll help Dr. Crowley with—"

"I want you as director."

"Fuck." I blew out a breath. I thought this might be coming. There was no way I was going to throw my best friend under the bus and rob her of her dream job. "No. This job is hers."

"I love Decca. You know I love Decca. She's brilliant in the field. The best of the best. But she lacks the leadership we need right now."

"You've all but promised it to her."

"I never have. I swear to God, Chris. I've never promised because it's not mine to promise."

"Just like it's not yours to promise me now."

"I'm not promising. I'm begging."

"Maybe not verbally, but you promised when you took Decca under your wing from the start. Keeping her there for years. Mentoring her. Training her to be *you* when the time came."

"The circumstances are different. This time the department doesn't need another *me*."

"No. You'll get my money. I'll ask my parents, but I can't promise anything. They went to Vandy, and they have pet projects they enjoy funding a lot more than rival universities. Especially when half of that money will probably end up going to the football team anyway. You want money? I'll pledge money. However much you want. I'll fundraise from the sidelines. But don't use my relationship with Daphne to blackmail me into robbing Decca of her dream job. The last thing this university needs is another white man as the head of anything."

"I don't want a white man either. But I want you, Dr. Carter, despite your race and gender."

I shook my head.

"She won't want this," Jeanette said.

"What do you mean?"

"Decca likes fieldwork. She just got married. She wants to stay with her husband and live her happy little life. She doesn't want a flashy job schmoozing with corporate sponsors. Can you even imagine her in business suits?"

Jeanette was right. Decca had flat out told me, several times, she didn't want this anymore. If the program was growing, bigger, better, brighter, it didn't need another hard-working academic. It needed someone like me. Someone who knew both forensics *and* capital. And honestly, I could see myself here. But not without Daphne.

"So let me get this straight: not only do you not want to fire me, but you also want to promote me to administration. After violating the code of conduct."

"The code only says you'll be sanctioned. Not terminated. As part of your sanctions, I'm urging you to take on more responsibility."

I stared at her.

"What about Daphne?"

"McKinnon? That's the student, I'm guessing."

I nodded. There was no point in keeping it quiet from Jeanette.

"Figures. Decca's protégé. You're together? Committed?"

"Yes." Even after four days of knowing her.

"How committed?" She chewed her lip.

"If it's her or the job, it's her."

"Okay. I'll work around it while I'm here. It's not ideal. For either of you. It'll be worse if you're seen together as soon as she graduates—with you as her program director the whole time... it's a bad look, Chris."

"No shit."

"Your testimony could be called into question."

"I'm well aware." I gritted my teeth.

"How did this even happen? Asking as a friend. Not as a boss."

"I had no idea she was a student."

"Shit."

"You can say that again. I've spent the past two days hating myself."

"Why two?"

I wracked my brain trying to remember all the events of the last two days. The wreath-making and the cilantro jelly—jelly she'd left in my car—the spider bite, and the 0.03% chance that it would affect her the way it had. "The infuriating woman makes friends wherever she goes, so it takes forever to leave anywhere."

Jeanette was almost smiling when I told her about the lap dance burgers. Of course that was the part she'd wanted me to elaborate on. "It sounds like a whirlwind few days."

"Insane."

"It also sounds like you found your balance."

"I have."

"Welp," she hoisted herself out of the chair. "I got to get this place cleaned up enough to pack it all up by May, so if you'll excuse me..."

"Of course. And thanks for supporting me on this."

"I'm not supporting you. This is incredibly unethical and I don't *support* any of it. But I'm old enough and I've seen enough shit. I know you well enough. Sometimes love is inconvenient. And you're not beholden to the pearl clutchers."

"I appreciate it just the same." I turned to leave, even more confused than when I walked in.

"Dr. Carter..." she called. I turned back. "There's nothing in the handbook that prohibits a faculty member's spouse from attending school." A slow smile spread across her face.

"Good to know." I smiled back at her. "Merry Christmas, Jeanette."

Chapter 21

Daphne

When Mom left, I tried to keep this house comfortable. I added small things here and there that Dad wouldn't think about. Getting new kitchen towels when ours got all threadbare and gross, or remembering that Mom never skimped on buying name brand toilet paper or laundry detergent, but wouldn't waste her money on something like fabric softener. Everything in the laundry aisle looked the same to Dad.

I'd taken pride in the way I cared for the house, but it was never mine.

Now I was back here, and it felt even less like home.

I wouldn't be home until Chris came to his senses, until I could throw my arms around him and plaster my body against his. The trouble was, now that I wasn't following him around, bugging him to want me, to love me, to touch me, he probably felt the opposite.

Relief. That was probably what he was feeling.

He'd gone back to his cat and his life and could hold his head up, knowing he hadn't sacrificed his ethics, and had extricated himself from a problem that would ruin his career. And his life.

Dad and I ate Christmas dinner as quietly as ever. Talking only minimally just to be polite.

I'd overcooked the turkey, then berated myself for it, nibbled on the sausage dressing and green bean casserole, and let my hot fudge sundae melt into glop. I didn't have room to swallow much besides my disappointment.

It had settled into my belly, rising higher and higher into my throat. Every minute, it threatened to well up in my sinuses and spill out of my tear ducts. If I started, I'd never stop. I needed a dam. A diversion of some sort.

While Dad played the new video game I'd gotten him, I retreated to my bedroom to mope until the start of the semester.

I sat cross legged on my bed, watching *The Muppet's Christmas Carol* on my laptop, but not even the *meeces with no cheeses* could lift my Christmas night funk.

I let the audio of the movie keep running in the background. It was precarious, doing that with old technology. It would likely crash my computer, but so what if I had to restart the ancient brick one more time? I had nothing better to do.

I opened the online copy of Journal of Forensic Science and searched for Chris. A listing of hundreds of results for Christopher Carter, DDS, PhD populated the screen, including thirty-seven articles where he was a lead author. Only Decca had published more. After Dr. Bass, of course. He was the scientist who'd started the field of forensic anthropology, so if you had to come in second—or third—he was the one you'd want to beat you.

I clicked on the first article. I'd read it before. Before we'd been something to each other. Re-reading about palatal rugae morphology in children aged eighteen months to thirty-six months wasn't alleviating the ache I felt for him. I didn't know what I was even looking for here. I couldn't hear his voice in his academic writing—only the rigor of his study. He was everything an academic should be—detached and removed from his subject.

And I'd tried to take him away from that. From a world that needed him.

My phone buzzed.

My heart rate increased. I was tempted to look at the screen, but it wouldn't be him. I knew better than to get my hopes up again. He wasn't going to talk to me for two years. By then, he'd probably find someone else. Someone older, equally illustrious in her career, who looked good on his arm and didn't fangirl over hot water or got grease under her fingernails.

I looked at the screen anyway. Decca.

I hope you're having a wonderful Christmas, my bright young anthropological shooting star!

It was sweet and almost maternal, and it almost brought a smile to my face. I double-tapped the text, hoping it wasn't too rude not to wish her a Merry Christmas. I just couldn't right now.

I sighed. I should probably call my mom. Talk to my brother and sisters. I scrolled through and clicked on her name.

"Hi, Daphne," she said.

"Merry Christmas, Mom."

"Livi, turn off the drone, I can't hear Daphne. Merry Christmas, baby! I miss you."

"I miss you, too, Mom." I gave her back the empty words I just needed to say and she just needed to hear. I'd stopped chasing after the love she'd never give me long ago, but sometimes I got caught up in her promises and forgot not to care. Like the other day, when she forgot I was supposed to go caroling with the family and they all left without me. Well, everyone except my stepbrother, Raleigh, who actively hated my mother. He and I had spent the afternoon before Decca's party watching movies and eating all the cocktail meatballs my mother was probably saving for Christmas Eve, when Steven's parents would come over.

They had traditions. Mom had taken ours with her when she left. Then acted like they were mine again whenever I came back to her house—her house that was definitely never my home.

"How was caroling?" I asked, knowing whatever answer she gave would be another stab to my gut. Maybe that was exactly what I was looking for now. The kill shot.

"Oh, it was a mess. Emma's soccer party ran late and she insisted she didn't need a coat because all the kids walk around with throw blankets over their shoulders these days. But guess what…? She got cold. Just like I told her she would. And the Clifton's dog pooped right on the Murphy's lawn during The First Noel, and Sheila was livid, because Debbie had nothing to clean it up with," She sighed.

"Sounds like it could've still been fun though."

"Maybe if Emma had actually sung, instead of just mouthing the words. She's the one in choir and she never wants to sing. It's a good thing you weren't there. It was so embarrassing."

Yeah, good thing, I almost said. But I didn't. I wouldn't give her the lie of polite apathy anymore.

"I wanted to be there, Mom. I was supposed to be there. You left early. Without me." It was brave for me to say even that much.

I took a deep breath and exhaled slowly, thinking of Chris's shocked face when I told him I was never *real* around my mom. I let myself be her friend, her sounding post for how she raised my sisters. Like I was in the thick of it with her. Bouncing back and forth from being something akin to a co-parent, when her life got hard, to her casual friend, when it was easy again.

"Oh, honey, it wasn't anything like I thought it would have been. We didn't sound good at all."

"I don't care. You should have waited for me. You always treat me like a guest instead of a real part of the family. *Your family.* That's how I refer to you all. I should be part of it, not someone Livi and Emma need to tiptoe around."

"It's because you're never here, Daphne. When you come, it needs to be special. Or else you might never come back."

"I don't know if you've ever paid attention to me, Mom. No... that's... not even fair because it's partly my fault that I hide myself from you... but I don't like perfect. I like off-key singing and laughing at dogs pooping on uptight women's lawns, and being forced to attend your stupid megachurch, even though I disagree with everything that pastor says, but at least it would seem like I'm a real part of your life. You always give me your social media life. Your highlight reel. I want the stuff you hide in your camera because it's not aesthetically pleasing enough."

"Well, honey... I didn't know you wanted any of that. You've always been so mature. So good. I didn't know you needed me for anything."

"I did though."

"Well, I'm sorry I wasn't good enough for you. I tried my best."

Did she, though? Maybe.

"I'm sorry I brought it up. I was just—" *no, not just.* "I was hurt that you didn't wait for me. You knew I was coming over."

"But honey..."

"What?"

"You're kind of pitchy."

"I'm what?"

"You sing off key."

"So what? It's neighborhood caroling."

"I wanted to make a good impression. The Murphys have their lights. And the Virenzis give everyone in the cul-de-sac a box of the most elaborate cookies."

"I don't think I want to hear any more of this, Mom. Merry Christmas. I love you."

"I love you too, dear. Oh, Livi wanted to ask you something, hang on..."

"Livi knows she can text me. I'm hanging up now."

By the time I pressed END, she was already yelling at one of the girls, as if our conversation, my first declaration of real feelings since I was a child, hadn't mattered to her at all.

I tossed my phone across the room. It landed somewhere in a heap of laundry. I didn't care if I never saw it until school started.

I lay on my bed and resumed the Muppets. Marley and Marley were singing their song when the doorbell rang. I cocked my head to the side. No one ever rang our doorbell.

"Dad," I called. There was no answer.

I wrapped my own throw blanket over my shoulders, for comfort more than heat, and shuffled to the front door that no one used.

Outside the window was a man in black. A man I hadn't thought I'd see for two years.

I opened the door tentatively.

"Chris?" I blinked. Maybe I'd fallen asleep and this was a dream. Maybe I'd left my wallet in his car.

He pointed to my wreath. The one from the workshop.

"I hung mine, too."

"I thought you already had a wreath."

"My new one has better memories. Besides, it's a Christmas tradition." He smirked, but his eyes were cautious.

"What are you doing here?"

"You forgot this." He pulled out my jar of cilantro jelly from his coat pocket. A different coat. Black. Engine grease proof.

"Oh." My heart deflated, despite how careful I'd thought I'd been not to let it balloon up.

"I couldn't let you go another night without giving it back to you. You might have needed it for your cream cheese."

"I'm kind of afraid to try it, now. After the spider."

"I don't think any of the radioactive venom made it into the jar."

"Not radioactive. Still no powers. See?" She made the Spiderman gesture.

"Too bad. I can think of certain positions where those webs would come in handy." He wagged his eyebrows.

"You don't get to come here and do that, Chris. You don't get to turn me on and leave again when you remember there are consequences."

"There are no more consequences."

"What do you mean?"

"I resigned. Just came from Jeanette's office."

"On Christmas?"

"I didn't want to spend another night without you."

"I thought you needed time to think."

"I had plenty of time. I walked into my apartment and all I could think about was you. I went to the piano and started playing your song. My parents want to take you to Germany with them this summer. Everything is you. Christmas isn't Christmas without you. Then Gita came and forced me out of my head and told me she'd never forgive me if I came back to my apartment without you."

"I think I like Gita."

"The feeling is mutual for her." He looked around, into my dark house, the dark exterior. "I— Can I come in? Or can you come out? This feels..."

"Don't say a word about the mess. I've been busy lately."

I grabbed him by the hand and pulled him through the house—just a few turns, unlike his family estate—and into my room, where...

"Wow."

"You said you wouldn't say anything."

"Right. I just don't quite know where to..." he leaped over a waist-high pile of half-dirty laundry and two smaller piles of all-cleans and all-dirties and stood in front of me. "Nice race car bed."

"Thanks."

"You didn't tell me you still use it."

"Still works. It's big enough for me. Dad built it to fit a twin."

"You're fucking adorable."

"So are you." I wanted to touch him, stroke his stubbled cheek and feel him drop the weight of his cares into my palm. But he needed to do this for me first.

"I keep thinking about today," he said. "With Carol."

"Yuletide Carol!"

He smiled and took a deep breath. "Today I got to really watch you in your element."

I winced. "Oh, God, I hope car mechanics isn't my element. I know I'm going from a dirty job to an even dirtier job, but at least dirt and decomp wash off." I held up my hands. "Unlike grease. This is why I paint my nails black, by the way. So you can't see what's underneath."

He looked at me like I had no idea how wrong I was about to be proven. "Watching you open up that engine and check the... whatever you were looking for—the best competency porn. But I don't mean just the car. I mean your kindness. You make friends with everyone wherever you go. From the guy at the rest stop, to Patty and her granddaughter, to Valentine the Stripper—"

"Exotic dancer and geriatric nurse."

"Right, I love the way you care about people. I think that might be what I love most about you."

"Even if I did get grease on your coat?"

"I don't care about the coat, Daphne. I love you. I'm sorry for not telling you twelve minutes after we met, but I'm telling you now and I'm not going to stop."

I said nothing. I was too stunned, too busy exploding with brilliant happiness to even think. I let his admission settle like—well, another blanket around my shoulders, heavy and perfect, until I could trust that I'd heard it for real.

"Every time I look at you it takes my breath away. I knew it was you. I knew it'd be you from the first time I turned my head and you were standing in front of me."

"Three days ago."

"Yes, three days ago. And look what we've gone through in three days. You said, earlier tonight, that we hadn't seen hardship. But that's patently false. We've had weeks, maybe months of hardship. Crammed into three days. We work together. We just do. We're two valves, calibrated in to mix the perfect amount of fuel and air for combustion... And yes, I looked that up before I came here, but it's true about us. The past three days have proven it over and over again."

He researched the fuel injection system; my heart could burst from that alone.

"Did I get the engine part right?"

A tear leaked down my cheek as I laughed. "Not really, no. But I love that you Googled engines for me."

"I'll get books. Big, fat textbooks on engine mechanics. I'll take classes. I want to know about everything you love."

"So, what happens now?"

His eyes flickered mischievously. "That depends on you, darling. I can stay resigned and be extraordinarily happy being your personal chef, sommelier, and sex slave."

"Sounds pretty good."

"Or..." he looked down at the pile of clothes. "Why do you have so many..." He reached down and grabbed an armful of clothes and shoved them on top of the other piles and I didn't care one bit.

"Or?" I said impatiently.

"Or..." he took another deep breath and knelt on one knee. "You marry me. Now. Before the start of the semester. We stay together. And we work together. As a team." He kissed my knuckles. "I'm sorry I don't have a ring. I couldn't wait until tomorrow when the jewelry store opens. I wanted to spend the last few moments of Christmas together."

I brushed his hair to the side and stared at his boyishly handsome face. "The second option *does* seem like a much better use of your degrees." He smiled his lopsided smile that told me he really would give it all up without any regrets. But I didn't want that. "I want so badly to be your team, Chris. I want to keep being your biggest fan. Read more of your research. Co-author with you. Learn from you."

He nodded as his eyes welled with tears. "You'll do it? You'll marry me?"

"On the other hand... I do like the sound of you as my sex slave."

He rose back to his feet. "Sweetheart, that's a given either way."

Chapter 22

Chris

"I KEEP THINKING ABOUT Winston." Daphne chewed on her lip.

"Winston's perfectly safe in the lab." I turned the wheel sharply to the left. "I made reservations at The Tennessee for later. They have the best wine list in town, but if you'd like something else—"

"Anywhere's fine," she said distractedly. "I trust you. Eating out for me is fast food, so I don't know any of the right places."

"Anywhere's the right place with you, sweetheart." I lifted her left hand to my lips and kissed the vintage gold band I'd placed on her finger less than an hour ago. She wanted something simple that she could work in. I'd relented and given her simple.

She didn't know it yet, but tonight, I was also giving her a four-carat, Gilded Age emerald and diamond "engagement" ring; a piece straight out of an Edith Wharton novel—along with some other vintage jewels—a diamond collar of stars that reminded me of our first night together, Mikimoto pearls in the same lustrous gray as her eyes, plus a first edition of *The Age of Innocence*. Once I'd realized how much fun it was spending my money on my wife, I'd gone a little overboard at the New York auction houses.

"But I'm not taking you to McDonald's for our wedding reception."

"Huh?"

"Nothing," I shook my head, smiling. Nothing could diminish the joy I felt this evening. Even work. "What exactly are you thinking about the skull?"

She gave me a worried glance. "Do you recall a Starving Time in Tennessee history?"

"What do you mean? Like a Jamestown situation?"

She nodded slowly. Intuitively, I knew what she was reaching for, but it was way too high on the shelf. "I was reading an article earlier and it triggered something."

"You were reading an article about starvation cannibalism on our wedding day?"

"No, I was reading an article about prion diseases on our wedding day and it made me think about the Russian famine, which of course, led me to starvation cannibalism in general. What else was I supposed to do while getting my nails done?"

"The idea is to relax."

"Reading is relaxing—"

"About the Russian Famine?"

"That part wasn't relaxing."

I chuckled and changed lanes. I knew exactly where this conversation was heading and there was no way I wasn't giving in to those big round eyes of hers when she inevitably asked if we could go to the bone lab instead of our wedding dinner.

Her phone buzzed. She looked down and dropped her phone back in her purse. "Decca's mad we didn't invite her."

"She didn't invite me to her wedding either."

"There's recent DNA evidence to suggest that our uncanny ability to resist prion diseases is because cannibalism was a lot more common throughout human history than we think," she said.

"That's only a theory," I said.

"So is gravity. No scientific theory can really be proven. But if it was common in human history, maybe it's not as taboo as we like to think it is. Maybe we've just stopped looking for evidence."

I sighed. "Cannibalism as the cause of natural resistance to TSEs needs a lot more study."

"You're only guessing the skull is a century old, meaning Winston has been deceased for that long."

"The soil samples might tell us more," I said. "Nothing's been run yet. Still on break. Remember?"

She paid no attention to my not-to-subtle hint that *we* should be on break as well. "One hundred years puts us at the Depression. That might account for it," she said to herself. "Besides, there are always people who snap and do crazy shit."

"Say it. Say it out loud. The thing you're thinking."

"You'll make fun of me."

"I might tell you it's wishful thinking that your first grad school case could end up something this... monumental, but I'd never make fun of you for throwing yourself into academics. I'd be a hypocrite."

She took a deep breath. "The marks on the temporal bone—if you think about it, that's the muscle insertion for a real meaty part of the face—the more I think back, the more they remind me of the serrations on Jane's mandible—Jane the cannibalized skull they found in the archeological dig at—"

"I know Jane."

"I know it's ridiculous, but I think Winston was also a victim. Is there any evidence of ritual cannibalization in North America?"

"Ritual? Not really. There's hearsay about certain Iroquois tribes practicing warfare cannibalism, but we only have secondhand accounts written by colonizers, most likely propaganda to vilify Native Americans. Even if it were true, it has no bearing on Winston. In this soil, he'd most likely be dust if he were that old. You're more on track with Jamestown."

Great. Now she's got me going with this insane hypothesis. "It's a stretch to assume those marks were made with the intent to consume. We'll never prove it. Jane had a lot more circumstantial evidence."

"I don't need to prove it. Just position it. Maybe an archeological team can find some circumstantial evidence."

I sighed. "If you're right, I can't wait to see the look on Decca's face. She's going to shit herself for giving up this case."

"We'll be sure to credit her in the paper."

I laughed. "That's my girl."

"Always, Daddy."

Fuck. She was going to get massacred tonight. My brain was already dulled from postmarital bliss, and it was supposed to be getting even duller after feasting on a good steak, great bottle of wine, and Daphne's juicy pussy. *Ignore throbbing cock... ignore throbbing cock.*

"First we need isotope dating to pinpoint the year," she said.

"The center's never going to fund that."

She smirked and waggled her eyebrows at me. "For headlines about cannibalism, they will."

"Shrewd. But you're getting too far ahead of yourself."

I pulled into the parking lot of the last place I thought I'd end up on my wedding day.

"Really?" her eyes popped open. She must have just figured out where we'd been going. "Are you sure? Chris, you don't have to do this. I was just talking out loud."

"Are you going to be disappointed if your findings don't support your hypothesis?"

"Probably."

"I'll rephrase. Will you still let me take you to dinner if your findings don't support it?"

"Regardless of what we find..." her hand slid up the inside of my thigh, "I'll let you do a lot more than that, husband."

"I LIKE THAT SUIT on you," she said, as we strolled hand in hand down the halls of the academic building.

"Thank you."

"Very ducal. But I like everything on you."

Her heels clacked on the terrazzo floors. Until today, I'd never seen her in heels. Only combat boots and the ratty pair of sneakers she wore during her morning runs.

She ran in the mornings. Like me.

She'd called it her medicine. If she didn't start her day without some kind of endorphin-dopamine cocktail, her cognitive skills were mush until she got some oxygen into her brain.

I loved finding out these things about her. And since I'd only known her a little over a week, I'd be finding them out for a very long time.

Eight days.

That was how long I'd known her. My wife, as of... I looked at my watch... forty-three minutes ago.

God, this was weird. Weird and good and it all still felt like a dream.

"I like that dress on you."

"It's not too short?"

A sound came from the back of my throat. "I don't know. I'll have to take another look." I dropped her hand and stopped. I nodded for her to stand in front of me. "Arms at your sides." She giggled and stood with her body erect, her arms straight as arrows. "Hm. Clearly that hemline doesn't come anywhere close to your fingertips. I'm going to have to punish you, Ms. McKinnon." I closed the gap between us slowly, taking my time, staring covetously at her thighs.

"I'm sorry, Dr. Carter." She bit her lip, stepping back as I advanced. "I'll be a good girl next time."

"Promise?" My fingertips brushed the satin hem. The silk flirted with her skin as I inched the fabric up and up, just barely brushing, dancing over the tops of her stockings.

"What are you going to do to me?" Her back hit the wall and I braced my forearm next to her face.

"That depends. Was it your intention to give me improper thoughts?"

Her eyes were big and wide, shining up at me. "No. I had no idea." She giggled as my hands found her ass. I slid my fingers under her panties and kneaded her muscle.

"You had no idea how uncomfortable it would be for me in these pants? Anyone can see what you do to me." I pressed my hips against hers and lifted her leg, tucking it around my thigh to open her up further.

"Dr. Carter, someone could see us *now*." Her pupils were blown wide the fuck open and there was a hitch in her voice that made me know she liked the idea.

I rolled my hips against hers. “You’d like that, wouldn’t you? To be caught with a professor. You’d have so much leverage.”

She shook her head.

“Tell me, do you want to be caught, sweetheart? Or do you want to be watched? Are you a little slut, Ms. McKinnon?” She gasped. I smiled as I said it. It was getting harder to play this role and not just give in to wanting her, but I’d play as long as she wanted.

“I’m a married woman.”

“A married woman who leaves the house in a dress that short? For your husband’s sake, I’m sorry.” I rolled my hips again. “You were asking for this. You know that, right? Teasing me. Tempting me. Knowing I’m off limits. A married professor.”

“I didn’t mean to, but maybe... you’re right. I am a slut. But only for you.”

I dropped her leg and straightened my body, exhaling like I had control over any part of this.

“But—” she complained.

“Bone lab,” I breathed.

“Are we...?”

“I need a minute.” I braced my hand against the wall and nodded, my gaze trained on the floor. I was one squeeze, one swish, one kiss away from coming in my pants. Straightening, I grabbed her hand and pulled her down the hall and into the empty room.

Everyone was gone between semesters, and it was mostly clean. The postdocs were always good about keeping the lab clean. And anyway, cleanliness wasn’t my top priority right now. I’d fuck her in a public bathroom if I had to. Hell, I’d fuck her if there were students here watching. Okay—I probably wouldn’t follow through in either one of those scenarios, but she made me feel like I would. She made me crazy with need for her.

I pinned her against the door, kissing her glossed lips and reaching under her dress to pull her panties down.

She moaned into my mouth. "God, yes."

"What do you want, sweetheart?"

"Put your fingers inside me."

I slid easily through her lips and groaned. I'd never get used to how wet she got. "You're already leaking all over my hand." I pulled it away and licked her off my fingers, then pushed back into her pretty pussy, back farther this time, inside her. "I love the way you taste. Like a storm on the ocean. Briny and sweet. Dangerous." Her eyes widened and she inhaled a gasping breath, rocking herself on my hand.

"I don't... Fuck, Chris, I'm gonna..." She held my wrist still, panting. "I don't want to come on your nice suit."

I needed her. Now. I loved her like this, slutty and squirting for me.

"Turn around," I said.

"But—" she started to protest but did it anyway.

I lowered the zipper of her dress and carefully lifted it over her head. Underneath, she was bare. Just stockings and heels. I hadn't realized she wasn't wearing a bra.

Her back was lovely and she shivered when I traced my finger up her spine, reaching around to cup her breasts and pull her against the front of my body. Her hair cascaded over her shoulder in a stream of silver. "You want to make a mess, baby?" I whispered in her ear.

She nodded and rocked her head back against my shoulder as I cradled her long arcing neck in my hand. "Please."

"Stay here."

She whined when my hands slid away from her body.

In the massive shelf-lined room in the back, I brought down the box I'd logged earlier. Case number 24-126. Winston.

"I'll let you do the honors." I said, referring to the box on the table.

"Can I have my dress back?"

"You said you wanted to make a mess. I don't want you to ruin your wedding dress."

"Chris! That's not what I thought you meant and you know it."

"But it's what I meant." I smirked. "I brought you an apron."

"It's see-though."

"The more you talk, the longer it'll be until we both come, so find me some evidence of cannibalism."

"Yes, Daddy."

"WE'RE SUPPOSED TO BE flying to New Zealand tomorrow," I said, pressing the ignition. The car purred to life.

"Yeah, about that."

"Yeah, I know."

"I'm sorry."

"If this is the discovery you think it is, this is career-making. History-making. Besides, we have the rest of our lives for you to fuck up our travel plans."

"Thank you... I think?" A devious smile spread across her face.

"I wish I had fucked you in the lab. Who knows how long I'll have to wait after your big discovery."

"Dr. Carter," she said. "If you think any old bones are going to keep me from boning you—probably several times a day—you've got a shock coming."

"That right?"

She climbed over the console and threw a leg across my lap and rocked her hips against my already hard cock. Of course it was hard. "I might have a lot of work to do, so I'm going to need your full support."

"I intend to give it." I adjusted my seat back as far as it would go. If this is what she had in mind, we needed the interior to be a lot bigger than this.

"I expect you to take care of our meals, because you love cooking and I hate it." She raked her teeth over my earlobe before sucking it into her mouth. *Oh, heavenly...* I was melting into the seat.

"I want to finish my program without any interruption."

"Of course, I—"

She pressed her index finger against my lips. "That includes you making excuses for me to your friends if I'm sick or late with an assignment. No donations made in my name to get me out of class. No easy grades. Not from anyone. I still need to prove I belong."

"You do belong." I captured her fingertip between my teeth, playfully, but of course she thrust her finger in deeper, making me suck on it.

"If I ever have a free weekend, or time off between semesters, I want to go sightseeing. I want to stop at every stupid kitschy roadside attraction along the way."

With her finger still in my mouth, I started to protest, but she only laughed, which made the angle of her hips shift even lower against my cock, aching to burst free.

"More than anything, I want you naked in our bed every night." She reached down and stroked me through my pants. "I want this cock rock hard and leaking for me."

"Darling—"

She kissed me. It was messy and fast and needy. Drunk on power, love, and an upcoming life-affirming, career-gold win. And I answered every desperate little groan of hers with one of my own.

My hands met her hips, grinding her body on my cock.

"We haven't..." she panted. "We've spent so long in this car and we haven't even—"

"Too small. Won't work."

"I'm limber."

I groaned. "Fuck, take me out."

Her hands were already unbuckling my belt as I fought the seat controls, moving the seat back and reclining as far as it would go, looking for every extra inch of space.

Before I had a chance to process, she'd squeezed herself into an impossibly tight space and took me into her mouth. "Oh, yes, sweetheart." I lovingly brushed her hair out of her face as her eyes met mine. She swirled her tongue over the tip, collecting the pre-cum that was leaking copiously. "That feels so good."

She popped off my dick and used her saliva to stroke me, moving my foreskin up and down as she watched. "I love your cock. It's so much fun to play with."

I laughed. "I'm a big fan of it, myself."

"I had a question to ask, but now I forgot."

God, even her hand felt fucking amazing. It was hard to think straight. "Ask when you remember."

She leaned in and licked a path from my base to the tip, swallowing me down. I groaned. "God, you're good at that."

She popped off again. "Oh! I remember now." Lick. "Remember in the building..." Lick. Swirl. "When you called me Ms. McKinnon?" Lick. Swirl. Suuuck.

"What? Uh... oh, fucking hell. Uh. Yeah." I was about to come and when I did it would spurt everywhere. Jesus.

She bobbed her head a few more times, swirling her tongue in a way that was making my eyes roll back in my head. Then she was pulling away again, using her hand as she thought aloud. "I think I want to change my name."

"What?" I was in a daze. Was she speaking words? Oh. Oh, yes. Name change. "To what?"

"Yours, silly."

"Oh."

"Would that be okay? I don't have to."

"Wait. What now? You want to be... *Jesus, had I heard her right?* Mrs. Carter?"

"Does it sound too much like your mom?"

"No!" I shouted. "Sorry, I just never expected... yeah, my God, yes. I would be honored if you took my name."

"Really?"

"Of course. I mean, fuck, that's..." I brushed my hand over my face. Incoherent as fuck. I didn't know why it felt like she'd given me a gift, but it was powerful. It reached into the recesses of my psyche and squeezed that shameful, deep caveman urge to possess and claim her.

Everything about Daphne turned me into a beast.

"Come here, baby." I brushed my thumb across her cheekbone. My touch was gentle, my tone was anything but.

"Yes, Daddy."

My cock pulsed.

Daphne climbed into my lap and held herself over me on her knees. She bent forward to kiss me sweetly. Achingly sweet. Just the lightest touch as she strategically planted kisses across my parted lips. I let her do it, not forcing anything, just savoring the feel of being cherished and cherishing her in return.

Her new perfume blended with the intoxicating, heady scent of her arousal and it was perfect. I knew she'd be wet even before I touched her, but when my thumb brushed through the cleft of her pussy, she was already flooding my fingers. Every slight amplification of her body was another twist of the key, winding me tighter and tighter. So tight I was going to burst.

"I need to be inside you, Daphne. Can you take me like this?"

"I think if I..." she shifted off her knees and onto her feet so she was squatting over me. "Oh, I think that might work. I like that."

"Where are your panties, sweetheart?"

Her cheeks reddened. "I never put them back on after the lab. Just in case."

"I love your contingency plans."

Her clit was so hard I knew I had to touch her delicately, or the stimulation would be too sensitive, but just below, in that slick smooth place between her clit and her vagina was exactly where she needed to be stroked.

I lined my cock up just there, massaging that place with my head until her cunt was dripping down my shaft.

She moaned when I slid through her wet folds and sank into her.

I forced my eyes open, watching her face soften our joining. Even rutting in a car was profound and sacred. We were meant to be like this.

"Daphne," I said.

But it was all I could manage to say.

"Me too," she said back.

Neither of us moved until she did, just to lean forward, resting her knees on my thighs. Closer. Close enough to feel her breath on my cheek, her fingers in my hair. Still enough I could count her heartbeat by watching the pulse in her neck.

I pulled her forward to kiss that spot. That warm, soft spot that smelled of ancient florals and sweet hay and her own delicious sweat. I devoured that scent, licking it up and scraping my teeth across her pale skin.

She whimpered. I had to move. I thrust my hips up, pushing myself in deeper before withdrawing. My dick glistening with her slick need. I did it again. "Oh, fuck," she cried. "This feels so good."

I held the back of her neck as I did it again and again. Slowly fucking into her perfect cunt and dragging my cock back out, each time slicker than the one before. "Oh, sweetheart. You're so fucking... I can't... Fuck."

"Harder. More."

"Oh, God, I can't... I'm gonna..." I thrust my hips against hers. "So deep. Darling. Are you okay?"

I was only half coherent. It took everything to hold myself back. The windows were covered in a haze of fog. My glasses were even half-fogged. Even in the cold car, our heat was too much. Sweat slicked the skin at her neck. I felt it sliding down my back as my hips pistoned into her wildly.

"Yes, yes, yes, like that. Harder, Daddy. Fuck me harder."

"Stop. I can't... hear... I'm too close..."

Her eyes and mouth popped open. "Oh, fuck, I'm coming. Oh, God oh God oh God. I'm sorry. I forgot. It's so..." she gasped as she squirted all over the front of me, flooding my cock and my pants and my shirt.

"Oh, shit. Daphne..." The sight was enough to make me come right along with her. I sank into her completely, pulling her as close as possible as my orgasm sent me into another dimension.

My sight was gone. Did I even need it anymore? I could only vaguely hear the sound of our breathing, but it wasn't immediate. Instead, it seemed to be coming from another realm. I was a cock. That was the only part of me that existed anymore. Maybe some other pieces would reattach, but as I lay there, unable to move, unable to do anything but feel my orgasm still coursing through me, my cum pumping deep inside someplace warm and happy.

"Oh, Chris, I'm sorry. I ruined everything. My dress. Your suit."

I said nothing. Still incapable of speech, or thought. I pulled her down farther and pressed her chest into mine, holding her against me. Mess or no mess, I didn't care. No. That was wrong. I did care. I loved her messes. "My darling." I wiped an errant strand of hair away from her face. "I wouldn't have you any other way. Because this is something spectacular your body does for me."

"Are you sure?"

"Fuck, it's such a turn-on. It makes me hard again, immediately after. You're going to kill me. Between making sure you eat during study breaks and being your on-call sex slave, you're going to fucking kill me."

"At least it'll be a good death."

"Mm," I murmured into her hair. Miraculously, I was softening inside her. I could go to sleep like this every night. "Promise not to consume the remains." She laughed.

Neither of us made a move to leave. "The holidays are over," she said.

I nodded. "You can't say we didn't make the most of what was left. I'd say a wedding anniversary is a pretty great holiday tradition."

"Chris, there is one more thing we haven't done that would make this year complete."

"What's that?"

"Well... I still haven't driven your car." She lifted her head and batted her eyelashes at me. "Please, Daddy."

"Did you fuck me so you could butter me up to ask?"

"No. I just thought I'd take advantage of the timing."

I sighed. "Daphne. Have I ever said no to you?"

I could see her running through the events of the past week before biting her lip and smiling with anticipation. "No."

I grabbed her by the ass and hoisted her off me, plunking her back into the passenger's seat, half wincing, half proud at the fluids dripping out of her along the way. I winked at her shocked face.

"There's a first time for everything, sweetheart."

Epilogue

Daphne

"Happy New Year, Dr. Carter."

"Happy Anniversary, Dr. Carter."

We'd snuck away from the New Year's Eve benefit to have this little moment to ourselves. To celebrate, just the two of us.

We raised our glasses without clinking them, which, I was informed, was not only uncouth, but bruised the crystal.

His parents had given us a fabulous set of vintage champagne coupes as an anniversary gift. They were horribly expensive, being that they were bought from Sotheby's and came with the provenance that proved they'd once belonged to Marilyn Monroe, gifted to her by Lee Strasburg, of the famed Actor's Studio, in celebration of her marriage to Pulitzer Prize winning playwright, Arthur Miller. It was pretty well known that Lee was at least tangentially responsible for Marilyn's emotional downfall. And her marriage to Miller was rocky, to say the least. But all that aside, I was thrilled to own a piece of history.

I sipped the champagne. It was a special bottle. A 1979 Krug Clos du Mesnil. That was the other half of our gift. The wine prickled with less effervescence than the one Marcia and I had chosen to serve the guests tonight—alongside the cilantro jelly and cream cheese wontons that everyone had been raving about—and I was told that was because it was cellared perfectly, the flavors naturally developed into something nuttier, richer, while the bubbles grew smaller.

"It's good," I said.

"Mm." Chris savored. "Nutty and biscuity, with well-developed dried fruit flavors."

"Where did you read that?"

He smiled. "*Wine Spectator.*"

I giggled and sipped again. I knew I was feeling more than the alcohol, since I'd only had a sip. I was buzzing with a different kind of high.

"Yeah. I can taste it. I'm getting notes of oatmeal cream pie, so I can see the comparison."

"Give me that." He lifted my coupe from my hand and set it down on the counter behind me. "Little Debbie." He shook his head. "If anything, this wine had notes of Pepperidge Farm Chessman."

"You're even bougie about your junk food."

"Of course."

I still knew nothing about wine. Only what I liked. And apparently, I only liked the good stuff.

I was enjoying the perks of being rich a little too much.

But not ostentatious rich. Subtly rich. Old money rich.

Drinking champagne that cost thousands of dollars a bottle while hiding in my in-law's butler's pantry with my husband rich.

I always said if I ever won the lottery (the only way I could have ever conceived of becoming this wealthy a few years ago) I wouldn't buy a McMansion. I'd buy a house from the nineteenth century with a fireplace in the kitchen and original wide plank floors. I'd plant a medicinal herb garden and hang bundles of flowers to dry from the beams of the low ceilings.

But I didn't win the lottery. And we were still more than happy living next to Harish and Gita.

So, the colonial house would have to wait.

Besides, since I married an almost-billionaire, I was still pretty broke. Relatively speaking.

I'd turned down my financial aid money to be supported by Chris's robber baron wealth. Actually, with the exception of an occasional gift he lavished on me, we lived off his income from his dean's salary and some smaller investments. Besides taking the directorship—after Decca had turned it down flat—he'd pledged the next twenty years' worth of his mind-bogglingly large dividend checks to help fund the new Forensic Anthropology Center, which was finally breaking ground this fall.

I'd been depositing my small teaching stipend into my dad's account. I felt bad he didn't have me there anymore to cover food and the little share of rent I'd been contributing since I turned eighteen.

I didn't see him often. I was working through my issues with my parents in counseling, and the truth was, I was in a good enough place to help financially, whether or not he deserved it or not. *Deserve* wasn't for me to decide anyway.

I saw my mom even less, and was okay with it. Now that my sisters were both at UT, we had a real relationship. With flaws. We talked about real struggles.

When Mom found out I was "married to money," she started coming around more. Calling. Caring. She'd done a one-eighty and had immediately become a shaky, blurry facsimile of the mother I'd always wanted, while trying to gaslight me into thinking that was how it had always been. Which proved she could have been a real mother to me all along. Without Chris's money.

And as *eat the rich* as I was, it was the rich who'd given me the love I'd always wanted. Not only from Chris.

To hear Marcia tell it, she and Brian had fallen in love with me as a daughter before they'd even gotten their bags off the luggage carousel when we'd picked them up from the airport four years ago.

Authenticity blanketed their shoulders like the softest, warmest cashmere. They had opinions, but they always shared them with kindness, and trusted Chris and I to make the right decisions for us. It had opened my eyes to just how much I needed to prioritize my healing.

But now, I was in a good place.

Too good of a place. Tonight, I was wearing a long black dress with a slit up to the top of my thigh and a neckline that plunged halfway down to my navel. It was sexy and elegant. And it could all too easily be pushed to one side or the other for easy access.

Because in our four years together, Chris and I were no less ravenous for each other.

And I had an important question to ask him.

Oh, but the way he was sucking on that spot under my ear... maybe it wasn't so important after all.

I moaned and pressed against his mouth, needing more.

"This dress has been driving me out of my mind." He said, kissing lower, bending me backward over the counter so he could reach my collarbones, the hollow between my clavicles—suprasternal notch, but that didn't sound sexy. His tongue dipped in there before his teeth clamped just gently enough over my collarbone. He knew every plane and facet of my body that got me panting.

"Wait until you find out what's underneath."

He pulled back. "Yeah? You buy some sexy little things?"

"Maybe." I smirked. "Or maybe it's what I didn't buy."

He sucked in a breath and looked down at my plunging neckline. It wasn't engineered all that well. Unlike some dresses that had illusion fabric or strategic boning to prevent embarrassing gaffes.

This was strapless. There was boning, but only in the waist, and only to hold up the cups that were cut to just barely cover my pierced nipples. My breasts had grown in the past few years. I'd put on weight while getting my doctorate. I was eating more and eating better. I wasn't running in the mornings on an empty stomach only to "fast" all day because spending money on food felt like a luxury. I'd replaced my beloved Mountain Thunder with scented sparkling waters. Chris packed us lunches like salmon salads with sesame dressing and made brownies for dessert.

His eyes darkened as he ran a finger under the loose cup. He did the same thing to my right boob. Then he lifted my boobs clear out of the bodice of my dress.

"Has it been this easy for your tits to pop out this whole evening? Talking to Jeanette, and Dr. Davies, and the Coughlins?" He rolled the delicate platinum barbells between his fingers and his thumbs, eyeing me with a predatory gleam. "Have your nipples been this hard, Sweetheart? So big anyone might have seen them?"

"Uhn." Was all I could say. My body had started its process. Turning off some functions to fuel more important ones. The wetter I got, the less cognition I could rouse.

"My slutty wife. You should have told me earlier how much you needed me."

"I need you now."

"I know, baby. I'll take care of you. I'll always take care of you."

He dropped one hand to the opening of my skirt, gently peeling the front panel up and to the side until he saw my bare pussy. No doubt glistening proudly for him. "No panties, either. Darling." He shook his head. "What am I going to do with you?

"Fuck me, please," I whimpered.

He was already kicking my feet apart, crouching down and spreading my lips apart with his thumbs. "Oh, look at you. My gorgeous girl."

I moaned. I was so full, so ready, it hurt to be so open. I longed to rub my legs together, for Chris to touch me.

"You want my tongue? Because I would love nothing more than to taste you for the rest of the night. To congratulate our biggest donors, and suck up to the ones who haven't given enough, all while knowing your cum just wet my tongue and quenched my thirst."

"Oh, God, yes. Please, lick me. I can't—"

"You know what I want, baby. Say it and I'll give you everything."

"Daddy. Oh, God, Daddy." I whined, writhing in my sky-high heels. But something...

Daddy...

Chris dove in with his tongue flat, rubbing his whole face into my pussy. Oh, fuck, he was soaked already and I hadn't even come. His nose was nudging my clit as his tongue was hard against the place between my clit and my vagina.

He was everywhere. Hitting everything, but right where I wanted. And he knew. He knew and he did it this way to tease me. And I loved it even more.

My legs shook and he hooked his arms around my knees to keep them still.

"Talk to me, Sweetheart. Tell me what you need."

"Just you, Daddy."

Daddy... *shit.* That's what it was.

"Pass me my glass." His nose glistened when he came up for air. And a drink.

He sipped, letting the bubbles linger on his tongue as he slid it back into me. Very calmly, between little licks up my slit, he said, "I need you to come for me now, Daphne. I want it all. Don't hold back."

"What if I get you wet?"

"I'll change."

"But—"

"Do you want my fingers inside you, sweetheart?"

"Yes, Daddy."

"Good. Now do as I told you." He licked again, reaching up and spearing me on his long elegant fingers, stroking my clit from inside my vagina in the place that made me spurt like a fucking fountain. I didn't know what he had in mind, but it was something, and knowing him, it was filthy. He always got quiet and cerebral when there was something up his sleeve.

I loved when he was like this. Calm and proper, with something feral about his eyes. Between his lips sweetly kissing my swollen clit and his fingers and thumb massaging the rest of my sloppy cunt, I was done for.

The pressure was building and building and oh, yeah it was right there and it was only lucky I could warn him in time to get out of the way.

"Fuck, it's coming. Oh, it's coming." My legs shook as he pushed me back against the cabinet. My whole pelvis throbbed as torrential flashes of pleasure crashed over and over me.

But he didn't get out of the way. He... oh sweet, merciful... he held his champagne coupe under my pussy, cupped over my lips as my cum rained into it, only a little splashing out the sides and down his hand as he continued to massage my clit, eking out the last drop of my pleasure with his thumb.

He stood. My boobs were still hanging out of the top of my dress, heaving with my breaths. His lust-drunk eyes pinned me down as he raised the glass up and up, touching it to his lips, tilting it back. His perfect hands, delicately holding the fine crystal as he poured my champagne-scented cum down his throat in one, two, three gulps.

Jesus.

I was dead. He'd killed me with his audacity. Who would have thought someone this aristocratic and gentle and refined and good could be so fucking filthy?

"Chris, I want you inside me."

He kissed me sweetly for that, but I knew he was turning me down. "What did you want to talk to me about?"

"Oh!" *Oh, yeah. That.* "Um... I think my defense will go well at the end of the semester."

His brows scrunched together in that quizzical expression. He was still so boyishly handsome, now with a few more gray hairs at his temples. More from the stress of this expansion than age alone. "I have no doubts about that."

"So, I had that doctor's appointment a few days ago. Remember how I didn't feel well after. For a little bit."

His face fell. "Daphne. What's wrong?" He gripped the back of my neck in the way he always did when he thought he needed to protect me from something. "Sweetheart. What is—"

"I had him remove my IUD. So, if you want..."

His face froze. His whole body froze. I counted the seconds. ...four... five... six... "Chris?" I lifted my hand to check for his pulse. He sucked in a breath and held my wrist, kissing my palm as his eyes closed.

When he opened them again, they were wet and glossy.

Finally, he inhaled a ragged breath. He licked his lips. "Turn around," he whispered, as if his voice would crack if he said it any louder.

I felt lighter. My skirt was gone, he'd lifted the material aside and draped it over his forearm as he gripped the counter in front of me.

I watched from over my shoulder as he pulled himself free and stroked once before sliding into my wet cunt, moving gently, but wasting no time. Both of us moaned.

God, the sight of us joining... nothing was better. Him disappearing inside me, the way his eyelids always closed at that first stroke. "I love you, Daphne." When he dragged himself out, dripping with my fluids, and said it again. "I love you. And I already love our baby."

Oh, god, I wasn't sure the way he'd reacted. Tears of relief streamed out of my eyes.

"Fuck me, Chris," I sobbed with need.

"You want me to give you a baby, sweetheart?"

"Yes."

He lifted my leg, opening me up, putting my knee on the counter, and from this angle—oh fuck, this angle—he was cleaving me in two. He jerked his hips into me again, harder, and I muffled my cry with my arm. "I can't wait to see your belly all big and round. Your gorgeous tits filled with milk... leaking... fuck."

"Chris."

"Do it, sweetheart." His hands were back on my pussy, my clit was such a rude little thing, sticking out so hard with my legs splayed wide, getting ready to splash on the marble tiles. "Come for me, darling." My pussy was filling up. More and more. Oh shit, it was too much... and he was fucking me so deep and playing with my pussy just where I needed him.

"Oh, fuck, there it is, baby," he said.

I was dribbling out onto his cock. "Oh, sweetheart." His hips lost control of the rhythm I needed as he chased his own orgasm, spilling his seed deep into me as my legs wobbled on my heels.

"Fuck, yes, Daddy, fill me up."

His hips jerked a final time and he collapsed onto my back. Panting and wrecked.

"Thank you, sweetheart."

When he pulled out, the rest of our cum gushed onto the floor with an obscene noise. Him, me. "I fucking love you, Daphne."

He pushed me forward onto the counter as he balanced on the balls of his feet and licked me clean. Then he grabbed a towel, and in his pristinely tailored tuxedo, he cleaned the floor of our mess.

When he stood, he turned me around and wrapped me in his arms and held me tight, watching me with a lazy smile.

"That might be my favorite holiday tradition."

the end

Please know that your review is very important to this indie author and Megan appreciates you sharing the word on as many platforms as you feel comfortable, including: GoodReads, Amazon, Story-Graph, BookBub, and all social media platforms.

Acknowledgements

As you can probably *(maybe)* tell, I've read everything in print about deathcare. I approached my Last Responders romance series (of which *The Remains of Christmas* is a spinoff) as though I was getting a master's in the history of mortuary science and the culture of deathcare workers. This is the most deathcare-light of my recent books.

While studying the work of death doulas for *The Bones of Love*, the book where Chris is first introduced, my research included a large amount of end-of-life confirmations and deathbed confessions. Again and again, lifelong spouses will say things like, "I took one look at her, and I knew." Or, "he asked me to the game, and I fell in love on our first date."

That's the kind of love I like to write about.

I LOVE instalove, and I'm a firm believer that that's what most of us are writing when we write romance. No matter the trope. No matter what you call it. No matter that it's really nothing more than a spark, at first, or a quick shot of adrenaline. It's all instalove to me. That's *why* the FMC's skin gets all red and she focuses her attention on the esoteric details during her meet cute at the diner. That's *why* his eyes zero in on her earlobes (or whatever body part) when she slips in the rain and he reaches out to catch her.

What is love besides making the choice to act on that magic? And making it again, and again, until you realize 50 years have gone by, and that spark might have waxed and waned as often as the moon, but you recognized it was there, even on the dark nights.

Remains is my tribute to instalove. My version of magical realism.

Oh! Also, real quick, before I forget:

Fiddler's Grove Historic Village is a real place, although I fictionalized aspects of it (Not the funeral home, though. That's there.)

My discovery that there is an annual drive-though light show called *The Dancing Lights of Christmas* was what turned this story from a short novella into a full-length novel. Something about that perfect, ludicrous name inspired Chris and Daphne's entire road trip. I changed it to The Merry Lights of Christmas in the book, but I'm sure it's namesake is a perfectly lovely holiday exhibit.

The Forensic Anthropology Center (The Body Farm) is very real. Founded by Dr. William Bass, the patron saint of forensic anthropology, the FAC was the first research facility of its kind: a 2-acre patch of woods in Knoxville, where scientists study the effects of climate, exposure, and other variables on donated corpses. The work has been, and continues to be vital for the codification of criminal investigation and postmortem examination techniques. For more information, my favorite forensic anthropology books are *Death's Acre*, by Dr. William Bass, and *Trail of Bones*, by Mary H. Manheim. And if you're new to nonfiction about death, I'd urge you to begin at the beginning, with *Stiff: The Curious Life of the Human Cadaver*, by Mary Roach. Roach is one of my very early writing inspirations. Her dry wit is always tempered with her respect for her inquiry and her subject: the dead.

Sadly for me, cilantro jelly is not real.

And yes, some people really do have crazy bad reactions to certain spider bites and are perfectly fine as soon as they get the antivenin. It's incredibly rare, but it's a real thing. And *of course* Daphne would be one of those people.

Thanks to my writing bestie and first reader, Piper Collins, for always being on the other end of a text, whether it's about face cream or freaking out over marketing. And for finding so many tiny errors my eyes can't see. (seriously. Who else catches extra spaces at the end of a line?)

Thanks to Rebecca, for your friendship (and beta reading)!

Thanks to my awesome group of readers, friends, and readers who become friends because I have no boundaries when it comes to people who DM me (you're automatically my friend at that point).

Vielen Dank an die Autorenassistentin Britt und die Lektorin Marie bei Obsidian Hearts Publishing für die Übersetzung und Veröffentlichung von *Remains* in Deutschland.

Thanks to Lemmy and Luna Literary Management for being a phenomenal PR representative and champion.

Thanks to Book Bunny Editing for the copyediting and proofreading. I'm so thankful I found you!

Thank you, Sarah Jane, for illustrating Chris and Daphne to perfection, and for seeing my vision and making it right.

Thanks to my husband, Johnathon, who always finds new ways to demonstrate his love (I love you, too) and to my son, who's always in good spirits, despite having a boring, grumpy mom who doesn't know it's probably inappropriate to teach kids about cannibalism and embalming.

The Merry Lights of Christmas: the playlist

Wu-Tang Clan Ain't Nuthin ta F'Wit,
Wu-Tang Clan

Hotta Chocolatta,
Ella Fitzgerald

Lully, Lulla, Lullay,
Philip Stopford

It's a Marshmallow World,
Jo Stafford

Angels from the Realms of Glory,
Trois Amis

O Tannenbaum,
Vince Guaraldi Trio

Atlantis,
Noah Gundersen, Phoebe Bridgers

I'm Getting Nuttin for Christmas,
Shirley Temple

Rattlin' Bones,
Preservation Hall Jazz Band

Stopping by Woods on a Snowy Evening,
Rebecca Dale, Robert Frost, Tenebrae, Nigel Short

Ceilings,
Lizzy McAlpine

Find the playlist on Spotify under:
The Merry Lights of Christmas

HOT CHOCOLATE FOR DAPHNE

1 serving | 10 mins

INGREDIENTS

2 cups half & half
4 oz. bittersweet chocolate, chopped
2 tbsp granulated sugar
1/2 tsp vanilla extract

PREPARATION

In your fanciest French saucier, heat half & half to scalding (180 degrees). Do not let it boil.

In a large microwave-safe bowl, begin melting the chopped chocolate on very low power.

When milk has reached temperature, remove pan from heat and incorporate the chocolate and sugar, whisking until smooth. Add vanilla extract last.

Serve immediately. Top with whipped cream or homemade marshmallows.

Substitute half & half with nondairy milk for an inferior experience.

Do not use chocolate chips or snacking chocolate. It will not melt as well and it may become gritty.

Use good quality baking chocolate (Chris recemmends Valhrona or Callebaut).

Optional add-ins include peppermint extract, cayenne & cinnamon, or a caramel drizzle. Chris does not recommend annisette extract.

adapted from fifteenspatulas.com

Also by Megan Montgomery

A Last Responders Romance:

Morgue to Love (B.R.A.G. Medallion honoree)

Undertaking Love (Rudy Award winner for contemporary romance)

The Bones of Love

a Small Town Chesapeake Romance:

Well… That Was Awkward

(Best Indie Book Award winner, IndieReader Discovery Award winner, B.R.A.G. Medallion honoree, and Page Turner Finalist for best book and best screenplay)

Please visit www.meganmontgomerywrites.com to sign up for the Morgue Newsletter or connect with Megan on social media!

Printed in Great Britain
by Amazon

54843349R00184